The Huntsman and The Heretic

The Hunter's Rose Series - Book 3 by:

Troy M. Costisick

DEDICATION:

TO ALL THE STUDENTS I HAVE TAUGHT, AM TEACHING, AND WILL EVER TEACH, THIS BOOK IS FOR YOU.

ACKNOWLEDGEMENTS

God, Rebecca Costisick, Aaron J. Etheridge, Emily Wiser, Kim Hardin, Rachell Anderson, Nathan Sobol, Joshua Jacobs, Stephen Livingston, Kevin Auberry, Amy Ohlinger, and the countless bloggers, YouTubers, and podcasters out there like Jenna Moreci, Ellen Brock, and K.M. Weiland whose tireless efforts in making the process of writing and publishing a book more accessible to all.

Dwarf Caves
The Merchants' City
Everpass Hold
Dreadstone Keep
Empyrean Falls
Tatterdemalion's Tower
Coal Mines
Safe House
Vitalba Village
Ruined City
The Furrows
Infuria's Den
The Slough
Hedge Maze
Celandine Valley

CONTENTS

Chapter 1:

SUMMONS TO THE LODGE

Faint echoes of panicked beating lingered amongst the walls of the stone room at the top of Everpass Hold. The red light of dawn eked its way past Tristan's eyelids as they fluttered open. Half-sleep and half-wake contended with one another. *Was there a pounding at the door? Are we under attack?* He jerked to his left. The room was silent. Among the ruffled folds of heavy sapphire-colored blankets trimmed with white fringe rested the stony face of Mikhelena. Her soft breathing made only the faintest sounds. Tristan's muscles relaxed. He caressed her flaxen hair, barely moving even a single strand. A smile worked its way across his lips.

Tristan rolled onto his back, nestling deeper into the mattress and covers. *Just my imagination. Who would come up here so early in the morning?* The first light of morning, reflecting off the Everpass mountains, streamed in through the translucent glass of the filmy bedroom window; giving the sparse, grey-stone room a skin of warm golden light. They had enjoyed themselves for two days in this private locale, free from the traditional wedding revels the townsfolk of Vitalba cherished so dearly. No werewolves or vampires stalking them, no dwarves playing tricks or warlocks calling down thunder. The refuge of Everpass Hold shielded the freshly made couple from all the horrors of the Celandine Valley.

Knock. Knock. Knock!

Except one: destiny.

Tristan clenched his fist. He'd left strict instructions with Lawrence, high-keeper of Everpass, not to allow anyone to disturb him and his bride. And yet, there came the knocking once again. Dismissing an inclination to just ignore the intrusion and suffer the consequences, he rose.

His body bore the emblems of many battles. Scars crisscrossed his back and bedecked his arms. Snatching a woolen robe from a chair, he draped it about himself and marched to the door.

The rapping came again, but Tristan flung the accursed door wide before the intruder could finish his staccato cadence.

Bitter cold air whipped Tristan across the face while the wavy locks of his dark hair flung backwards revealing stern eyes and set jaw. "Lawrence," Tristan growled as he stepped out onto the balcony looking over the razor-tooth range. "What do you want?"

The slight man wrung his hands together, "I-I'm sorry. I've been told to summon you."

Tristan closed the heavy door behind him. "No one is to bother us."

"I know, I know. I wouldn't have, except…"

Tristan waited impatiently, folding his arms on his chest and raising his eyebrows. "Except what?"

"Huntsmen from the Lodge have come to collect you. They say it's urgent and wouldn't let me go until I agreed to come up here myself."

Tristan folded his arms and stared down at Lawrence.

Lawrence shrugged and took a step back. "They're afraid to come get you themselves. Not everyone will climb the stairs you did to find this place, Tristan. I don't even like it. This part of the keep was forbidden for many years." he said.

Tristan turned his eyes to the gold and ruddy clouds dancing among the peaks. "Why would a place of beauty and joy like this be so forbidden?"

The other huntsman adjusted the runic ring on his finger, the symbol of his position at Everpass Hold, and said, "The huntsmen who closed it off said an ascetic lifestyle is more befitting our creed."

Tristan waved his hand and looked over the sea of jagged mountaintops. Their white faces refracted the sunlight in every direction. The wind, constant and cool, beat upon Tristan's exposed chest and whipped his long brown locks across his face. Autumn was nearing its end.

"Leo promised us ten days away from all this. We only just arrived here the day before yesterday. What do they want?" Tristan asked.

Lawrence put up his wispy hands and shook his head. "Not sure. They simply stated that it's urgent, and I can't leave until I get an answer and to tell you—"

"Is it Mersha? Did she come to arrest me again?" Tristan asked, peering over his shoulder.

"No, she's not with them."

Tristan turned and studied Lawrence. *Mersha didn't come? She still won't leave the village, even for this?*

"Tell them I do not want to come. Tell them I want to be left alone," Tristan stated with all the authority he could muster.

Lawrence stared at the ground. "They told me if you said that, I was to say that you would be putting the whole village in danger."

Tristan ground his teeth together. "Always urgent. Always an emergency. Always the village in danger. Why is it, that even with almost two dozen new huntsmen added to the Lodge in the last year, they need me?" Tristan looked at the dejected face of the huntsman still standing next to the door, knowing that questioning this man was useless. Lawrence delivered a message, nothing more. Tristan's blood cooled, and he looked away. "I'll come. In an hour."

"The Cause keep you," Lawrence said with a slight bow and scampered off. The mere presence of that tremulous man was enough to set Tristan's nerves on end. *Thaul was wise to set him in charge of this place where he'd stay out of trouble.*

Tristan went inside the room and pressed the door closed. Mikhelena still slept in the bed, though she had turned on her other side. He sat on the straw mattress with his back to hers and began dressing himself.

"What's wrong?" came a tired voice.

Tristan grunted. "Someone's here to 'collect me,' according to Lawrence. Urgent, he says. You can go back to sleep if you'd like. I'll shoo them away and come back to join you."

"Is Mersha with them?" she asked, rolling towards him.

"No."

"I'll get dressed." She got up and wrapped a robe around herself. The cold air from outside sucked all the heat from the room. All of a sudden, he felt a delicate finger tracing one of the scars on his back. Electricity.

"Whatcha doing, bright eyes?" he asked.

"I remember this one," she said. "It was one of the worst you got when you fell through that porcelain wall in the ruined city."

He looked up. "Heh, yeah, I forgot about that. It was the first time you ever—"

"And this one." She ran her fingers over a series of pale colored dots on his shoulder. "That one came from our fight with the wolf-queen."

"Her teeth dug deep. I didn't realize at the time how dangerous that was."

"None of us did."

He cradled Mikhelena's left arm and rotated it up, exposing a shiny patch of bumpy skin midway between her wrist and elbow. He stroked it with a finger in a circular motion. Electricity. "You got this one in the vampire tower."

"Zorn," she said with a shutter. "But thanks to you, we won't have to worry about him anymore."

He moved his hand down to hers and caressed the tiny stump where the end of her index finger used to be. "I remember when a dire wolf bit you here."

"I've adjusted," she said with a shrug. "At least it's on my shield hand. Besides, his hide furnished us with a fine set of clothes for the Spring Carnival, didn't it?"

Tristan laughed. "I never had such nice clothes to wear. Father never let me go to the carnival. Said it was frivolous."

"Remember how I got these on my shin?" she asked, raising her foot to the bed. She swiped her finger over an arcade of chevron shaped scars.

"Mastiff," he said. "Bit right through your armor."

She stared at the marred skin for a moment. "Surprised me just how deep his teeth could cut."

"We've faced a lot of surprises over the last three years."

"Mmm-hm. Here, you were stabbed by a dwarf," she said, rubbing a vicious looking scar across his left ribs. "Six weeks after the carnival. I hated him. The 'magic fire rocks' he gave people burned down their houses. So many families were cheated by him. I'm glad he didn't relent. I'm glad we destroyed him."

Tristan looked away. "It would be best if all the Unhallowed abandoned their ways and rejoined our village. You still think about your sister sometimes?"

"Of course. I still love Sidaxa, my father, all of them. It's not their fault they're Unhallowed, and it doesn't change how I feel. I would think you, of all people, would know that. Your father..."

Tristan nodded and pulled her into his arms. "Someday, we'll bring them back. I promise."

She stroked his arm with her hand. "I know."

Tristan reached down for his broadsword. He grasped it by the scabbard and held it up. "Think I should bring this? This Eldanar metal can't hurt anyone who came for us, but maybe I can scare them a little."

She giggled and gave his shoulder a playful shove. "Leave it here."

Tristan stared at it. "I suppose I will. I can't get used to a double-edged weapon anyway. I miss my paramerion."

She wrapped her arms around him from behind. "We'll get it back someday. I know we will."

He bowed his head until his lips touched her hand. "Yes. Someday."

An hour later, they descended the spiraling steps leading from the forbidden outlook of Everpass Hold and into the keep proper. The breathless grey stones of the ancient corridors held no answer as to why Tristan had been summoned, so they proceeded to the great hall. The roaring blaze in the massive stone fireplace, well stoked that morning, crackled and popped. Smells of burning oak filled the room, reminding Tristan of the beloved kiln lost to him when he was seventeen.

Sunlight streamed in from the high, multi-colored gothic windows; casting light and shadow across tight woven rugs on the floor. Each one depicted huntsmen in battle; waging war in bright yellow, red, green, and silver hues against the varied Unhallowed that haunted Celandine Valley. Lawrence placed a tray of small refreshments on a table between two supple brown leather chairs. Two other huntsmen offered a friendly smile.

Tristan pointed at them and said, "Which one of you has the courage to tell me that I have to leave on my—"

"Tristan, just wait. Lise and I came—"

"You," Tristan growled at this red-haired huntsman. "Yanis, isn't it? Didn't I help rescue you last year from Tatterdemalion's tower? Is it so important for you to impress Leo that you'll come to hound me about some mission any other huntsman could do?"

"Eet ees not like that," said the black-haired huntress in a soft but heavy accent standing next to Yanis.

"Not like what?" Tristan demanded.

"Eet has nothing to do with a mission." Her eyes seemed sad to Tristan, but when he took a step closer for a better look, she shrank away.

"Not a mission? Then, why did you come? If you wanted a chat, you could have at least waited until we came down for breakfast."

An uproar from outside the keep interrupted their conversation. It grew so loud Lawrence raised his hands to his ears.

"Shouters," said Yanis.

"Deesgusting creatures," replied his companion.

"What do you know about them?" Tristan growled, taking another step closer. When they acted as if they couldn't hear him, he raised his voice as loud as he could. "What do you know of them? What they suffer, who they used to be? You don't have any idea about their pain. They used to be—"

Mikhelena gave Tristan's arm a gentle squeeze. "It's alright. They don't know about my father. Don't tell them."

His muscles relaxed, and he gave her an understanding nod. "Shouters are too far beyond the walls of Everpass to bother us, anyway. They're none of your concern right now."

The roar from outside quieted somewhat. Tristan put his hands on his hips and glared at the two hunters.

"Tristan, I am deeply sorry to disturb you. Lise and I were sent to get you—"

"Why can't Leo just give me one week alone? Can't the Lodge get along without me for that long? What does he want, anyway?"

"Well, that's just eet," Lise answered. "Leo ees dead."

Chapter 2:
OF SHIELDS AND FANGS

Mikhelena gave a slight gasp and covered her mouth. Tristan stared closer at them.

"He's dead! How?" he asked.

Lise glanced at Yanis then, back to Tristan. "He passed een hees sleep. As no white rose has appeared yet, we can only assume Thaul ees steell alive een Tatterdemalion's tower. The troupe leaders have called a counceel. The counceel weell decide who shall lead us."

"I'm not a troupe leader. Why summon me?" Tristan growled.

"You were requested to come by troupe leaders Hedvidge and Valere and by Aranka, too," Yanis said.

"Look. Why don't they just go rescue Thaul? We've got more huntsmen now than we've had in a long time. Tell the council to attack Greyfell Tower and bring Thaul back."

"Huntsmen do not go looking for a fight, Tristan," Lawrence said quietly.

"I don't know what they're going to do. All I know is that we were ordered to bring you to the meeting. We aren't going to leave until you agree to come," said Yanis, walking over to the tray of food and putting a grape in his mouth.

Tristan stared at Mikhelena. His eyes told her *"I don't want to betray our time together."*

Her eyes answered, *"I know, but they wouldn't have come if it wasn't urgent."*

He straightened his shoulders and turned to them. "Since you seem intent on ruining my happiness, we will return to Vitalba, but I won't forget what you took from me."

Yanis gave him a plaintive smile. "I really am sorry, Tristan, but once you get—"

"We'll meet you by the front gate when we're ready."

Tristan and Mikhelena returned to the chamber. A small mountain fowl chirped tender notes nearby. Late morning crept upon them. The heavy, sweet scent of mountain mist hung in the air. The soft sunlight and still air could not cool Tristan's mood. He stuffed his gear into a backpack while Mikhelena neatly folded her clothes nearby.

"What could they want with me?" he asked aloud.

"They're probably just getting everyone together. Strange they didn't mention Mersha. Wouldn't she want you there?"

"You know her better than I do."

"Not really. I just spent more time with her is all. In all those years, she never really said much to me; no matter how hard I tried to impress her."

"She's got a hard edge," Tristan said, shaking his head.

Mikhelena laughed. "True."

"I hate this, Miki. I'm so sorry this is ruined for us. You deserve better." Tristan said as he tossed his pack over by the door.

Mikhelena stepped behind him and put her arms around his waist. She laid her cheek against his back. "I knew what I signed up for, Tristan. I chose the life of a huntress."

Tristan placed his hands over hers and tilted his head back until it touched her golden brow. "Those in authority have no problem imposing themselves on the regular folk, but any time one of us asks for something, they act like we're demanding the moon. It's a double standard, and I hate it."

Mikhelena squeezed him tighter. "I know."

"There's nothing holding us here. We can leave Celandine Valley, go to the Merchants' City, and find the huntsmen that bring back the refugees from the wilderlands."

Mikhelena let go and went back to folding her last garments, though she kept her eyes with Tristan's. "Is that what you really want? To leave the village?"

Tristan averted his glance. "No. I still want my home. *Our* home." He paused for a moment. "I, too, have chosen the life of a huntsman. Regardless of the circumstances, this is what I signed up for."

Mikhelena pressed her lips against the prickly stubble of Tristan's cheek then double checked her pack. After an hour passed, they were ready. Outside the keep, Tristan turned his eyes toward the peaks of the Everpass Mountains, straining to see the outlook they had just left behind. It was just after midday, and the blaring rays of the sun chased away his glance. Lise and Yanis had brought ponies for them to ride. Gear secured; they started south for Vitalba village.

At first, Lise and Yanis tried to strike up idle conversation, but Mikhelena's demure nature and Tristan's smoldering demeanor quashed any exchange before it began. The only sound was the hard echo of the ponies' unshodden hooves colliding with the mottled stone path that led away from Everpass Hold.

Night came and they camped in a dense patch of forest just off the main road. A secondary and seldom traveled path intersected it here. It was once a great road connecting the western part of the kingdom to the east. A violent storm ages ago caused a landslide, cutting off the pass through the mountains in the west. No attempt had ever been made to clear it; the landslide had been so disastrous, no one knew how.

Tristan took the first watch. The intrusion of two other huntsmen on what should be a private time kept him too agitated to sleep. He spent the night next to the dying embers of the fire, grinding a fist sized sharpening stone against his sword. On one particularly rough downstroke, his sword made a strange sound. It was more of a rustle than a scrape. He looked at the bottom of the stone. Nothing unusual. He tried again. A second rustle. He tried sharpening the other side. This time, there was a rustle and a growl. It wasn't the stone. *Something's found us.*

He placed the stone on the ground and grabbed his shield. Moving as silently as a panther, Tristan crept toward the disturbance. He discerned voices now, whispers.

The path ahead was dimly lit by a crescent moon. An undulating shadow moved about. At first, Tristan thought it was a single giant beast of some sort but soon, the figures made themselves distinct. There were three dwarves, a man, some creature hunched over, spiders, and the largest wolf Tristan had ever seen. *I know what that is. It's the Vekkenwulf. The father of all dire wolves. His hide would be worth a small fortune.*

Tristan crept back to the camp as quietly as he could - but not as quietly as he should have. His lust for the rare hide clouded his senses and the sounds of dry autumn leaves brushing against his armor and twigs snapping beneath his boots failed to register in his mind.

He found Mikhelena first and gently rubbed her shoulders. Electricity. "Miki, wake up. The Unhallowed have found us."

He moved to Yanis, and then to Lise.

"What's going on?" Lise asked.

"Shhhh. Unhallowed. They've got us. We have to fight," Tristan answered.

"Where are they?" she whispered.

"A little ways there. Just past those scraggly shrubs. Four or five, I think," he said pointing into the bleak night.

"They haven't attacked yet. Perhaps we should hide and let them pass," offered Yanis in a low voice.

Tristan would not hear of it. "No. They'll have us surrounded and maybe bring reinforcements. We need to hit them before they hit us."

"I'm with you," Mikhelena said, drawing her scimitar.

Tristan nodded then motioned the others to follow. They crept along, barely out of the campsite when the figures came within view. The hunters poised for their charge but halted. A shrill voice broke through the misty night air.

"Gimme the packages. Gimme the packages!" came a high-pitched cackle in the dark.

"Dear me, calm yourself!" came a rich, courtly voice. "What has gotten into you all of the sudden?"

Tristan recognized the second voice as Drastist the warlock, his old tormentor from the swamps in the south. The young man's blood boiled; his muscles tensed. He crouched for a charge. Gathering his strength and courage, he lunged to make his move, but a thorny branch had surreptitiously snagged his leg. Just as he emerged into view, he stumbled to the ground.

"Kill the huntsmen! Kill 'em all! Gimme the packages. Gimme the packages!" came the shrill, almost delirious voice once again.

Half a moment later, a shadow flew through the air. Tristan flinched and jerked his shield up to block it. The object slammed into the wood and metal frame as darkness turned to light. Fire exploded in all directions. Flames clawed through the slit in Tristan's shield, scorching the cloth on his banded sleeve and burning a streak of skin on the right side of his face.

"Again, again! Gimme the packages!" called the laughing monster.

Tristan stood tall. "Charge!" he cried.

The four huntsmen crashed through the bushes and launched themselves into battle. The misty darkness of night was chased away as Tristan's broadsword glowed with blue fire; Mikhelena's with red. Yellow and green flame from their compatriots' weapons illuminated the faces of their Unhallowed foes in an array of hues. The throbbing burn near Tristan's eye angered him and emboldened him more. Boots stampeding against the hard autumn earth, he engaged his enemies.

The startled dwarves dropped their brown paper parcels and scattered. The recognition that his fury proved enough to intimidate the Unhallowed brought a smile to Tristan's face. He had a reputation among them now.

He swiped at a dwarf as it scrambled away, but it somersaulted over the blazing sword. Tristan spun around for a second swipe and raked the razored edge down the back of the runty abomination. The dwarf hissed and leapt into the trunk of a nearby tree, vanishing from view. Tristan skidded to a halt. He cursed it for its cowardice.

Just then, Drastist appeared before him in a puff of smoke, holding his gilded serpentine staff. The aged warlock raised his profane weapon for battle. Tristan ducked, slid on his knees, and thrust his immolating sword under the staff and into the magician's gut. The image of his long-time tormentor shimmered and disappeared. A mirage.

"Have you learned nothing these past three years, young man? A warlock is not so easily slain," called the sultry voice of the magician.

Tristan hopped to his feet and wheeled around to face Drastist only to be tackled by a giant wolf. The huntsman barely raised his shield in time to fend off its gaping jaws. Foul breath smothered Tristan's face. His lungs burned with acidic vapors. The Vekkenwulf drove him backwards, digging deep ruts into the ground where Tristan's feet braced against the charge of the corrupted creature. The force would have crushed any other man.

Lise gashed at the Vekkenwulf with her cutlass. The monster flinched, then grabbed her by the arm and flung the huntress to the ground ten feet away. Tristan lunged with his burning broadsword; driving it just under the brute's left shoulder blade. A gale force howl shattered the night. The world grew dim. Even the light of his sword seemed less brilliant. Spots clouded his view and he lost his grip on the sword as it clattered to the ground. The wolf charged him again.

His ancestors' blue shield jolted upwards as the slavering jaws of the massive lupine beast clamped over the top of it. Tristan dropped to a knee and frantically groped along the ground for the handle of his weapon. The barking, growling, hollering of the Vekkenwulf grew ever more boisterous. The odor of a thousand opened graves blasted from its mouth. Tristan held his breath, lest he be overcome by the smell.

At once, Tristan felt the pommel in his hand. He snatched the blade up. Before he could ready it, the massive beast rolled over his hand, taking the weapon with it. His sword was lost once again and Tristan backed away as the father-wolf screeched and scrambled to its feet.

Tristan glanced at Yanis. "Keep it busy for a moment."

Yanis charged. Tristan slung his shield over his back and raced to a nearby ash tree. He snatched one of the low-hanging limbs, ripping it from the trunk. The splintering left a nearly sharpened point at the base of the limb. He grabbed the dagger from his boot and finished fashioning a point at the end, transforming it into an even more dreadful weapon.

"Miki, I need you!" he called.

Lise dashed in to take Mikhelena's spot in fighting the werewolf. Mikhelena joined Tristan as he cleared the small branches and twigs from the limb.

"I need Eldanar on the end of this," he said.

Pulling a vial from under her belt, Mikhelena loosed the stopper and applied a viscous substance to the carved point of the makeshift spear.

"Quenium: Eldanar dust mixed with oil. I use it for healing, but it should work," she whispered.

"Good. Go help Lise with the werewolf," Tristan replied.

"I'd rather stick my blade into a dwarf," she said.

"They aren't the real threats right now. Worry about the lycanthrope first."

Mikhelena placed her hand above the quenium and chanted, "Though made to heal our allies, now bring harm to our enemies."

Instantly the wood burst into purple flame. Tristan took up his improvised weapon and charged the Vekkenwulf. The abomination swiped Yanis's legs from under him; knocking the huntsman prone to the ground. With fangs salivating, the great beast went for the kill.

Tristan bore down on the great monster at full speed and jammed his shield between the jaws of the monster the very moment they were about to end the life of Yanis. The Vekkenwulf reared back with a howl and clawed at Tristan. He dodged, putting himself between the wolf and Yanis, who scrambled away.

The sounds of splintered metal and wood filled the air. The father-wolf's jaws slammed shut. Tristan feigned left, then launched an attack with the flaming spear to the right, but the giant wolf proved too quick. It swiped at the legs of the attacking huntsman, knocking him off balance. A second strike of the wolf's heavy paw snapped Tristan's handmade spear in two. Tristan's body hit the ground with a thud. He tried to recover, but a pair of massive jaws clamped down on his back. The Vekkenwulf shook Tristan like a ragdoll. The huntsman could only hear the scraping of teeth on his armor.

With the snap of its head, the Vekkenwulf flung the hunter to the ground. Tristan thought sure his spine and ribs were broken, but there was no pain. He leapt up and ran his hands across his chest and abdomen. There was no blood, no punctures in his armor. He exhaled, thanked The Cause, and re-entered the fight.

He spotted the burning end of the spear lying to his right. Tristan raced to the half-spear, but something dragged behind him, knocking against his heels. It was his ancestors' shield. The strap had somehow snagged his leg in the tumult. He slid off the strap and it clattered to the ground in a heap. He didn't have time to check it, only to grasp hold of the spear and once again turn to his enemy.

Yanis had reengaged the beast and was holding it off as best he could, but the Vekkenwulf charged and knocked him to the ground. The monster opened its festering jaws to put an end to the huntsman when Tristan grabbed it by the fur under its chin. With a powerful thrust of his fist, Tristan drove the remnants of the flaming branch through the bottom of the titan-wolf's jaw and into its brain. The Vekkenwulf reared back, then fell to the forest floor with a shudder.

Tristan found his broadsword protruding from father-wolf's shoulder; from when the beast had rolled over it earlier. He yanked out the blade and surveyed the battlefield. The spiders were motionless; curled in on themselves. Two dwarves lay on the ground. He thought they might be changing back to their human forms. Lise lay unconscious, while Mikhelena had chased the werewolf into a tree. It was dancing and howling among the branches.

"Help me! Help me, friend Drastist! Help me!" yelped the werewolf that hung upside down from his perch.

Tristan ran to Mikhelena. "I'll give you a boost up!"

Tristan sheathed his sword and interlocked his fingers down by his knees. Mikhelena stepped into his hands. Tristan launched her up into the tree as if she weighed no more than a simple clay jug. The werewolf shrieked and dropped to the ground.

"She's going to get me! Help, friend Drastist!" the mad lycanthrope called, racing toward the warlock.

Yanis began his pursuit of the unhallowed fiend, only to have the werewolf toss another exploding package into his path. Yanis dodged out of the way and into a barberry bush. The thorns snagged and pulled at his surcoat as he struggled to free himself.

"The huntsmen are surrounding us! We must get the packages through!" exclaimed the last remaining dwarf.

"Very well, you weakling. I suppose you will have to fuel the transportation spell," replied the warlock.

"No, no Drastist, no!" the pint-size fiend pleaded.

Mikhelena dropped to the ground next to Tristan. "I've got my wand, Tristan. I can draw the leylines to stop them," she said.

Tristan nodded, but before he said anything, Drastist interrupted, "I see what you hold in your hand, huntress. This warlock is not blind. Sadly, I must bid you adieu. You have won this round. But I'll have you know that a reckoning is coming. Not quite yet, but soon. The seed is almost sown, and once it finally blooms, you will not escape its horns of destruction."

The warlock slammed his gilded staff into the ground just as Tristan reached him. A ring of green flame exploded outward from the dwarf, throwing Tristan backwards a dozen feet. Yanis had freed himself from the shrubbery, but the flick of the warlock's hand tossed him aside.

The werewolf came scampering on all fours. The next moment, he vanished and reappeared next to the magic user. Tristan dashed to Yanis's shield side. The two huntsmen stood, staring at the Unhallowed while Mikhelena began tracing her lines on the ground with her wand.

The werewolf snatched a package from the nearby cart and hurled it at the huntsmen. Tristan caught it in his left hand and flung it back, but the two Unhallowed shimmered and vanished. The package exploded in red fire filling the cool night air with the acrid odor of burnt sulfur.

The Unhallowed were gone.

Mikhelena replaced her wand into her belt and rushed to Lise. She began examining her, checking her eyes, breathing, and wrists.

"Tris, get over here and help me," Mikhelena yelled.

Tristan rushed to her side and knelt down. "What do you need me to do?"

"Open my satchel. Lay out all the vials and get a fire going. Quick. It doesn't have to be big, just an open flame. The venom is in her arm, and if I don't get it out, she'll lose it."

Tristan dashed back to camp. He rummaged through Mikhelena's pack until he found a leather satchel with a golden latch in the shape of an aloe plant. He grasped a burning branch from the fire and rushed back to the injured huntress. Mikhelena had removed Lise's gauntlets, armbands, and several other pieces or armor. Yanis hunched over her, his face contorted with worry.

Flinging open the satchel, Tristan arranged the eight different vials in order. He set the burning log to the side and looked at the fallen huntress. Mikhelena chose the second vial, removed the stopper, and poured its contents on Lise's wound. The oozing blood foamed and turned white.

"Good. Get that fire going," ordered Mikhelena.

Tristan and Yanis added grass and small twigs to the burning log. Soon a small blaze was going.

Mikhelena added a second compound to Lise's arm. The blood foam crackled and sputtered, then turned a deep orange color.

"It's working. I'm drawing the poison out of her arm toward the wound, but I still have to get rid of it. Tristan, hold this flask while I suck the poison from her arm."

Tristan took the tin from Mikhelena's hand. She leaned over and wrapped her mouth around the wound. Moments that seemed like hours passed. In a sudden jerk, Mikhelena straightened up, snatched the flask from Tristan's hand, and poured it into her mouth. She crouched by the feeble fire and blew into it. The spray ignited in brilliant light. Mikhelena held her mouth agape. Flames danced on her teeth, tongue, and lips. Tristan's eyes widened, expecting her entire face to ignite. In a moment, the flames ceased and Mikhelena collapsed to the ground coughing and choking.

Tristan tried to help her up, but she gasped, "No. Take some bandages from the satchel and wrap her arm. Quickly. Before infection sets in."

Tristan nodded and mimicked the bandaging he had seen Mikhelena do so many times. When he finished, Mikhelena had regained her strength and she rolled over to examine his handiwork. She nodded in satisfaction.

Tristan slid his arm under her and helped her to sit up. Her body was trembling. "Are you going to be alright?"

Mikhelena nodded and smiled.

Yanis moved next to Lise. "Is Lise going to be alright?" he asked.

"I think I got to her in time," Mikhelena said in a raspy voice.

"Spiders?" Tristan asked, helping Mikhelena up to her elbows.

Mikhelena nodded again. "Just nicked her arm, but that was enough. Then the werewolf knocked her out. I've never seen that one before. Who is he?"

"I've seen him," said Yanis. "He was kept in Tatterdemalion's tower: a prisoner. In fact, I think those two that fell over there were prisoners with us, too."

Mikhelena placed her hand on Tristan's shoulder and rose to her feet. "A prisoner? Why would a vampire keep a werewolf prisoner?" she asked.

Tristan got up next and went over to the fallen Vekkenwulf and began examining its corpse.

"His name is Gibbous, and wherever he goes, bad fortune follows for huntsmen and Unhallowed alike. He's pure chaos, and it is said anyone who sees him will have nothing but tragedy in their lives for the next twelve years," Yanis replied.

"I guess mine is starting now." Tristan said, holding a pile of debris in his hands. "My ancestors' shield. It's destroyed."

Devereaux

Chapter 3:

RESTORATION OF A COUNCIL

Mikhelena and Tristan tended the two slain dwarves. They had, by now, shed their dwarven skin and chosen to take back their humanity from the corrupted Unhallowed form. The hunters made them as comfortable as they could, then moved those two recovered villagers on to stretchers. When they finished, Tristan took out his boot knife, ignited the flame, and removed the hide from the Vekkenwulf. He sliced it off, inch by inch, and admired it.

"My first pelt in almost a year," he said, holding it up so Mikhelena could see it.

Mikhelena ran her hand through the fur. "Very nice. I'm happy for you."

Tristan folded the pelt carefully. "This one is a treasure. All those months of guard duty in town instead of out hunting… We've hardly anything to show for it."

"Mersha's not been the same since we failed in Greyfell Tower," Mikhelena said as she turned to pack her gear.

He bowed his head for a moment. "I wish we had gone back. I wish we had gotten Thaul."

Mikhelena placed a hand on his shoulder. "I know, but no one regrets what happened there more than her."

Tristan nodded, then stood. Taking a deep breath, he said, "I understand, but regrets have a way of paralyzing you."

They returned to the others. Yanis held Lise gently in his arms as she fought to regain consciousness.

"Yanis, my watch is next. You want to get some sleep? I'll stay with her," Tristan said as he walked toward him.

Yanis didn't look up. He brushed his hand through her sweat-soaked hair. "No. You sleep."

Tristan patted Yanis on the shoulder and said no more. He rebuilt the fire, then slung the Vekkenwulf skin above it to dry it out. He didn't get much sleep that night. He rubbed his hands over the fine wolf fur, admiring what a unique trophy it would be hanging in his storeroom at the Lodge.

The sun peeked above the horizon late that morning. Great, heavy clouds lurked in the eastern sky. Yanis served a savory breakfast of salted pork and hard biscuits supplied by the storerooms in Everpass. Tristan's attention turned to the two unconscious men lying on the ground, wrapped in hunter's cloaks. Carrying them and leading the ponies would be difficult. His eyes moved to his pack. His wrecked shield lay in a pile next to it. Only the Eldanar boss from the center survived unscathed. *I wonder if they would have just left us alone if we hadn't attacked. If I hadn't woken the others.*

Lise woke with a start.

"You're fine, Lise," Yanis said. "Mikhelena! She's awake."

The huntress left her meal next to Tristan and knelt beside the injured huntress. Mikhelena checked Lise's bandages, then nodded with a smile.

"What happened?" Lise asked, sitting up.

"It was a gloomweaver. A fang just barely punctured your armor, but we got the poison out. You're gonna be just fine. You'll have to avoid combat for a couple weeks, okay Lise? Another hit to the head might do permanent damage," Mikhelena answered.

Lise nodded and said, "What ees eet you are eating? I'm starveeng."

"Here, you can have mine," Yanis said, handing her his tin plate of half-eaten food.

"Will she be able to carry a stretcher?" Tristan asked.

"Probably. At least for a bit. We'll have to take it easy and not push her too hard," Mikhelena said.

Tristan kicked a clod of mud near his heel. "That's fine. I wasn't excited about getting back to town anyway."

As he spoke, the sound of hooves sauntering along the nearby road caught their attention. Tristan set his plate to the side and motioned to Mikhelena to follow him. The two snaked their way amongst the bushes concealing the camp from the road. A tall man with long dark hair, well-trimmed goatee, and sharp nose was riding south. The horse was old and pale, but the man carried himself with regal posture upon a light green saddle.

"Is it a merchant? A spy?" Mikhelena whispered.

"Don't know. We should find out. If he's not a spy, maybe he can help," Tristan replied.

The huntsman stepped into the road, Mikhelena close behind, and raised his hand. "Hold!"

The man pulled the reins of his aged horse and peered down at Tristan. He cleared his throat and smiled from under the rim of a black plumed hat. "Ah, how very good. Greetings, fellow huntsman," he said in a deep voice.

Tristan failed to recognize the figure. The stranger dismounted and approached. Tristan cocked his head to the side and asked, "Do we know you?"

"Most likely not," the man said, grasping Tristan's hand and giving it a hard shake. "I've been in the wilderlands for years, sending as many as I could toward the valley. But one can only spend so much time away from Celandine's beauty. I've returned to bring back the knowledge I've gained in the wider world to Vitalba and help in any way I can."

The man wore old, banded armor. It looked undamaged but discolored from rain and sun. A cudgel, crudely laced with Eldanar, hung from the right side of his waist. The rose on his chest, bright and new, looked freshly picked though the petals were bespeckled with black spots. Tristan smiled.

"Then, you'll have your first chance to help right now. Nearby we have two rescueds, and one of our own is injured. We'll need help getting them and our ponies back to the village. My name is Tristan, by the way, and this is my wife: Mikhelena."

"Pleased to meet you both," he said, vigorously shaking Tristan's hand again and then softly taking Mikhelena's. The huntress made a face of discomfort and yanked her hand back. Tristan stared at her, trying to read her mind. "I am Devereaux. Let's find your friends."

The three hunters passed through the bushes to find Lise and Yanis packing the ponies. Tristan introduced Devereaux and preparations to leave were completed. The two rescueds were strapped into the expandable bamboo stretchers. Tristan and Mikhelena hefted their man into carrying position.

Tristan looked at Devereaux. "You going to help Yanis carry his?"

"Uh, I thought I might perhaps lead my horse and the ponies to the town. Sheepshear doesn't care for strangers, and I am afraid he may buck when Lise grabs his reins. As she is injured, I do not wish her any further harm, of course."

Lise knelt down at the head of the stretcher. "I'm fine, Tristan. I can carry heem."

"Allow me to take your pack, madam," Devereaux said to Lise, holding out his hand.

She passed him her things and he secured them to Sheepshear.

"I'm ready now," Lise said.

"And, so it goes," Devereaux said with a tip of his hat.

It took another five days for the huntsmen to reach Vitalba Village. The going was difficult for Lise, for they had to stop to give her rest every so often. Once or twice, Sheepshear broke free from Devereaux's grasp and had to be recaptured.

They took the two rescueds to the infirmary of the Huntsmen's Lodge. Darian wore his usual melancholy expression as he applied salve to one of his patients. As Thaul's personal healer, he enjoyed the power and prestige that came with that position. Since Thaul's imprisonment, however, he went about his duties in the Lodge infirmary barely saying a word.

"You need to hurry to the library. The meeting has started," Darian said to Tristan as he knelt to examine the first man.

"What meeting?"

Darian just shrugged. Tristan rolled his eyes at him and turned to Mikhelena.

"I need to help care for the wounded," she said.

"Mind if I observe, at least until the meeting is over?" asked Devereaux, removing his hat.

Mikhelena looked across the mostly empty beds. "I don't mind, I guess," she said.

"I'll be back soon," Tristan said.

"I'll be here," she replied, putting her hands on his chest and standing up on her toes.

A quick kiss, and she was off. Tristan left the infirmary and passed through the corridors of the Lodge until he entered through the double doors of the library. Several other huntsmen were sitting around the great oaken table in the center. He hesitated at the door. They looked like a crowd of mouths all open and screaming at one another. *This looks like fun. They might as well be Shouters.*

Around the table sat Aranka the librarian, Nicole the lead healer, Patric the Lodge's lawyer, Eldo the gatekeeper, and Halbert and Valere: both renowned troupe leaders among the huntsmen.

"So, it's settled then?" asked Valere.

Tristan shut the door behind him, allowing it to close just hard enough to draw their attention.

"About time. We should have started without him," grumbled Patric, flicking his long golden hair behind his shoulder.

"We did," said Aranka. "Tristan, please take a seat. Eldo, will you fill him in on what is happening?"

"Gladly," said the gatekeeper, rising to his feet.

Tristan took the empty chair next to Eldo and gave the gatekeeper a dubious look as the old man began to tell his story.

"Last week, we buried Leo. No white rose has appeared, and so we must believe that Thaul is still alive and uncorrupted in Tatterdamalion's tower. The Lodge cannot thrive without leadership. Wouldn't you agree, Tristan?" Eldo said.

Tristan could not imagine why his assent would be needed, but he played along with a nod. "Yes. Of course."

Eldo again took a seat in his chair and folded his hands on his chest. With a deep breath, he said, "What we are going to do is something that has not been done in over an age. There wasn't always a white rose. There wasn't always a singular man or woman that led the huntsmen. Once upon a time, there existed a group of elders that made decisions for the 'Blessed Ones,' as huntsmen used to be called. Each member of the group sat in charge of one aspect of huntsmen life: healing, learning, patrolling, and so on. It wasn't until the people asked that one individual be put in charge that the white rose appeared. Of course, he did not last long, but his grandson was the great builder-huntsman, Osmajure."

Tristan nodded. "I'm not the greensword I used to be. I've learned the stories. The Sun's Council met in the very first village established in Celandine Valley. No one knows where that is now."

Eldo smiled. "That village had to move several times, but under the guidance of the council, it prospered and grew. Since the line of Osmajure is broken, or at the very least in absentia, we are temporarily returning to that ancient tradition until such time as Thaul is freed or a new white rose appears."

Aranka broke in. "Each member of the Sun's Council had a specific task: healer, builder, provisioner, treasurer, warrior, guardian, administrator. While you were coming, Tristan, we assigned roles to everyone you see at the table. Nicole, naturally, will oversee the healers. Halbert is taking builders. Eldo will become the provisioner. Patric will be our treasurer. Valere shall lead the troupes as warrior. You have been assigned the sixth position: the guardian."

Tristan's eyes narrowed. "That sounds like a position here in town, not out in the wilderness," he said.

"Indeed!" Eldo said, pointing at Tristan. "As the guardian, you will be in charge of village safety, and I am taking on administration. That doesn't put me above anyone, you understand Tristan? I am just the person who tracks what each member is doing and makes sure everyone has what they need in order to fulfill their roles. Do you understand?"

Tristan leaned back in his chair. "Not really, no. Why pick me as guardian?"

"You are one of the youngest in the Lodge. We wanted someone from your age group to be represented. We did not want…" Aranka's voice trailed off and she glanced at the others. Patric made a sound like a horse snorting.

Valere leaned forward and said, "We didn't want anyone in the lodge or outside it to get the impression we are lording over them. We are just a temporary fill-in for the white rose until it returns. We are not better than anyone else, and we are not demanding anything except that people fulfill the roles they are already in."

Tristan leaned in and folded his hands on the table. "I understand, but I'm not sure I'm the best one to be gatekeeper."

Eldo tapped the table with his fingers and pointed at Tristan. "Well, you're in luck. My son, Markus, is taking over my station at the gatehouse. He will report to you. You won't have to watch the gate. Julia oversees watching the steamworks. Shamir is in charge of the cages and will be your liaison to the mayor and his council. I manned the gate for many long years now, and that is why it's time to move on to something else. It's been far too long since my feet have traveled in the Deeping Wood or crested the hills in the Furrows. I'd like to see Everpass once more and traverse the delta archipelago in the east and watch as the many rivers trace over the edge of the valley there and evaporate in the Congregational Falls. I'm old, Tristan, and soon I'll retire."

A deep sigh escaped Tristan's lips. "Not sure I'm ready for this."

"No one ever is, my boy," Eldo said with a pat on Tristan's shoulder. "No one ever is, but The Cause calls us to the positions and places where we are needed."

Tristan nodded and rubbed his chin with his hand. The stubble had grown into full length whiskers. His beard was coming in, finally.

"Very well, then. All in favor of adopting what we have discussed, say aye," Aranka said.

The huntsmen all gave their consent, though Tristan's 'aye' came last and hesitantly. He looked around the room. The faces seemed so optimistic, so confident.

"I'll show you to your new quarters," Eldo said, rising from his seat.

"Quarters?" Tristan said without moving.

"Yes, young man. Now that you are part of the council, you must take your place in the counselors' quarters," Eldo replied.

Tristan pushed his chair along the wooden floor and rose to his feet. Eldo exited the library and Tristan followed with furtive steps. Along the passages and up the stairs they traveled until they entered the hall where Leo had taken him last year to present the scimitar Thaul had made for him. Eldo led Tristan past the door with a dove perched in the branches surrounded by persicaria flowers; past the noble ram overlooking a mountain range; past the third door engraved with an eagle in fight; past the fourth with a fox surrounded in flames; and, finally, to the next where a great steed in full battle regalia stood outside a stone wall.

"I'm the horse?" Tristan asked, crinkling up his face.

"Indeed. This is yours now," Eldo said with a laugh as he grabbed hold of the latch.

Eldo placed a key in the lock, turned it, and pushed open the door. It led to a large room, richly appointed. At the far end, squatted a small fireplace with an iron grate in the center that showed a fair bit of rust along its edges. An expertly taxidermied head of a large buck gazed toward Tristan from above the fireplace. To the left, sat a bed—a real bed—with feather-stuffed mattresses and pillows. To the right, a chest of drawers and dresser were arranged with a clay pitcher and water basin that looked familiar to Tristan. He walked to them, lifted the water basin, and examined the bottom. His own initials stared back at him.

"It is very nice," Tristan said, setting the water basin back on the dresser.

"Very comfortable for the two of you," Eldo said.

"I don't think I'm ready for this," Tristan whispered to himself.

Eldo placed the key on the dresser and took Tristan by the shoulder. "You seem to be conflicted, Tristan. I do understand. If it helps, I've found that opportunity never waits until you're ready. It presents you with a challenge, and then you grow into the person you've become."

Tristan's shoulders slumped. "One last question."

"What is it?"

Tristan turned and looked Eldo dead in the eye. "Why wasn't Mersha chosen instead of me? I mean, she's a better leader, a better warrior. She knows more about huntsmen lore than I could ever hope to learn. She's got more experience and had more success. She isn't much older than me, so if you needed someone from my age group, why not her?"

Eldo's face turned serious. He seemed to search for a reply, then finally broke through and said, "All of that is true. She is all those things, but she's seen as abrasive, impulsive, self-righteous, and aggressive. You are far more agreeable. The honest truth is none of the other members wanted to work with her."

Chapter 4:

LOSS AND GAIN

Tristan left his quarters, intent on finding his captain. He knew the most likely place to find her would be in the practice yards, so he set his gait in that direction. The clanging sounds of swords on swords, axes on shields, and spears on armor filled the bright autumn air. The sky burned an azure blue with fast moving clouds chasing each other in the high-altitude currents. A chill wind washed over Tristan, prompting him to hunch up his shoulders. He saw his troupe captain ahead and marched toward her.

Mersha stood, arms folded on her chest, outside one of the practice circles. The bright sun gave her long auburn hair a halo effect. Lise, with fresh bandages, sat next to her poring over a thin book with red leather binding. She turned the pages, staring at each one intently. Yanis maneuvered in the round practicing his swordplay with Filippos, another new recruit from Garrov's workshop.

"Remember to guide your enemy's attack away from your body. Quickly swing your sword down and back at your enemy," Mersha commanded.

The men nodded and resumed their practice. They were both older than Tristan but weren't the most experienced, he could tell. Not the strongest, either. Tristan imagined himself in the ring. With his strength, he could just bully both of them and have his way in combat. He looked to the west and shook his head. *Stuck in the town now. How am I ever going to get my own home; how am I ever going to get my father back?* The men stopped for a breather, giving Tristan a chance to approach his captain.

"Mersha," he said, trying his best to sound tough and authoritative.

She didn't look at him. "What do you need, Tristan?"

His full name: Tristan, not 'Tris.' This was a bad sign. She only used his full name when she felt aggravated with him.

"I, I was hoping to talk to you for a minute." Tristan folded his arms on his chest, then moved his hands to his hips, then finally clasped them behind his back.

"Oh? About what?"

Coyness. Another bad sign.

He had been through this sort of banter many times now. The familiarity of it bred enough contempt that he lashed back at her with, "I think you know."

She turned on him, eyes narrowed. *Oops.*

"You mean about how you got selected for the leadership council and I didn't? How I've been workin' my way up in this Lodge since I was a kid, never askin' for anythin,' and somehow a greensword with only two years' experience gets picked ahead of me?" She took a step closer. "You mean how that sleaze Patric, and that recluse Aranka are going to decide everythin' now?" Another step closer. "That what you wanted to talk about, Tristan? Was that it?" She was nearly nose to nose with him.

He raised his hands in protest. "Hey look, I never asked for it. I never wanted to be on a council."

She pointed up at him. "Don't lie. You wanted this. You know you did."

Tristan shrugged. "Maybe. But I can't do this alone. I'm not a born leader. Not like you, anyway."

Mersha turned her attention back to the practice round. "At least you understand your own limitations."

Filippos and Yanis finished their next set and took a moment to regain their strength. Lise rose with a soft grunt and brought her husband a waterskin. He accepted it from her and they touched lips.

"I was just hoping you'd know why they chose me," Tristan continued.

She gave a sarcastic laugh. "Cause you're easy to manipulate, Tris. All Patric has to do is accuse you of somethin' and you cower in a corner. All Aranka has to do is quote one of the ancient texts and you clam up. All Valere has to do is brag about his kills and you run back to your trunk, countin' whatever you've got left in there. They just wanted somebody who'd go along with the group. That's all."

Tristan thought her words would hurt, but they didn't. It was all true, and he did not care. His objective had always been to buy his home back, not to win the respect of his Lodgemates.

"I'm sorry they didn't pick you," Tristan said, moving his hands back to his hips.

She shrugged and turned back to Yanis and Filippos. "Enough resting. Back to your practices."

"The reason I came to see you is I want our troupe to stay together, even if things are changing all around us. I've been put in charge of village defense. I was wondering what station you'd like to have. I'll let you pick whatever you want," Tristan said.

At this, Mersha burst into laughter. She doubled over and clutched her stomach. It unnerved Tristan the way she gave herself over to mad jocularity.

"What position *I* want?" she gasped.

Tristan nodded. A smile crept across his lips. "Yeah. Anywhere in the town guard, whatever you want."

She rose up and shoved him. His body barely moved. "I'm not takin' a position in this town! You think I'm gonna to stay here and let the likes of you, Patric, Valere, or anyone else tell me what to do? Never! I'm a troupe leader, and I'm gonna stay that way. I'm headin' out."

"We haven't left town in over a year, so——"

"Now's a good time to go."

"Where you gonna go, then?"

"West, far into the west. The mountains most likely, past the mines."

"Not much happens out that far. I don't know of anyone who patrols so deep in the range," Tristan said.

"Good. I doubt we'll cross paths with any other troupes, and that's the way I want it," she said as she pointed to where Filippos should stand next.

"But why, Mersha?"

She clenched her fists until her knuckles turned white, her breathing heavy. Tristan thought she might slug him. Then, all of a sudden, her hand loosened, her posture relaxed, and her breathing quieted. "I failed, Tristan. I was sent to get Thaul, and I failed. Not only that, but Mathias also died, Syra got turned into a bloodborn, and Miki almost lost her arm. That's on me. So how can I ever be trusted with a mission again? It's best if I just go and find my own way with a few people I trust. We won't cause any trouble out in the Betherian Mountains. Nobody else'll get hurt."

"That seems like such a waste. So, you didn't bring Thaul back. It was his choice. Your fighting skills are unmatched in the Lodge. If we lose you, we'll lose a lot."

"You don't know that. Besides, no red-rose like you is gonna to give me an assignment. We're equals. You have no real power. Aranka and Patric think they can run this place. Feh, their roses are no whiter than mine."

"Then, stay for me. Stay for our friendship."

"Again!" she shouted at the sparring huntsmen in the circle.

"Isn't that enough?" Tristan added, glowering at the side of her face.

"The apprentice becomes the master, eh?" Mersha said, putting her hands on her hips. "No. You secretly want this, Tristan. I know you do. Otherwise, you would have fought it. I'll not be commanded by anyone 'cept Thaul or whoever The Cause chooses to replace him."

"But-"

"That's the end of it, Tristan. Go away," she said.

"Mersh."

"Go away!"

His face flushed as his anger rose. "You know what? Run away. Abandon your post. Abandon those who care about you. Run to the mountains and hide from the horrors you now fear."

Mersha tried to shove Tristan away, but he remained unmoved. He folded his arms on his chest and looked down at her.

"I fear no Unhallowed," she hissed. "Only myself."

She whirled around and walked away. Tristan reached out for her to try to stop her, but something deep within stopped him. Her long, tightly woven braid swayed back and forth along her back like a pendulum warning him to stand down. His heart hurt, for he knew this was the end of their friendship.

"The Cause keep you out there," he said, then turned to the others. "Keep her safe. The Lodge is going to need her even if she doesn't think she needs us."

"Yes, sir," they said in succession.

Tristan turned and made for the Oak Sprig Inn. He mounted the steps of the front deck and nodded to a pair of gentlemen who were commenting on the weather. At the threshold, he paused and placed a hand on the door post. A half smile came across his face. He patted the doorpost like an old friend, then proceeded inside. Bindle, the village bard, was playing a merry tune on his egg-shaped ocarina. Tristan made his way to his usual table in the corner and asked one of the maids to bring him whatever was fresh. In a few moments, she returned with a steaming bowl filled with a curdled yellow mixture. Tristan dabbed a spoon in it. The goop was spongy and released a heavy odor of smelly feet.

"I wouldn't eat that," came a deep, strong voice.

"Okacheybay, what is this?" Tristan asked.

Okacheybay's dark, sinewy hand reached for his scabbard and unhooked it from his belt. He clapped it on the table in front of Tristan and took his seat. "Your cousin calls it 'cheese chowder' or some nonsense like that."

"Never heard of it," Tristan said. He dug the spoon in deep and let the canary-colored gloppings dribble into the bowl. Pools of brownish oil collected in the dimpled valleys of the porridge-like substance.

"It is something he has cooked for himself. He thinks others will like it, too. Now that he will be running the inn, he is pushing it on every unsuspecting customer who dares to walk through that door. I honestly wish he would not make it. Stinks up the whole kitchen."

"Yeah, it smells - wait. What? Who made this? Tristan asked, leaning over the table.

"I did," came an old, familiar voice.

"Michael!" Tristan bolted up from his chair and wrapped his arms around the man who had just walked up to his table.

"Good to see you, cousin," Michael replied.

Tristan took a step back. "I can't believe you're back! You look different. Your skin is pale, and your hair is lighter. What happened?"

Michael took a seat next to Okacheybay. "Side effects of some of the things I did in the Merchant's City. Nothing to worry about, though. I'm glad you came in today. Oak told me you would."

Tristan returned to his seat as well. "When did you get back?"

"Three nights ago."

"You didn't come find me?"

Michael put his hands behind his head and leaned back. "You weren't here, and I wanted to find my father first. Of course, he's gone. I was surprised to find Oak, but he took me in, fed me, and told me about your dad and also... about my dad."

Tristan nodded and looked down at the table. "I went with him, Michael. To Empyrean Falls. I was there until his last moments. Your dad didn't—he wasn't alone."

"I know. Thank you," Michael said, folding his hands on the table.

"So, what are you going to do now?" Tristan asked.

"Take care of the inn," he said with a terrific grin.

Tristan turned to Okacheybay. "He's gonna be running the inn? I thought my uncle gave it to you."

"He did, and now I am giving it to the rightful owner. Michael has worked hard this past year to get here, and this place should go to him. I promised his father I would return it if he ever came back, and so he did."

"But what will you do, then?"

"I am hoping, my friend, you will select me as a retainer."

Tristan probed at the porridge-looking slop in front of him again. "I don't understand. What are you talking about?" "I have joined the huntsmen. I am to become one of you now. Since I have not been assigned a troupe, I was hoping your troupe would select me."

Tristan cleared his throat. "Things have changed a bit. I'm now part of the leadership council. I won't really have a troupe. Instead, I'll be charged with village defense."

"A very auspicious position, my young friend."

"I meant to tell you congratulations when you first came in, cuz," Michael said.

"What do you mean?" Tristan asked.

Michael pulled his chair a little closer to the table and nodded to the left. "Patric and Halbert came in just before you, talking about it.

Tristan looked in the direction his cousin nodded. Patric, Halbert, and Devereaux were sitting at a table sharing drinks and laughter.

"I see. Well, that means I'll be stuck in town a lot more," Tristan said, turning his attention back to his chowder.

"That means I'll get to see you more often," Michael added.

"Indeed. I'll stop in regularly."

"Food and drink are always on the house. For you, too, Oak. I know my father would have wanted that," Michael said.

"Very kind," Okacheybay replied.

Tristan folded his arms on his chest. "Why join, Oak?"

Okacheybay leaned in. "I owe my life to the huntsmen, and I want to work as one of them to bring back others who were under the same curse as me. I have felt the power of the Unhallowed and the despair that comes with that life. I want to free people from it. There was no life for me here in this inn. It was just something to sustain me until I realized my true calling, and now I have!"

Tristan smiled. His own heart was stirred by Okacheybay's words. "Well, I can't say I'm disappointed. Just shocked is all, but how many times do I have to tell you? We didn't save you. You made the decision to accept a second chance. That took real courage. Anyway, if I have the power to appoint you as my retainer then, by all means, you shall be!"

Chapter 5:

THE MISTY WOOD

Tristan left the inn a few hours later and returned to the Lodge. A half-moon dimly lit the street on a cloudless night. The massive headquarters of the huntsmen appeared as a grey shadow, its carved animal heads bleakly staring out over the town.

He went to the storeroom in the barracks and slung the door aside. Empty. It wasn't his anymore. He turned and looked back across the rows of cots in the barracks. A half dozen huntsmen sat mending their gear or talking. One huntsman looked up at him then averted her eyes as if she did something wrong. Tristan felt a moment of disgust. *Three years and I still don't feel like I'm part of them, and I know they feel the same way. Now, I'm a leader, a member of the high council. I can't imagine I'll ever be fully accepted. At least my new room still keeps me separate. I don't think I could ever sleep out here with all the madness and commotion.*

He drew in a deep breath, nodded to a brother-sister pair of huntsmen who just finished packing up. Tristan headed for the exit when Mersha entered. She didn't look in his direction but marched straight to her trunk. Tristan followed her. He watched as she opened it. The trunk teemed with gems, pelts, wands, braids of giant's hair, spider fangs, and coins of all sorts and colors.

"Your trunk is stuffed!" he exclaimed, unable to contain himself.

Mersha jerked around with an angry look. "What's it to you?"

Tristan put his hands up. "Nothing. Nothing at all. I'm just, surprised. How have you been able to accumulate so much? I always see you selling what you take."

Mersha erected herself and faced Tristan. She began popping her knuckles one by one. "It used to have more. I sold some this past year since we stayed in town so much. Still, you'll not find too many other trunks as full as this. Half of it came from my grandmother, Deborah. I've only kept the best of what I take and sold the rest. Everythin' I have in here helps me, empowers me to take on the Unhallowed."

Tristan looked down. "Several new recruits have recently joined the Lodge and have very little stored away. I'm surprised you sell so much when others are just getting started," he said.

Mersha kicked the trunk lid shut and slammed the lock closed with the top of her boot. "They'll fill their trucks as time goes and as The Cause gives them opportunity. Part of the power we have comes from takin' these things from the Unhallowed, from learnin' how to fight, then decidin' what to do with the spoils. I sell what I take to provide for those who've lost someone in the Lodge. Phen, Deserie, Cienna, Pierre, Julio – they all had families. Things have gotten better lately, but the town is still stretched thin. How would they be provided for if not for those of us in the Lodge?"

Tristan nodded. "How will you get your treasure to them now that you're leaving?"

He hoped his question, a last-ditch effort, would convince her to stay and help him run the city guard.

"A plan is in place, Tris. I have to get going."

They clasped arms together. "I hope to see you again," he said.

She shrugged. "I'm sure you will. Life is long, and no one knows where we'll end up."

"Very true."

They released one another, and Mersha left the room cradling a few artifacts from the trunk in her arms. *She'll be back. Once winter comes and cold descends on the mountains, the snow will pile high, and she'll come back.*

Tristan ascended to his new quarters. Eldo was just leaving the room with the eagle door. He wore a huge smile and nodded at Tristan.

"I'm leaving the city guard in good hands," he called as he walked by.

"Thank you, sir. Good luck on the trail," Tristan replied.

Eldo began climbing down the steps. "I appreciate that. It's been many years since I left Vitalba. Going to need all the luck I can get."

Tristan entered his room. Mikhelena had not yet returned. He placed his new shield over by his sword and opened his own trunk. The contents were meager, and he could not help feeling jealous of Mersha's fortune. He left the trunk and went to his dresser, placing a hand on the broken shards of his ancestors' shield.

A sudden tiredness overwhelmed him. The air in the room was thick and dusty. The bed looked so inviting. Clouds moved in and covered the moon, changing the colors of the room from pale to dark. *Laying down couldn't hurt. Miki will be back soon anyway, I'm sure.* He kicked off his boots and laid down. Resting his head on his pillow, he breathed in sleep.

Tristan's eyes adjusted to the darkness. The room was gone. Cold, damp air clung to his skin like a blanket, and his lungs ached from breathing in the frigid mist. High shagbark hickories spread their hands above him blotting out the sky. Only the faintest light broke through, casting feeble rays on a rough and knobby forest floor. Tristan scanned in all directions for any sign that may tell him where he was, but this forest was entirely unfamiliar.

He rolled over and moved up on one knee. His hand instinctively reached for a nearby tree trunk. The dry bark crumbled to splinters as he pressed against it. Beneath the desiccated bark, the slimy decayed wood of a dying tree clung to his palm and fingers. He scraped the rank sludge from his hand on a jagged piece of flagstone nestled between two bulbous roots.

Sounds of nocturnal beasts filled the air. Howls of coyotes, hoots of owls, and screeches of bats enveloped the huntsman. He crept forward, placing hand over hand on the swollen roots and fallen branches, feeling his way along what once might have been a path. *How did I get here? What is this place?*

An interminable time passed when he came to a clearing. He might not have noticed if not for spiky leaves on the ground poking into his hands. He held one up to the dim starlight. It was a holly leaf.

Tristan stood to full height and wandered into the circle of bushes. Each stood as tall as a house and was laden with red, orange, or yellow berries, barely discernible in the moonless night.

"Tristan," a voice called.

The huntsman whirled around on his heel. At the opposite end of the clearing, just inside the holly trees, stood the pallid glowing figure of a young girl.

"Justina?" he gasped.

It was her. She held up a hand, warning him not to come closer. "I have something to tell you. You've moved close to finding me, but the Unhallowed will make it harder."

"What? How? Where are you?" he asked, taking a step in her direction.

"Here are three things you must know: First, you will be betrayed by three people."

As Justina spoke, ghostly images of three men flashed before Tristan. Their faces were blank, no features, and their forms faded in, then out of view.

Taking another step closer, he held out his hand and said, "Who? Who will betray me?"

"Second, you must go to the one place you fear most."

A glowing image of a vortex with fangs rushed at Tristan, swallowed him. He ducked, and the image vanished.

Tristan rose and again moved closer to Justina. "Where's that? Underground somewhere?"

"Third, you must win against a foe that's never been defeated."

A phantasm in the shape of a great castle with a massive wall sprang up from the ground all around them. It vanished with a wretched scream. Tristan crouched, readying to lunge himself at Justina, to grab her and hold on so he could bring her back, but something brushed up against his arm. He looked. There was nothing.

"Come with me," he said to Justina. "We're here now. We'll find a way out just like we did in the slough. Grab my hand."

He reached out for her, but that same sensation of something rubbing up against his arm returned. He flinched and looked in all directions but saw nothing.

"Stay true to the path you're on, Tristan. Should you stray, return to it again as soon as you can. We're waiting for you. I know you can find us."

"Us? Who's us?" he asked.

Something grabbed his arm. "Tristan," a new voice said.

He lunged for Justina and, just as his arms closed in around her small frame, his eyes opened, and he was in his bed. Mikhelena laid next to him, gently caressing his arm. Electricity.

"Finally," she said. "You worried me."

Tristan sat up and looked around the room. His mouth was dry, and his lips cracked. "What do you mean?" he asked at last.

"You've been asleep for more than a day. I couldn't wake you. You're cold and damp. What happened?" she said while massaging his shoulder.

Tristan rubbed his hand across his face and looked up into her emerald eyes. "A whole day? I was having a dream. It… It was so real."

"Are you strong enough to move? The council has called a meeting again. You're needed in the library."

Tristan sat at the edge of the bed and collected himself. He then arose and began changing his clothes. Sunlight through the window cast a red gleam upon the wall. His gaze followed it to the ruby centered in his new shield leaning against the wall in the corner. He turned his back to it. On his dresser were strewn the pieces of his old one. He stared at them for a time.

"I was thinking about your uncle's shield again," Mikhelena said.

Tristan's eyes narrowed. "I know. I should get a new one. I just haven't visited the armory yet. This shield was important, is important to me."

She moved behind him and wrapped his arms around his waist. "It's damaged beyond all practical repair. You would spend an enormous amount of resources trying to piece it back together."

His shoulders slumped. "I know."

"It's important to me, too. Let's place it in your trunk along with your other treasure to remind us of how it brought us through dangerous times. This way we don't lose the wisdom it brought but still remain open to what comes next."

He nodded and took her into his arms. "That's perfect. You are blessed with such wisdom."

"Not always," she replied in a humble voice.

He released her. "So, what next?"

She broke and skipped across the room. "I'll show you."

Tristan followed her to the opposite side of the bed. Mikhelena stooped down and pulled a rectangular-shaped package wrapped in vellum from under it. She placed the package on top of the bed and said, "It's for you, Tristan. I've been waiting for the right time to give this to you. I thought I might wait until the Winter Holidays, but I think this is a good time."

Tristan rotated the parcel and began unwrapping. "Thank you! What could you have gotten me-"

The wrapping revealed a silvery shield embellished with a cross pattern of Eldanar. In the center was an ellipse outlined in sacred runes. Affixed in the ellipse was a huge red jewel.

The gem reflected Tristan's image back to him. He stood up, took the shield in his hand and held it up. It was surprisingly light. He waved it back and forth, raised it above his head.

"This is amazing," he declared. "How did you get it?" "The gem I took from Zorn in Tatterdemalion's tower. Garrov's been working on the shield for months now. He only finished it yesterday."

Tristan lifted the shield and fitted it to his arm. It was light but powerful.

"Thank you," he said.

"You're welcome. I'll place the old bits in your trunk, but you better get to your meeting."

Tristan entered the T-shaped Library. The familiar smell of musty books and scrolls greeted him. The proud glass windows, standing two stories high on the far wall, let the sunlight in and painted the room a warm golden color. It became the temporary meeting hall until an adjoining room could be made more suitable. Aranka was escorting out a few of her pupils, replacements for Syra who succumbed to vampirism the year before. The other five members of the Sun Council burst into laughter around the grand oak table, patting each other on the backs, and talking in loud voices.

"I remember that time, Eldo," said Halbert. "Infuria sent her prized three-headed wolves to test your gate. You proved your mettle that day."

Eldo grinned and looked to the ceiling, as if he were trying to bring back a memory. "Indeed. It was a fine battle, but it wasn't just me. Thaul was there, too. He slew many that morning."

An uncomfortable silence hushed the room. The hunters at the table shifted their casual postures into more formal erectness.

"Patric, will you call the meeting to order?" asked Aranka as she finally settled into her seat. She took the end of her braided cornsilk hair off her shoulder and let it drop behind her back.

"Very well. All take your seats. There is something we need to discuss," said Patric. Tristan couldn't stand his voice. It was weak, rat-like. Not surprising for a lawyer.

"I have something I'd like to start with," Tristan said, raising a hand.

Patric straightened up and pointed at him. "Out of order!"

Aranka rolled her eyes and shoved his arm out of her face. "Oh, let him speak. What is it, Tristan?"

Tristan shuffled in his seat and placed his fingers on the edge of the table. "Well, we have a huge stockpile of Eldanar sitting in ingots, unused. Also, in the last year, we've had a good number of new recruits join us from Greyfell and the village. Their equipment is old, worn out, or even non-existent. I say we let Garrov start outfitting the lodge. Thaul did nothing with the Eldanar, and it's done us no good."

"He must have had his reasons," Patric said, cocking his head to the side.

Valere cleared his throat. "I think it's a fine idea. We barely have enough to go around as it is. I'll second the motion."

There was silence for a moment. "Patric?" Aranka asked.

"Oh. Yes. All in favor say aye," he said in a monotone voice.

The motion passed and a wave of pride washed over Tristan.

"Next, we have two retirements to recognize. Julio, Mila, please come," Patric commanded.

Two huntsmen stepped forward. They looked as if they were in their forties. *Kinda young to retire. Younger than my father, and he was still plenty strong. I wonder why they're going.*

"Yes, it is time for me to go. I've seen enough violence and loss for a lifetime. With the white rose lost to Tatterdemalion, I feel it's a sign for me to chase new horizons," started Julio.

Patric flung his long golden hair behind his back. "Where will you go? Out of curiosity."

"To the Hermitage in the North Ridges. I have nothing else," said Julio with a shrug.

"And you?" asked Patric, turning his pointed nose to Mila.

A grimace spread across her sharp features. "My daughter lost her husband to wolves. He was a woodsman. She needs someone to help her with the children. I've plenty saved up from my days here in the Lodge, so I'll be moving in with her."

Nicole pressed her fingertips together and bowed her head toward Mila. "Your skills as a healer will be greatly missed. So few of us remain."

"The Cause will provide," answered Mila with a bow.

"Indeed, but I will miss you both," chimed Eldo.

The two retirees shook the hands of everyone at the table and left the library. Devereaux, with his long wavy black hair and an equally black beard on his chin, glided forward. He stood straight and tall, but his smile drew Tristan in with its charm and warmth.

"This is the next order of business," Patric said, waving his hand casually at the man. "His name is Devereaux, and he has a request. Sir?"

Devereaux cleared his throat. "In my travels abroad, I saw much suffering. The wider world is full of destitution and pain. Those who have not left the valley cannot imagine it. In fact, I could only endure so much, and upon witnessing the suffering of children abandoned by parents and forced into slavery by merchants and demagogues, I was forced to return to Celandine. Much to my dismay, I also see suffering here. Not to the same degree, you understand, but suffering none-the-less. Take the daughter of the woman who just left. Her husband died while he was simply trying to provide lumber for the town. Tragic! Her story is not unique, I fear. There are many in this town who suffer just the same."

"What is it you want from us?" Aranka interrupted.

"Permission, mainly. I want your permission to collect from the townsfolk and visiting merchants. The money would be used to purchase food, warmth, and medicines for the suffering," Devereaux said with a slight bow.

"The gardens can provide food for those who need it, and townsfolk are always welcome here if they get ill," responded Nicole.

Devereaux bowed to her. "Indeed, madame. But today I spoke with many in the town. They feel a certain, erm, sense of shame—shall we say—while picking from the gardens, and there seems to be a degree of distrust for the Lodge. I have not been in this town for many years, so there is much I do not know. Yet, the disappearance of the White Rose, the attacks on the village, rumors of betrayal and theft, not to mention the legacy of the dark huntsmen in ancient times seems to play a part."

"What makes you think you can overcome that, then?" Tristan asked.

"Young sir, I am an outsider," replied Devereaux, placing a right hand over his chest. "They do not see me in the same way they see you or any of the other esteemed members of this council who have served as Huntsmen for so long. Unfamiliarity, in this case I believe, will breed a sort of trust, while familiarity in your cases, with all due respect, has bred contempt."

Tristan leaned back in his chair and looked over at Nicole with a skeptical glance. "Is it not the church's responsibility, then, to provide those needs? Perhaps you should ask the priest Juanitos—"

Devereux scrunched his face and held up his hand. "Frankly, madam, if the church had been doing its job, I never would have noticed this suffering to begin with. Think about it. I've been in this village less than a few days and already I've witnessed a huntress have to quit her station in order to help provide for a family in destitution. Where are the ordained when it comes to that?"

Tristan grabbed the end of the table and leaned forward. "You'll not speak of pastor Juanitos that way. He's a kind man, a good man. One of the very few who ever showed me what compassion meant."

The outsider bowed in Tristan's direction. "I meant no disrespect, and I am sure Juanitos has a very kind heart. But he seems impotent to solve the village's problems."

"Misfortune can never be eliminated altogether. Even the shepherds in the furrows lose sheep to death and accidents from time to time," said Eldo. "True, but perhaps we can alleviate it some. How can you oppose that? Isn't it worth the effort?" Devereaux responded.

Silence descended on the meeting for a moment. Then, Eldo asked, "How can you be sure you'll collect enough to do any good?"

"The truth is, I can't. I did not come here to ask the huntsmen for money or material support. Just permission. If I am asked about my activities, I want to be able to say I have the council's support, otherwise it could sow dissension and suspicion - two things I dearly wish to avoid. I ask you to search your hearts. Do you not care for these people around you? Do you wish their suffering to continue? Are you so unwilling to let me try to help them?" Devereaux asked, his arms stretched wide.

The council members glanced at one another. Tristan scanned their faces trying to get a sense of which way they were leaning. Their faces were stoic, lost in concentration save Patric. He was resting his head on his left hand, a placid smile across his face.

"I like this man," Patric said, breaking the tension.

"We'll discuss it in private," Aranka said, "then, give you our answer soon."

"And so it goes," Devereaux responded.

Devereaux bowed to the council and took his leave. Two hours later, Tristan delivered the answer. Despite reservations from Nicole and Eldo, the council voted in favor of granting Devereaux the permission he wanted. His charity could begin.

Chapter 6:

AND THEN, WINTER CAME...

Snow fell early that year. The last of the merchants had barely left Vitalba's gate before the first flakes wended their way toward the village grounds. The clanking, fizzing, whistling, grinding of the steamworks rose with sudden urgency as Garrov pushed the furnaces to keep the village warm.

Winter for the people of Vitalba was a time for rest and reflection. The harvests have been brought in, the timber felled, the last coal shipment—dragged back by weary miners—stored for the long, cold season ahead. It was also a time of celebration. The villagers had three weeks from the first snow to prepare for Winter Holidays, and already mothers and fathers were busy hanging the starcrest from the corners of their homes. Most were made from simple twigs, shaved of their bark and tied together with colored thread in a ✳ shape. The wind blew them, spinning the decorations in all directions. While the rest of the valley turned grey and barren, the homes of Vitalba village bristled with color.

Tristan admired these decorations as he inspected the wall on the east end of town. He paused for a moment to examine one in particular. Some artist had taken a large starcrest made from Eldanar and turned it horizontally. From each of the ends hung smaller starcrests tied to the first by purple, white, and pink ribbon.

"This is my favorite time of year," Tristan said to Okacheybay who strode by his side.

Okacheybay let out a long, satisfied breath. "Mine, as well. Before my family moved from Celandine, I would make dozens of these with scraps I found in the forest. Then, my sister and I would sell them for two coppers each."

"It's a shame we didn't know each other growing up. I think we would have been good friends," Tristan said.

"Indeed, but the opportunity for our friendship has been presented to us anyway. I, for one, am glad," he said, placing his long fingers on his chest.

"Same here," Tristan said as he raised his hand and put it on Okacheybay's broad shoulder.

"Why do so many of these hang from the homes and stores?" came a voice from behind.

Tristan turned to see Devereaux closing in on them. Tristan returned his eyes to their former preoccupation. "They're the symbols for the Winter Holidays."

Devereaux cleared his throat. "Ah yes, I remember now. It's been many years since I spent a winter here. They've grown in complexity since I left."

"What's it like out there? On the outside." Tristan asked, looking to the north.

Devereaux's right hand grasped the end of the cudgel hanging from his waist. "Beautiful. Gorgeous. Prosperous. There is far more outside the valley than in. Us Celandines have cut ourselves off from so many pleasures by fixing ourselves to this valley."

"We stay in the valley to protect what's outside from the Unhallowed," Tristan said, and with that he and Okacheybay continued their stroll to the eastern wall.

Devereaux followed. "They are not entirely defenseless."

"Do they have Eldanar?" Tristan asked, looking a bit over his shoulder at the persistent huntsman behind him.

Devereaux shadowed them with his hands behind his back. "Um. No, they do not."

"Then they are defenseless," said Okacheybay.

They quickened their pace, but Devereaux matched it.

"Where are you going on such a brisk morning?" Devereaux asked.

Tristan shrugged. "To the wall. I try to check one section at the beginning of each week."

"I've often wondered," Devereaux said, pulling even with Tristan and flashing him a knowing smile, "if it isn't our strange customs that keeps the merchants and travelers away from Vitalba during winter."

Tristan cast a sideways glance at Devereaux. "I think it's the winter that keeps them away."

Devereaux laughed. "Indeed. Our winters can be harsh, but I've also witnessed the merchants travel through swamps and jagged mountain ranges, dragging cart and goods through terrain I thought impassable, just to find a new market for their goods. It's quite incredible, even admirable, how persistent they can be."

What is this man getting at? Why is he talking to us about this? "Any of them die that way?" Tristan asked, hoping to end the discussion.

"Yes," Deveraux said with a heavy breath. "Some do. They enjoy the experience, though. Something has to be said for that, wouldn't you agree?"

"Not really," Tristan remarked, but there was a part of him that did admire it. He, too, would be willing to wade through swamps and over jagged mountains to get the coin he needed for his home. In fact, he had done those things. Yet, he had little to show for it in his own estimation.

"Until you see it, you wouldn't know," Devereaux mumbled.

Tristan shrugged again. "Perhaps. But my cousin just returned from the Merchants' City. Said the people there only care about themselves. They lack compassion and are blown about from passion to passion based on whatever seems most profitable at the time."

Okacheybay nodded in agreement.

"I knew your cousin. Michael DeSavoie, correct?" Devereaux said.

Tristan stopped. With a surprised look upon his face he said, "Yes, that's his name."

Devereaux cocked his head to the side with a sheepish smile and said, "He worked at one of the taverns in the city. I talked to him on numerous occasions, told me all about his family and his life here in Vitalba. And I fear that's what held him back."

"Held him back. How?" asked Tristan gruffly, placing his arms across his chest.

Devereaux continued in his superior tone: "He had too much of Celandine in him. To succeed in the broader world, you have to leave your legends and superstitions behind. Talk of what the huntsmen, what *we* huntsmen do, frightens the outlanders. The simple values of Vitalba are of little use there. There is an unimaginable amount of wealth to be had, but the wide world requires sophistication and no small amount of deceit to be successful."

"Michael has returned to the village, and he has his own inn now. He will find plenty of success here," Okacheybay said.

"Yeah. He's going to be just fine," Tristan added in a choleric tone while taking a step closer.

Devereaux said as he held up his hands in defense. "Yes, of course. And I am very glad he has returned. Like I said, he has much of the valley in him. But the people outside, when they see our Winter Holiday symbols, when they hear the huntsmen's chants, or hear the priest drone on about The Cause—they, well, they regard our kind with suspicion. What I am saying is, if we made less of a spectacle of ourselves, perhaps the merchants would try to come year-round, and would not that be good for the village? To have wealth and prosperity brought in the whole year instead of tossing away a third of it?"

"C'mon, Oak. Let's check that wall," Tristan said, turning away from Devereaux.

"Indeed," Okacheybay said as he followed.

The two of them walked on, but Devereaux followed closely behind, prattling on about the customs and observances of the Merchants' City and the nomads in the Land of Grey Sands. Tristan blocked out his voice from his mind and concentrated on his inspection behind the village gardens. He slid his fingers down the posts feeling for rot. The motion brought back memories of forming pots on his wheel. Over two years had passed since he last had his hands on wet clay. The memories of forming something useful from a misshapen lump began to fade. The methods of pottery he knew from childhood dangled by their last threads in his heart and mind.

Something snagged Tristan's foot, and he went tumbling to the ground. He jerked around and looked back. A small statue of an angry man holding two shields squatted amongst some thorn bushes. They had reached the gardens.

"Allow me to help you, young man," said Devereaux as he rushed to Tristan. He offered Tristan a hand, but Tristan grabbed Okacheybay's instead.

"There you are, my good friend," said the sable huntsman.

Devereaux examined the ground nearby. "What do you think tripped you?"

Tristan brushed himself off. "This old statue. I've fallen on it before. I should've remembered."

Tristan scanned the area. The gardens were barren and lifeless except for two pairs of young siblings playing amongst the dried vines near the entrance, pretending to put each other in cages. Their childish squeals filled the air.

"Lucky you weren't hurt," Devereaux offered.

"Yeah," Tristan said. His eyes spied an open area along the road nearby. He studied it for a moment. No house, no foundation marred the ground. It was unused, untilled. "Oak, you know anything about that spot over there?"

Okacheybay peered in the direction Tristan pointed out. "That empty plot? No, I know nothing about it."

Tristan adjusted his sleeves. "Me, neither. I wonder who owns it."

"I'm sure the town council would know, or the mayor," Okacheybay said.

There is an unimaginable amount of wealth to be had... Deveraux's words echoed in Tristan's mind. He gazed at the empty lot, wondering, imagining what might be. "I want you to check it out for me. Would you? Find out who owns this plot?"

"Of course. It would be no problem at all."

Just then, thunderous, droning notes ripped through the air. Tristan's head snapped to attention, and Okacheybay looked toward the center of town.

"Is today the start of the festival?" Tristan asked.

"Must be," replied his friend.

"I had no idea. Snuck up on me."

"Indeed," replied Okacheybay, turning to Tristan with raised eyebrows and a smile.

A grin worked its way across Tristan's lips as the bombastic chords of the hurdy-gurdy wrapped him in a sonorous embrace.

"It sounds dreadful," complained Devereaux, covering his ears.

"Let's go, Oak," Tristan said as he raced off to the commons of Vitalba.

As he dashed past darkened houses and empty streets, he came to the crowd gathering in the brown grass of the commons. A fiddle, dulcimer, sitar, and flute joined with the hurdy-gurdy in striking up the traditional bygdedansar dance that commenced the Winter Holidays.

The townsfolk, bedecked in greens and browns, joined their hands in two enormous circles. The married couples on the outside turning clockwise, the young folk in the middle going counter. Their bodies matched the rhythmic tunes of the instruments, and the human undulation took on the semblance of a pine forest swaying in the wind. The children made their own small circles on the outside while the eldest in the village, smiles beaming upon their hoary heads, stood close by and watched.

Tristan spied Mikhelena not far away, standing outside the circle, clapping her hands and laughing. He skulked his way past the buoyant bodies of the dancers and snatched her hand. Electricity. She jerked back with a start, then embraced him. He pulled her arms away from him, linked his hand with hers and seamlessly joined the outer circle of revelers.

They raced around the apprentices and maidens in the middle, holding tightly to one another. The gleeful din of the musicians overwhelmed every sense, except that special sense two people share when they truly love one another. When the notes came to a crescendo and ended, everyone in the village doubled over, hands on knees, breathing out heaves of steam into the cold winter air.

Tristan's face burned red with heat, and he noticed Mikhelena's gilded hair matted to her forehead and face.

"First time I've ever been on the outside circle," Tristan panted.

"First time I've danced at all," she replied.

The band resumed their merry peels and the townsfolk aligned themselves into two straight lines. Men on one side. Women on the other. Then began the do-si-dos of Vitalba's Winter Greeting: a dance where every able member of the village said hello, good-bye, and "I wish you well this winter," as they passed up and down the chain of dancers. Then, in the second bridge, all those too injured, lame, or unable to join were hoisted into the air by the strongest of the village and honored for their service and their examples as ones who persevere despite hard times.

At the end of the dance, Tristan, Mikhelena, Okacheybay, and another woman from the village took steaming mugs of hot wassail and rested on fresh cut logs. Woodsmen had dragged massive tree trunks to the center of town to serve as benches for dance-weary partiers, and later, yule logs for the village bonfire.

Okacheybay wagged a finger in Tristan's face and said, "You are quite light on your feet today, my friend."

"You weren't so bad yourself," Tristan said, giving Okacheybay a slight elbow to the ribs.

"Who's your friend, Oak?" Mikhelena asked with a flaring smile.

Okacheybay turned to the two huntsmen and said, "This is Janelle. She is a refugee from the Wilderlands. Eldo helped her make the journey here last month."

"How do you do?" Janelle asked, flashing a bright smile.

"I'm well, thank you. I didn't realize Eldo left the valley," Tristan said.

Janelle nodded. "Oh yes, he found me in the Sethaydren Desert many leagues south of your valley. A windstorm scattered my tribe, and I was alone, ready to die. By chance, he was passing through, on his way to the ancient caves beyond the sands. He asked if I would like to come back with him. I said yes, and here I am."

"We're glad to have you," said Mikhelena clasping her hand.

Just then, Nicole Predresoin walked by, checking her healer's pouch and counting the number of vials inside out loud.

"Nicole!" Tristan called.

She came closer to him, not looking up until her counting was finished. "Yes, what is it?"

"Did you see Mersha in your travels this fall?" Tristan asked, taking a sip of his wassail.

Nicole closed the flap of her case and pushed it behind her lower back. "I was in the Betherian Mounts two weeks ago, finishing my winter harvests. I saw her and camped with her troupe the night before I left. I know what you're wondering. I did ask if she was coming back to the village for the winter. Something flashed across her face. I couldn't tell if it was anger or sadness. But, she said no. She intends to never again leave the mountains."

Chapter 7:

THE SNOW FELL HARD
OUTSIDE THE VILLAGE

The next morning, A thunderous knock upon his door roused Tristan from sleep. It was a panicked pounding; someone was desperate to get in. *Again?* Tristan grunted and rolled to his right to leave the bed. A delicate hand clasped him by the forearm and pulled him back.

"Want me to get it this time?" Mikhelena asked.

He took her slender fingers in his hand and pressed his lips to them. "I'll get it."

Tristan trudged to the door, wrapping a woolen robe about himself. Cold seeped in from the windows and ceiling. Having his own room, a large room, on the top floor of the Lodge had its advantages. Keeping out the winter drafts was not among them. Tristan unlocked the bolt and pulled the door open.

"You have to come to the wall!" a young recruit said, his dark brown eyes wide in fear.

"Why?" Tristan asked, rubbing the crust from his eyes.

"Snow! Snow everywhere!" the young man continued.

Tristan started to close the door. "There's snow every year. Go back to bed."

The young man pushed against the door, squeezing his head through the crack and letting his long sable locks of hair dangle toward the floor. "Not like this, sir. Not like this."

Tristan relented and let the door fly open. The youth tumbled to the floor, striking his chin against the boards. Mikhelena sat up in fright at the intruder and pulled the covers up to her eyes.

"Fine. I'll come. I'll meet you at the door in thirty minutes. Dragen, isn't it?" Tristan asked.

"Yessir, it is," he said, rubbing his jaw.

"Thirty minutes."

"Yessir."

The youth scampered out. Tristan shoved the door closed, then went to his wardrobe. He pulled out the warmest outfit he had, a rich blue gambeson and wool leggings to go underneath.

"A bad snow?" Mikhelena asked.

"Apparently. I don't know why they'd need me to see it. The gates are shut. No one leaves the village this time of year anyway," Tristan said with an annoyed shrug.

"I suppose I'll get up and check the infirmary. We had a couple villagers come after the festival last night. Sweating through their clothes," Mikhelena said.

"You know what it is?" Tristan asked as he slid on his outfit.

Mikhelena slid out from under the covers. "No, but Nicole was going to stay up with them. She's seen more diseases in her time than I have."

Tristan turned to her and pulled her close. "Just let me know if there's anything you need or anything bothering you. I have a position of power now and I can—"

"Easy there," she said, turning away. "That's hubris. You're on a council, where many share equal power. If I need something, I know how to get it. And I know that you'd move Everpeak Mountain itself or march on Dreadstone to get it if I asked."

Mikhelena mentioning the name of the dark lord of the valley made the chill in the room just a bit colder.

"Good. I have to get going. Hope everything goes well in the infirmary. See you soon. There's someplace I want to take you later today."

"Oh? Where is it?" Mikhelena asked, taking a step closer and grabbing his hand.

He knew she would get the information out of him if he stayed any longer. "Not saying yet," Tristan answered with a coy smile. "But you'll see."

They parted ways. Tristan descended the stairs to the main corridor. Waiting at the bottom was Okacheybay, tightening up the last strap of his overcoat. Tristan nodded to him, and his friend returned the gesture. They passed through the empty great hall of the Lodge and met Dragen at the front archway of the Lodge. The three of them trudged toward the stockade. The streets were thick with mud as the underground pipes from the steamworks kept the village warm and thawed. Dragen kept a few paces ahead, furtively looking back at Tristan.

Finally, Tristan grew tired of the looks and asked, "What is your hurry?"

"The snow. It's bewitched!" Dragen answered.

"Bewitched," Okacheybay cried with a laugh.

"Indeed!" the distressed huntsman answered.

Tristan rolled his eyes and continued toward one of the ladders that led to the parapet atop the stockade.

"Lead the way," Okacheybay said to Dragen in a dry tone.

The youthful huntsman hurried ahead while Tristan and his friend lingered behind. Several times, Okacheybay opened his mouth as if to say something then shook his head.

"Something on your mind, Oak?" Tristan prompted.

Okacheybay grimaced. "Yes, but it is a silly thing."

Tristan raised his eyebrows as his feet sloshed in the wet mud of Vitalba's main thoroughfare. "I've never known you to be silly."

"Not me. Some villagers. They say they have seen a giant bat flying about their houses at night. They say it makes a creaking noise, almost like the steamworks in the air. I dismissed it at first as cabin fever getting the best of them. But enough have described the beast to me in the same way, I thought I would bring it to your attention."

Tristan turned his eyes to the clouds above. "Anyone hurt by it?"

"No. It just wakes them in the night."

"Any huntsmen see it? I mean, that you know of?"

Okacheybay shook his head. "No."

Tristan shrugged. "Could be just an illusion."

"Perhaps, but we have seen stranger things in this valley."

Tristan wrapped his cloak around him tighter. "Bitter outside today. I wonder what has happened to the snow to get Dragen so agitated."

"Someone is up there on the wall," Okacheybay said pointing up to the stockade.

Tristan could see a lonely guard, standing at the top. He thought it was Eldo, the former gatekeeper. Tristan pulled himself up the ladder. His foot slipped on the fifth rung, but he caught himself before falling off completely. Grumbling to himself, he finished his ascent and stood next to the aged huntsman. The sun was blinding. It had only just fully risen above the horizon and reflected off the snow in a blazing array of oranges, yellows, and reds. Tristan's suspicions were confirmed. Eldo was standing atop the wall, gazing out over the valley. In a moment, Okacheybay and Dragen were standing there with them.

"Morning, Eldo. What brings you to the wall today? You're a man of the wilderness now," Tristan remarked.

Eldo rubbed his chin. "Came to see if the rumors were true."
"Rumors?"

"That," Eldo said, pointing over the wall and out into the valley.

Now that Tristan's eyes adjusted, he could see what concerned Dragen so much. The snow was packed almost to within arm's reach of the top of the stockade. There was hardly anything to see except the tops of leafless trees and clear, red skies. A full eighteen feet deep it must have been. It glistened in the new morning sun, silent as a grave.

"It's not just the depth, which is definitely bad. It's also the color," Eldo added.

"The color?" Tristan looked out. The sun painted the snow a variety of summery colors so discordant with the biting cold outside. "Bah, that's just the sunrise reflecting off new fallen dust, Eldo. Nothing strange here."

"No, my young friend, you're wrong. By now the sun should be high enough the snow should be white or maybe blue. But it's not. This is bloodsnow, sent by Lord Dreadstone himself. I've seen it once before, when I was young. Mark my words, come springtime, these timbers will be rotten."

"Bloodsnow does that?" Tristan asked, continuing to scan the brilliant horizon.

"Yes. We're lucky the steamworks keep the village so warm, or every home and store would be under the same curse."

"All those pipes," Tristan said, looking back over the wall into town.

"Yes, running underground, keeping the earth warm and whisking away the water into the aquifer. No telling where we'd be without that."

"If the wall is going to rot, we'll be defenseless!" Dragen exclaimed.

"Calm yourself," Tristan said without looking at the recruit.

"But sir, we've got to do something. We're in trouble. This is an attack!" Dragen continued, pounding a fist into his hand.

Tristan held up a hand to the excited young man. "Panicking will do us no good. What do you suggest, Eldo? You've been on this wall longer than any of us."

"My grandfather served as gatemaster long ago when this happened before. He organized the huntsmen in the spring to help the woodsmen bring back fresh cedar timbers for the wall. I think you'll need to do the same."

"So right now, there is nothing to be done?" Tristan asked.

Eldo moved toward the ladder. "Not during the winter. Right now is the time for patience."

"Yessir," Tristan said with a nod. He peered out into the white-dusted forest, already searching for cedars that might be close by. His eyes turned to the multitude of posts that made up Vitalba's stockade. He gave up counting at two hundred. *So many. It will be the biggest project the huntsmen have done in a generation.*

"Thank you for the advice, Eldo. I'll be looking forward to the first thaw, so we can begin," Tristan said.

"Good luck, young man. I'd be lying if I told you I wasn't relieved to have someone else in charge of the wall instead of me. I've gotten too old to oversee this kind of thing. Not sure I have much left in me at all to be honest," Eldo said, starting his descent.

Tristan watched him go. "You're far from being too old to be useful. Stay strong, Eldo. Trust The Cause."

"Where are you going next?" Okacheybay asked while resting an elbow against the parapet.

Tristan looked up at his friend and said, "To find Miki. There's something I want to show her. There's nothing to be done about this now. I'll tell the council, but It'll have to wait 'till spring before we get started."

Tristan slid down the ladder and bounded back to the Lodge. *If trees must be felled, perhaps I can go out and oversee them and do some hunting at the same time.*

The prospect of hunting, getting out of the village in spring sparked a flame of hope inside him. In his mind, he told himself over and over: *This is going to be my chance. It has to be. My chance to get what I need to have a home.*

His conviction grew stronger as he burst through the Lodge's front door and scampered up to his room. It was empty. The bed was neatly made, and the washbasin was still damp from recent use. Tristan turned and checked the feasting hall, but Mikhelena could not be found. It wasn't until he remembered she was going to the infirmary that he was able to locate her.

He entered the sick room. A couple villagers rested on a pair of sweat-stained cots. Another sat hunched over in the corner. Tristan approached Mikhelena and waited for her to finish washing her hands in a basin.

"Hello Tristan," she said without turning around.

He wrapped his arms around her and whispered in her ear, "I have something to show you. Can you get away for a bit?"

"Something upstairs?"

Tristan laughed. "No, in the village. I've found something I want to share with you. Are you free?"

"These two are fine," she said, pointing to the nearest villagers. "The other... It's interesting. His lungs are congested, but there are no other symptoms. It's not something I've seen before. I don't think he's in any danger, though. Devereaux brought him in, just in case."

"I won't keep you long. Promise."

Mikhelena looked at the resting villagers, then nodded her head. Tristan took her by the hand and they left the infirmary. Mikhelena wrapped herself in a heavy cloak and scarf, then followed Tristan out of the Lodge.

"It's cold out today," she said.

"Very," Tristan agreed. "The reason they came and got me was that there's a problem with the snow."

She pulled her hood down lower. "What sort of problem?"

"Eldo called it bloodsnow. Says Lord Dreadstone sends it our way every generation or so. It eats away at the stockade and rots the wood. Next spring, we're going to have to replace many of the posts that make up our wall," Tristan said.

"Is the snow so deep they can't be salvaged?" she asked.

"Almost to the top. I've never seen anything like it. If you jumped over the wall, you'd be buried in eighteen feet of dark pink snow."

By now, they had made it halfway across the village. Several of the townsfolk were out conducting their business. Many homes were still adorned with starcrests celebrating the Winter Holidays. The news of the bloodsnow outside the village either hadn't reached them or they were unconcerned. Tristan expected a lot of questions about the stockade, or even a summons to the mayoral mansion to discuss what to do, but nothing of the sort came that morning.

At last, they reached the gardens. Winter had killed the plants inside. Dead, grey vines and lifeless brown stems looked like frozen snakes forever captured in the final throes of death. Tristan guided Mikhelena to the empty plot of ground nearby that he and Okacheybay had discovered just before the festival.

"This is the place!" Tristan said, pointing to the empty parcel of land.

Mikhelena peered in the direction his hand showed. She straightened her back and gave him a strange look. "I don't see anything," she said.

"That's right. This land doesn't belong to anyone. The village still owns it."

"How do you know?" Mikhelena asked, leaning to her side.

"I had Oak check into it for me. So, do you know what we could do with this?"

Mikhelena shifted her weight to the other foot and shrugged her shoulders. "No, I have no idea."

"We could build a house!"

"A house?"

He spread his arms out over the lot. "Yeah, think of it. We could have our own place. The apartment in the Lodge is nice, and certainly better than that old storage room, but this would be ours. We could build a family here, and it's so close to the gardens. It's the best place in town. What do you think?" Tristan asked.

She brushed a strand of hair covering her face behind her ear. "But what about your old one?"

Tristan shifted his weight and looked toward the eastern part of the village. "I don't think I'll ever get it back. The tenant potter doesn't know who owns it, and it seems Patric is the liaison between the owner in the Merchants' City and Vitalba. I'll never get anything out of *him* concerning my house."

"It's a big lot."

Tristan smiled and said, "It is. We'd have plenty of room."

Mikhelena stared at the emptiness for a moment, then perked up. "Could we have a glass room where I could grow herbs year-round?"

"Of course!" Tristan answered.

"And what about a room, a small room, for one patient who needed close care. Could we do that? Just for one?"

Tristan turned to her and took her hands. "Yes, anything you want. I'm going to have to oversee collecting new cedars for the stockade. It will be hard to get the lumber for a house, and expensive, but I think we can manage it. I have no doubt that Dreadstone will send his Unhallowed to harass the woodsmen. There'll be plenty of treasures to collect."

"It sounds wonderful, Tristan, but," she hesitated.

"But what?"

"We're already well provided for in the Lodge. You have a position of leadership now. Shouldn't we stay close to where we're needed?" she asked, staring up at him.

"It's a small town, Mik. If they need us, they'll find us easily enough. Ever since I joined the huntsmen, I've wanted my own place. This plot will be cheap. I think we can do it," he said, clenching his fist in excitement.

"So, you're certain of giving up your old home then?" she asked.

Tristan's shoulders slumped. "I think I am. The kiln has been upgraded so much, it'll cost a fortune to buy back. It's way more than anyone would need for this little village. Why's the owner putting so much into it? It doesn't make sense. It's almost like he wants to taunt me."

"You really think that?" she asked, taking his arm and pulling him close.

"No, not really. But I've just come to accept I'll never get that home back. I think we can get this home. I don't know if I'll ever go back to pottery, but I do know, if I have a home, I can have a family. And I want a family, Mik."

Mikhelena stood on her toes, cradled his head, and kissed his cheek. Placing her temple against his, they stared at the empty plot.

Chapter 8:
ENEMIES WITHIN AND WITHOUT

The snows melted and warm weather returned. Spring descended on Celandine Valley on the first day of the fourth month; brushing aside the bitter winter and replacing it with the songs of birds and rustling of breezes. The sun's golden rays, so long hidden by dingy clouds, bathed Vitalba village in their life-giving warmth. Old joints loosened, young children came out to play, and the woodsmen filled the forest in search of precious cedar timbers.

The walls of Vitalba had indeed been weakened by the bloodsnow. The once proud red timbers were blackened with mold and rot. Fortunately, though, Tristan discovered only a fifth needed replacing, and most of those stood on the western side of the wall. As soon as the road leading from town dried enough to support the weight of wagons, Tristan ordered timber be brought into the village for the carpenters to hew into posts for the stockade.

Tristan woke up early one day. Mikhelena was already in the infirmary concocting potions and salves. He wondered if she even came to their bed that night. Getting dressed and having a quick breakfast, he left the Lodge to inspect the wall, Okacheybay at his side. As they drew nearer to their destination, he heard someone speaking in a loud voice off in the distance.

"Who is up so early yelling at the villagers?" Tristan asked.

Okacheybay looked in the direction of the sounds. "I cannot tell. Devereaux perhaps?"

Tristan changed course and followed the voice. As they drew closer, he saw Devereaux atop a wooden block, speaking to a small crowd.

"If only you just believe in The Cause and keep its commands," Deveraux was saying, "you shall inherit riches beyond your imagination. Look who we have with us today: a farmer, a cobbler, a weaver, a miner, a hunter, and more. Obey, and all your needs will be met. Your change purses will overflow with silver!"

The crowd responded with positive assent.

"And to show you that I speak the truth, Halbert—one of your fine huntsmen—is here to share his great fortune! He recently sojourned into the forests and came across a small trunk of coins, just by chance! Had he not been faithful to The Cause, he surely would have lost instead of gained," Devereaux said, pointing to the huntsman sitting amongst the crowd.

"I've had a rough year, and I've barely got two coppers to rub against each other. How can I gain?" asked Resivere, a cooper in the town.

"If you lack coin now, it is because of unfaithfulness on your part," continued Devereaux on the block. "Something hidden in your soul that must be expunged before your wealth can flow."

The words grated at Tristan. His skin burned. "Have I something hidden?" he spoke up.

Devereaux flinched and spun around. "Oh. Tristan. I did not see you coming."

"Answer my question. Have I something hidden in my soul?"

Devereaux slumped and gave him a gracious smile. "How can I know? Each man must, um, search his own heart."

Tristan took another step closer. "I don't believe that I do. I serve The Cause. I have fought many monsters, slain many enemies. I have aided many villagers. Do all of you know that?" Tristan asked, pointing to the men and women around Devereaux.

"I saw you fight once, atop the stockade," said one woman.

"I saw you rescue a girl," piped up another man. "You and your whole troupe saved her from wolves."

The others joined in, but Tristan raised his hands. They grew quiet. "I have served The Cause as best I can, Devereaux, yet I cannot seem to fill my purse. Why do you suppose that is?"

Devereaux stood straight. His eyes became stern. "Perhaps your blessings have not yet arrived. Do you lack the faith to wait for The Cause to bring them to you?"

"I—"

"Are you so hot to have silver and gold that you forget the virtues of patience and will?" asked Deveraux.

"The Cause blesses whom it will. I'm convinced there is no forcing it whether through deed or prayer," said Tristan. Okacheybay grabbed his arm and gave it a tug.

Devereaux laughed. "I am not so convinced. It is justice that those who work hard should be rewarded. It is justice that those who are faithful should be rewarded. What proof do you have that it is otherwise."

"You are needed at the stockade, Tristan," Okacheybay said, letting loose of Tristan's arm.

Tristan turned to his friend. "Yeah. Almost forgot."

"And so it goes," Devereaux said.

Tristan nodded to the villagers as he turned his back to Deveraux. He straightened himself to full height and marched toward the wall. Behind him, he heard Devereaux resume his speech.

Just then, an alarm sounded from the northern part of the stockade. Tristan and Okacheybay glanced at each other, then sprinted toward the bell. Soon the church bell rang, as well, alerting the town. The gateguards were pulling the great doors of the village shut.

"No! No!" cried Tristan as he passed. "Let the hunters out. Let's face them in the field!"

The gatesmen stopped pulling, and all but two joined Tristan and Okacheybay as they ran outside the village. When the five of them rounded the corner, the attackers came into view. Two huntsmen atop the wall were doing their best with their bows to drive off a company of dwarves who were laying packages at the base of the stockade. When the handful of diminutive grey-skinned folk saw Tristan coming, they scattered back into the woods.

Tristan halted at the pile of parcels, figuring the dwarves retreated in order to use their ability to leap from tree to tree in other dimensions. Tristan examined the brown bundles while catching his breath.

"I imagine they explode, like the ones you spoke of last fall," said Okacheybay.

Tristan nodded. "I was thinking the same thing. We'll let Garrov dispose of them."

A crashing sound from the woods jerked their attention from the packages. A half dozen dwarves astride spider mounts charged forth. The green arachnids hunkered low as they skittered toward the huntsmen, their yellow eyes aglow.

Two fiery arrows from above pierced the first one in the head, instantly killing it. The dwarf who mounted it tumbled forward and was instantly pierced through its heart by Okacheybay's broadsword. Tristan dashed past him, drawing his sword and shield. The next enemy reared up in front of Tristan. The spider's fangs glistened with venom, but Tristan rolled under the attack. He slashed the beast's belly, spilling its vital fluids on the soggy earth. The dwarf jumped down and swung its axe at Tristan's head, but the nimble huntsman raised his shield, blocking the blow.

Standing to full height, Tristan brushed aside a second attack of the dwarf; throwing the enemy's stubby arm wide apart from its body. Tristan counter-swung with quick jabs, one-two-three, into the villain's chest. The tell-tale blue blood of the dwarf oozed out from the cuts with the consistency of pottery glaze. The Unhallowed dropped to his knees, then fell face-forward into the mud.

Not waiting to see if the dwarf would rise a second time, Tristan sped toward another at the wall. A gatesman was fending off the fangs of a spider and the mini-lance of the dwarf at the same time. Tristan leapt atop the spider, no taller than a pony, holding his broadsword like a dagger. Tristan drove his flaming blade into the dwarf's ribcage. The Unhallowed shuddered, then crumbled to the ground. The spider bucked wildly, throwing Tristan off at an awkward angle.

The huntsman tried to break his fall with his shield arm but jammed his wrist as his full weight came crashing down. Tristan squirmed off his wrist just in time to use his broadsword to catch an incoming axeblade on the haft. The dwarf he killed earlier, besmeared with greasy blue blood, had risen to resume the fight.

Tristan lay on his back. The half-size unhallowed tried to jump on him, but the huntsman slammed him with his shield and rolled away. Shockwaves of pain shot through Tristan's wrist. He growled and shut it out from his mind. Rising to one knee, Tristan protected himself from a flurry of axe blows. When the dwarf paused for a moment, whether from fatigue or from devising a new line of attack, Tristan lunged with his blue-flame sword. The blade plunged deep into the monster's belly. A flick of the wrist twisted the weapon, and a hard yank upwards spilled the infernal creature's guts in a cascade of entrails and blood.

Tristan scanned the scene. One of the other slain dwarves appeared to be shuffling off its Unhallowed form. Only one spider remained alive, flanked by two dwarves.

Just as confidence was creeping up on Tristan, a new sound echoed on the battlefield. A pack of dire wolves rushed from the foliage to join the fray. Tristan braced himself once again, but a hail of arrows downed most of the pack before they even reached him. More huntsmen from inside the village were coming. Just then, two werewolves leapt out. One wore a red ribbon on its left arm, the other a blue.

"The twins, Jean-Paul and Jean-Jacques!" Tristan called out, rushing to Okacheybay's side.

"The wolf princes have returned home," his friend added.

"I hoped it would have been as huntsmen instead of like this," Tristan said.

He ducked under a charging wolf, bouncing it up in the air with his glowing shield. He whirled right and decapitated the beast before it fell. Turning toward the wolfmen, Tristan charged with bared teeth.

"I'm coming for you. I'll set you free," he yelled.

If Tristan's words had any effect, they only served to enrage the werewolves. They charged back, flanking Tristan and Okacheybay at full speed. Tristan feigned left, then struck right with his sword. He gave the red-furred lycanthrope a searing gash across its back.

Tristan turned and raised his shield just in time to intercept the attack of the other wolfman. The abomination grasped the steel bulwark, and the flames from the Eldanar burned its paws. It staggered back in pain.

Tristan attempted a lunge, but two powerful claws seized him from behind by the arms. Tristan ducked, twisted his body, and rolled his arms up and around. The maneuver freed him from the werewolf's clutches, and he again attacked his foe.

"Oak! I need you," Tristan yelled.

"Dealing with the wolves at the moment, Tris," he yelled back.

Tristan executed a series of crisscross slashes at the neck of his red-ribboned enemy. Each time, the Unhallowed ducked and dodged. Tristan retreated a step, inviting the wolf-prince to attack, but Jean-Paul maintained a defensive stance.

Two iron-strong arms wrapped around Tristan from behind once again. Jean-Jacques had snuck up behind him. Tristan's weapons were pinned against his chest. Tristan pushed against the werewolf's arms, slowly forcing them apart when Jean-Paul leapt to attack. Tristan relaxed; the hairy arms slammed back against him. Tristan used his captor's own strength as leverage to draw up his feet and slam his boots into the chest of the oncoming wolfman.

There was a crunching sound as Tristan's heels sunk deep into the oncoming attacker. The werewolf reeled back, hunched over, and clutching his chest. *A couple of broken ribs, I bet.*

As Jean-Paul staggered backwards, Okacheybay's flaming broadsword came careening down on Jean-Jacques. The lycanthrope flinched and managed to avoid most of the strike. It merely opened a cut in the werewolf's left arm. The lupine abomination hurled Tristan to the ground, reared back, and belched a massive cloud of smoke and fire into the air. The foul mixture engulfed Okacheybay. Tristan jumped to his feet to attack, but the other werewolf let loose his smoldering breath, as well.

The hunters, momentarily blinded, flailed away with their weapons. When their sight returned, the battlefield stood empty, save the corpses of those defeated.

"They flee?" Tristan asked, maintaining his battle stance.

"It would appear so," Okacheybay answered.

Tristan turned to look at the top of the stockade. "Archers! Why did you stop loosing your arrows at the enemy?"

The two bowmen at the top of the wall looked blankly at each other. One turned back to Tristan and shouted, "We ran out."

Tristan shot his friend an aggravated glance. "Carry more in the future!"

Okacheybay sheathed his sword. "We need more weapons, more hunters."

"This was a pretty daring attack in daylight but not massive enough to really threaten the village. What was the purpose?"

"Terror?" Okacheybay answered.

"Perhaps, or maybe to draw us out."

Halbert

Chapter 9:

AN UNWELCOMED REVELATION

Several days later, Tristan was brooding in the library over a stack of reports. The reconstruction of the wall was making progress, and the troupe leaders had submitted their needs assessments for the Lodge. Aranka busied herself cataloging in a corner far away. Tristan shuffled the papers, glancing left then right then left again.

He slammed them to the table. "I should be out in the field, not stuck in here."

"It fell to you to serve as Guardian," Aranka replied from afar.

"I didn't choose it," he said, leaning back.

"There are many things you didn't choose, Tristan. Would you give up everything you have now in exchange for being able to choose your fate two and a half years ago?"

"Hmph," Tristan replied.

"Well?" she pursued.

Just then Darian opened the double doors to the library and led a man from the village into the brightly lit room. Tristan, thankful the intrusion saved him from Aranka's question, hailed them.

"Tristan, this is Parnell, head of the woodsmen's guild. He says he needs to speak with you," Darian said.

Tristan looked up. "How are things in the infirmary?"

Darian shuffled his feet. "Your wife works very hard, sir. Too hard. I worry sometimes. More and more villagers are coming to us, sick. We can't figure out why."

Aranka came over to the table where Tristan was sitting. "Any huntsmen falling ill?" she asked.

"No. Not to this anyway," Darian answered, motioning in the general direction of the sick-room.

Tristan turned his attention to the woodcutter and asked, "Parnell, what can I do for you?"

Parnell took his hat off, then put his fists on his hips. He stood up straight and said, "My workers aren't getting paid for their timber nor their labor."

"Halbert is in charge of paying you. If you find him, he'll give you what you're owed," Tristan said, shrugging his shoulders.

"I know, but no one can find him," Parnell said.

Tristan leaned back in his chair and folded his arms on his chest. "I just saw him the day before yesterday. I'm sure he's around; go look for him."

Parnell's expression turned serious. "I wouldn't have bothered you if it were that simple. He was supposed to meet us yesterday evening. He didn't show up. Patric told me he would meet us this morning at the Oak Sprig. He wasn't there. Darian said he hasn't seen him. I take it you haven't either?"

Tristan glanced over at Aranka.

"Don't look at me. He's not been in the library," she snapped.

Tristan returned his gaze to Parnell. "Well, I guess I can pay you. How much silver do we owe you for the first load?"

"Eighteen," the woodsman replied.

"That's simple enough. Come, let's go to the treasury. Aranka, I need your key. I only carry one," Tristan said, rising from his seat

Aranka flipped a thin, gold chain with an iron key attached over her head and tossed it to Tristan. He snatched it from the air then nodded to the exit. The two men passed through the corridors of the Lodge. Carvings of animal heads grinned at them as they passed. The iron-barred windows let in the pastel spring light. One of the kitchen boys darted across their way from an intersecting hall.

"Hold, boy," Tristan commanded. "Wait up!"

The young man returned to the huntsman at once, eyes cast to the floor. "Yessir?" he asked.

Tristan put his hands on his hips and stared down at the lad. "Have you seen Halbert this morning by any chance?"

The boy shook his head. "He asked for trail provision two evenings past. I wouldn't expect him to be back yet."

"Trail rations. How much?" asked Parnell.

"Five days' worth," the boy said.

Tristan scrunched his eyes together. "Thanks. You can go back to whatever it was you were doing," he said.

The boy scampered off down the hall. Parnell looked over at the hunter.

"Why would he leave?" the lumberjack asked.

Tristan grunted. "No idea. I'm going to find out, though. Let's get to the treasury so you can be on your way. I want those timbers here as quickly as possible."

"Understood."

They came to the apartments allotted to the council members. Tristan checked his door to see if Mikhelena was there, but the room held nothing but still air and silent furniture. He frowned. A look of concern washed over his face. They continued to the door marked with the lion. He placed his hand on the brow of the beast and waited a moment. A quick snapping sound told him the lock undid itself.

"The treasury is here. Please wait while I get what we owe you," Tristan said with a faked smile.

He ambled over to a heavy iron chest. A year ago, Leo had given Tristan a new scimitar in this very room. *I wish I were anywhere but here. I belong in the wilderness. Managing inventories and paying woodsmen is a job for a clerk not a warrior.*

Tristan inserted the keys into the locks and turned them. The top jumped open. It was empty. Tristan's eyes widened. He scraped his nails over the sides and bottom, hoping there was some secret compartment. Nothing. Beads of sweat appeared on his brow.

"How could this be?" Tristan whispered to himself.

"Everything alright in there?" called Parnell from outside the room.

Tristan kicked the lid shut. "One moment."

Did someone move it? How could it possibly be gone?

He shuffled through the door and closed it behind him.

"I can't pay you today, Parnell. You'll just have to wait," Tristan said.

Parnell shook his head. "Can't do that. I got men needing to feed their families. The merchants just arrived, and that means all the woodcutters are anxious to buy. Workers gotta get paid, sir, and if you can't buy my time, there's plenty in the village who can."

"You can't give me a few days, two days even?"

"No, sir."

Tristan folded his arms on his chest and looked away. His mind raced. *Where can I come up with that now? I can't ask anyone else. If I fail in this responsibility, I'll never be trusted again.* Then an idea struck him.

"Follow me," Tristan said as he brushed past.

They returned to Tristan's apartment. He went to the foot of his bed and opened a massive trunk at the end of it. He laid his hands on two fresh wolf pelts and pulled them out.

Pressing the pelts into Parnell's chest he said, "Here. Take these. Just got 'em a couple days ago. That's at least twenty silvers right there."

"Fine specimens. These will work," Parnell said, pulling the pelts close to his nostril and sniffing them.

Tristan reached down into his trunk again and pulled out a bundle of long silver braids: giant hair. He piled them on top of the pelts.

"Another twenty, maybe thirty. That will take care of the next shipment and more. Deliver your wood to the gate and the northeast section of the wall. Those are the two places most in need. Got it?"

Parnell bowed his head. "It'll be there."

They left the room, and Tristan locked his door behind him. "Can you see yourself out Parnell?" he asked.

"Sure enough," the woodman said as he sauntered down the hall.

"Good. I have something I need to attend to."

Parnell left and Tristan tromped off to the library. *I've got to find Halbert. Maybe he knows what's happened. How could the entire treasury be gone? It must have been moved without my knowing. He shouldn't have done that without informing the council first.*

"We have to find Halbert," Tristan announced as he burst through the doors of the library. "He's moved the treasury.

"How do you know it was him? Aranka asked.

"He's the only one who carries a copy of both keys. I had to pay Parnell out of my own pocket, for which I WILL be reimbursed. Can you send out birds with messages to the troupe leaders in the field? Tell them to send Halbert here if they see him."

"Halbert's outside the village?" Aranka asked, setting her pile of books down.

Tristan nodded. "I think so. One of the kitchen boys said he took five days' worth of provisions and left."

"He might be coming back then. When did he leave?"

"The day before yesterday. Just after I saw him, I imagine."

Aranka cleared a space on the table near a vase of white catchfly blooms. Then, snatching up a parchment and a charcoal pencil, she began writing. Tristan placed her key on the table then and turned toward the windows.

"I'll send the messages, but it is possible he is on his way back. Better inform the gatewatch to be looking for him," she said.

Tristan rolled his eyes and left. He took a detour to the infirmary. There, he discovered Mikhelena kneeling over a woman from the village. The villager was pale, clammy. Her skin glistened like wet, unfired porcelain. Tristan knelt next to his beloved.

"She looks bad," he whispered.

"Shhh. She'll be alright. This is the worst of it," Mikhelena said, continuing to dab at the woman's forehead with a cloth.

"I came to check on you. Are you okay? Do you need a break?"

Mikhelena bit her upper lip. "I'm tired but doing okay. These people need me. I can't figure out what's wrong, though. Darian and Josiah have never seen anything like this."

"You need to rest."

She gave him a furtive smile. "I will. I promise. Just not now. There's so many all at once and there's nothing that seems to connect these people. One's a farmer, another is Damion the cobbler, Resivere is a cooper, Melinda is a weaver, Harlan works in the mines. Damion is well off, Harlan is poor. I don't know what's caused this,""

"Resivere? I saw him, and several of these others, with Devereaux near the commons the other day. In fact, Halbert was with them, too. Is he here by chance?" Tristan asked.

"Haven't seen him."

"Devereaux?"

"He left when Juanitos showed up," Mikhelena said.

Tristan moved closer to her until his shoulder touched hers. "What can I get you?" he asked, hoping to catch her eyes with his.

"I'm trying to think of some root or berry that might help them. If I come up with something, do you think you can get a party to go and fetch it for me?" she asked, continuing her work.

"I'll do all that I can and more," he said.

"Thank you," she said, standing up. "I need to go check on that one in the corner. I'm just glad none of the children have caught this yet. I don't think their little bodies could handle the strain."

She stretched for a moment then gave him a quick peck on the lips. Electricity. Tristan nodded and watched Mikhelena go. He imagined himself holding her in his arms, the smell of her hair, the intimacy of her breath on his neck. She seemed so far away now.

Tristan spied Juanitos in his priestly garb, praying over another of the sick villagers. Tristan soft-stepped his way toward the minister, weaving between the half-conscious patients.

Placing a hand on the minister's shoulder, he said, "Pastor?"

Juanitos flinched and looked up at him. "Sorry, my son. I was deep in prayer. What can I do for you?"

Tristan helped the old man to his feet. "Have you seen anything like this before?" the huntsman asked.

The gentle priest shook his head. "I've seen many diseases, but none like this. There's no fever, no spots. What is ailing them?"

"I wish I knew," Tristan said, pausing for a moment. "Have you seen Halbert DeLongue?"

"Not in some time," Juanitos said, collecting his holy implements from the bed.

"I must speak with him. If he comes by your church, can you send someone to get me?" Tristan asked.

"Of course, my son. Is something troubling you?"

Tristan stared out the window on the opposite wall. "Not yet. Maybe soon."

"A cryptic answer," Juanitos said, leaning on his back foot.

"I'll let you know, Pastor. Thank you," Tristan said with a smile.

He gave Juanitos a pat on the arm and left the infirmary. He marched to the gate. Markus, the new gatecaptain, standing watch in a small tower built into the western gatepost waved as Tristan drew near.

"Any news?" Tristan asked.

Markus looked out over the top of the archway into the nearby forest from his perch. "Nothing yet, sir.'

Nothing yet. "If you see Halbert come through here, tell him to report to me immediately. Got that?" Tristan said, pointing at him.

"Of course. Anything the matter?"

"Just some misplaced items. Make sure he comes to me. Send someone with him if you have to."

Markus saluted. "It will be done—hey, isn't that him now?"

Tristan shot a glance to the road leading from Vitalba. Trudging his way toward the gate was the missing huntsman. "Halbert, where have you been? Get over here, I need to ask you something."

The man looked startled and ran.

"Halbert? Halbert!" Tristan yelled and the two of them gave chase. Tristan hopped a fallen log just off the path with Markus following close after.

They gained ground on Halbert who stole a glance backwards. That momentary lapse of attention to his direction caused Halbert to miss a divot in the mud. The fleeing huntsman tumbled to the wet ground. Tristan pounced on him, jerking him up by the shirt collars.

"Halbert! What were you doing? Why were you running away?" he growled.

"I'm so sorry, Tristan," Halbert said, holding his hands up in defense.

"For what?"

I didn't think I could possibly lose it all. I wanted to—I had faith in The Cause. I was going to win so much we'd never have to worry about money ever again."

"What are you talking about?" Tristan demanded.

"The treasury. I've lost it all. Every single coin is gone."

Chapter 10:

TRUTH OF THE MATTER

Tristan leaned on an elbow on the great oak table of the library across from Aranka. Patric dug something out of his fingernails to his right. Off in a chair near the great glass window of the library, Devereaux reclined with his cap pulled low over his face.

"We're all here, Tristan. Those who could make it, anyway. What's so important that we had to call a meeting of the council so soon and without the full membership being present?" Patric asked.

"Halbert, come here and explain to the council what happened," Tristan called, digging his nails into the arms of his chair.

Halbert entered the library, hat held in shaking hands, and approached his fellow council members. He stood still for a moment, as if he didn't know what to do.

"I thought he was out of town," Patric hissed.

"He was," Tristan answered.

"Well?" Aranka asked, glaring at Halbert.

Halbert inhaled deeply but never took his eyes off the floor. He began, "When I was put in charge of the builders and had to pay the woodsmen, the carpenters, and the workers who are fixing the stockade. I got to see how many of them lived. You know, we're so lucky in this Lodge. We have everything we need. Many of them don't. I wanted to help. I heard Devereaux talking to a group of villagers a few weeks ago—"

At this, Devereaux cleared his throat from under his feathered cap. He was fiddling with a small wooden trinket in the shape of a bull, holding it up to the light. Tristan turned his eyes to him, to see if he might say something, but Devereaux never uttered a word.

Halbert continued, "I was struck with a powerful urge to help them. A couple of days before, I overheard one of the new merchants tell about a man far in the south of Celandine Valley who can turn small amounts of wealth into large riches. So, I took some money from the treasury and went to see for myself. I found him, deep within a garden near the great slough."

Tristan straightened up in his chair. "You didn't mention he was in a garden before. Did the garden have a high wall with no gate around it? Maybe some old, dilapidated sheds or outbuildings?"

Halbert shook his head. "No, it was surrounded by beautiful, well-trimmed hedges. I found him in the center. All around him were piles of gold coins, works of art, bars of silver! I thought I had found the answer to all the workers' problems. He showed me many magical devices. One was a hollowed-out tree. Another was a box lined with golden cloth. He had me place my bag of coins in the box. He shut the lid, turned it over, then opened it again. Inside was a new bag with three times the coins."

"Sounds like dark magic to me, Halbert," Aranka said, adjusting her specs.

He nodded. "I realize that now, but I saw the money. I brought it back to town. Deveraux called another meeting, and I passed out the coins because he said it would bring the people faith—"

Devereaux cleared his throat a second time.

"Something to add?" Aranka asked in an annoyed tone.

"Not at all Madam, I am merely suffering from a little congestion from all the pollen," he answered.

"If you please, then, stay silent," Aranka growled, turning her attention back to him.

"And so it goes," Devereaux replied.

"Go ahead, Halbert. Tell them the rest," Tristan said in a soft tone.

Halbert flashed a nervous smile and rotated his hat in his hands. "I figured if a small bag could produce so much coin, a large bag would be enough to last us years. Maybe longer. So, I took the rest of the money. I never thought we'd need to pay the woodsmen so soon. I thought they'd work at least a week before they'd ask for any, so I didn't leave anything behind. I'm so sorry. Tristan, Patric, Eldo, Aranka, I'm so, so sorry!"

"Nevermind that. Tell us what happened," Patric demanded, shifting his eyes from person to person in the room.

"I went back to the garden. It was harder to find the man in the middle this time, but I got there. I placed the sack of coins in the box. He turned it over, just like before. Nothing changed. Everything happened the same way, but when he opened it, it was empty. Nothing. I looked at him for an explanation, but he only smiled and said sometimes fortune smiles and sometimes it frowns. I asked for my money back, but he refused. I looked for a pile of gold or some bars of silver to take, but all the treasure that had been lying around before was gone. The garden was empty, barren. I panicked."

"For what reason did you think this would be wise, Halbert?" Aranka growled.

Halbert stared at the floor. "I thought I could be a hero. I wanted to do something that everyone would remember and sing about for ages to come. It seemed simple, a guarantee. I didn't know what would happen."

Aranka leaned back in her chair. She closed her eyes and slowly shook her head. "No one ever sings about great treasure, just great deeds, Hal. Where is this garden?" she said in a low, angry voice.

"West and south of the swamp."

Aranka looked at Patric and said, "We have to reclaim our treasury. Sounds like a warlock, or some human trickster masquerading as one."

Patric put his hand on his chest. "I can't go. I leave tomorrow for Everpass."

"For what?" Tristan asked.

"I don't have to answer to you," Patric clapped back. "I have to go. That should be good enough. I think more needs to be done to protect travelers as they pass the Shouters from outside the valley on their way to Everpass Hold. I'm meeting a cadre of merchants there to see what can be done."

Aranka rolled her eyes. "Tristan?"

"What about Valere, Hedvidge, Eldo, Nicole? One of them should do it, especially Valere since he oversaw the warriors. I'm in charge of village safety, remember? The stockade is my job right now."

"I've seen to it that, going forward, the woodsmen will be paid from my own pocket, Aranka," Patric said.

Aranka nodded. "Tristan, the others are out on patrol. Nicole is in the mountains, gathering medicine for what is attacking the villagers' health. Hedvidge and Valere are in the north, trying to stop Gibbous and Drastist from helping the dwarves get whatever it is they are using in their explosives. Eldo is outside Celandine, and I cannot leave the library unattended, so you must go."

Secretly, Tristan's heart leaped. Halbert mentioned piles of treasure somewhere in the garden maze. He was dying to get out of the village and on an adventure. "I just don't want you to feel like I'm abandoning my post," Tristan said.

"You are not. Take this foolish huntsman with you so he can show you the way," Aranka said, pointing to Halbert. "Deveraux, do you want to accompany them?"

The huntsman sat up in his chair. "No, no I think not. I wouldn't want to be tempted to, um, to go out with this cold. I may get worse, you know. What sort of huntsman would add another patient to the infirmary right now?"

"In that case, The Cause be with you, Tristan. Choose your team and leave immediately. Who knows how long this character will remain in the garden?" Aranka said.

"And so it goes," added Devereaux with a tip of his black-plumed hat.

Tristan rose and brushed past Halbert without saying a word. He made his way to the infirmary to find Mikhelena.

"Darian, where's Miki?" he asked.

Darian shrugged his shoulders. "I think she might be sleeping. She looked exhausted, so I told her I'd handle the sick for a while."

"How are they doing?" Tristan asked, eyeing a sleeping young girl on a nearby cot.

"Stable, I think."

Tristan nodded and went up to his apartment. He cracked open the door, doing his best not to make a sound. With silent steps, he slid into the room.

"Hi, Tristan."

He froze. "Did I wake you?"

Mikhelena appeared from behind the screen in the room, just buttoning up her shirt. "No, I was just getting up. What did you need?"

Tristan settled on the edge of the bed. "I'm being sent out on a hunt," Tristan replied.

Her face grew a tired smile and she said, "That's what you've been wanting. I'm happy for you. Where to?"

"A garden Halbert knows of."

"Be safe, my love," she said, finishing her change of attire.

"Well," Tristan started, rubbing the back of his neck. "I was hoping you'd come."

She paused and stared at him. "Tristan, I have much to do here. The villagers are ill."

"I asked Darian. He said the villagers are stable. We're going to need a healer. Nicole is off collecting. I've never trusted Darian all that much in a fight. You're the best we've got."

She sat on the bed and looked away. "What if one dies while I'm gone?"

He crawled over to her. "Could you save them if you were here?"

"I don't know," she said, biting her upper lip. "Maybe."

"Miki, I really need you. Halbert took the entire treasury there and lost it to a wizard or dwarf or something. We have to get it back."

"A dwarf?"

"Possibly."

"If it were a dwarf, for certain, then I wouldn't hesitate. But let me decide. Don't force me."

Sensing her angst, he backed off the mattress and stepped away. "I wouldn't, and I'll support your choice. You know what we need. It would be better for us to have a healer we can trust, one with field experience. Darian and Josiah have little time in the field. You decide, though. We're leaving out in an hour. If you choose not to come, send Josiah. He'll do. He's good with a mace."

"He's not fully trained," she said solemnly.

"He'll do. I don't wish to take you away if you'd rather not."

She didn't answer.

Tristan left and went to the provisioning room. He packed two weeks' worth of rations and an extra blanket. He picked up his sword, freshly sharpened by the Lodge weaponmaster. He then went to the practice yard and recruited four hunters to go with him. When he got to the great room, Okacheybay was waiting for him with Halbert and Mikhelena.

Tristan smiled at Mikhelena. "Glad you came. Let's go."

When they left the village, Halbert was put in front of the group with Okacheybay and Stanislav, a veteran recently returned from outside the village. Emma and Analor, two huntresses, traded stories about archery and fletching while Tristan and Mikhelena stayed in the rear.

"No progress in curing the villagers?" he asked her.

She shook her head no.

"I'm sure you and Darian and Nicole will come up with something eventually," he said.

Again, she shook her head no.

Tristan reached behind his pack and pulled out a lump of bread filled with raisins, nuts, and dates. He tore off a chunk and handed it to her. She nodded, took it, and began putting small bites inside her mouth.

Spring was rising from the south. The air smelled of fresh rain and wet wood. The sky, dotted with puffy white clouds, adorned itself in a deeper shade of blue than just a month before. Swift breezes caressed Tristan's face, tracing quick paths through the wispy hairs on his chin and neck. A golden afternoon sun laced the road ahead in iridescent light revealing damp earth and the first green of the season: lime-colored mosses burgeoning on the borders of the pathway.

Tristan was grateful for the end of winter. The cold seeped into his bones that year. There was no escaping its icy grip. He felt trapped, and now with the coming change in the weather, he welcomed a change in his surroundings.

The huntsmen marched along Benegore's Road toward the crossing. One of the younger huntsmen asked Okacheybay to tell them stories of when he was a werewolf. Tristan could tell his friend was uncomfortable talking about that time, but Okacheybay obliged anyway. Tristan bowed his head, and his heart beat faster as his friend spoke about the moment he turned away from the Unhallowed life and re-embraced his humanity.

"There is no servitude worse than being a slave to one's fears," Okacheybay said.

"Why's that?" asked Emma, catching up to him.

"Hmph. Fear comes from your own mind, and how do you defeat your own mind?"

"I don't know," she replied.

"The only way I know is with the help of another. In my case, it was Tristan and Mersha who gave me the chance to decide what I wanted in life. I could have stayed in my wolf form. The power it gave me was so easy to have, easy to control. Or so I thought. The truth is, it controlled me. I gave it up, though, for the life I have now."

"Glad you did," said Stanislav.

"Me, too. So, while I could tell you of midnight raids against the vampire or the—"

"You fought vampires when you were a werewolf?"

Okacheybay paused for a moment. "Yes, some time ago. Years and years ago, before they started working together."

The questions zipped back and forth for hours. Finally, it was time to make camp. The hunters took refuge alongside the trail behind a small knob that would protect them from the night wind.

Tristan got only two hours of sleep when Emma woke him for his turn on watch. He sat up, head groggy, and smiled at her through filmy eyes.

"How'd everything go?" he asked.

She brushed a strand of long, dark hair behind her ear. "Just fine. Quiet really. I'm just glad I get the whole night to sleep now."

"This your first time on the trail overnight?" Tristan asked, rising to a knee.

She shook her head. "No, I've gone to the safehouse and back to the village a few times escorting coal carts and merchants."

Tristan grimaced and nodded. "It's best, on watch, to keep your hair pulled back until you sleep. Having it over your ears can dampen the slightest sound a wolf or raven makes on approach. The wind could blow it in your eyes just when the hounds of a sorceress or the constructs of a warlock might flash into view."

Emma's face was suddenly lined with worry. "Oh. So sorry. I didn't mean to..."

Tristan smiled and nodded. "No need to apologize. I've made plenty worse mistakes on the trail myself. You're doing better than I did. Just put it in your mind for the next watch."

"Thanks. I think I'm going to like it on the trail," she said.

Tristan gave her a slow nod then gazed off in the distance. "Good night," he said.

She nestled into her bedroll, and Tristan was alone. The valley seemed unusually tranquil. Even the chirping crickets were muffled in the chilly spring night. When he woke Mikhelena for the third watch, he stayed up with her for a bit.

"You were quiet today," he said.

"Yeah." Her voice was dead, emotionless.

Tristan hoped his observation would prompt her to explain, but he could see she was going to force him to ask.

"Why was that?" he asked, leaning forward, attempting to make eye contact.

"I'm, I'm just disappointed in myself," she said, hunching over a bit more.

Tristan raised his eyebrows. "In what? How's that even possible?"

She shifted a little away from him. "I don't know if I made the right choice to come."

Tristan moved closer. "I'm glad you did."

"I'm sure you are," she said, then kicked at a stone with the heel of her boot.

He put his hand on her back and gently rubbed between her shoulders. "Why are you unhappy about that?"

"How can you know what's the best course?" she asked, finally looking him in the eyes. "If I stay to make the sick happy, I fail you. If I leave to make you happy, I fail the village. So, what's a person to do? How do I know who to let down, and who to please?"

The song of a nightingale took Tristan's attention away for a moment. Mikhelena returned her gaze to the starlit blanket of night.

He looked back at her and said, "I don't think it's possible to make everyone happy. It's hard enough just to make *one* person happy. I spent years trying to please my father, and it seemed like I never could. Besides, you wouldn't have failed me If you chose to stay. I would've known you were making the right decision. I trust your intuition, Miki."

"Thanks, but I'm not sure. I don't want to disappoint anyone. How can I *fail* to *fail* one side? I just want everyone to get what they need."

"Tonight, you are here. In that, you are doing something good."

"But is it the *right* good?"

"We'll make it the right good together," he answered.

Tristan took her into his arms and held her. He squeezed her tightly. Electricity. Mikhelena began to sob. Her mourning echoed in the black sky of night.

At first light, they started off once more and reached the safehouse by lunch. From there, Halbert led them south. Recollections of past traumas in the great slough in the southern reaches of the valley crept over Tristan.

He remembered his first encounter with Drastist. He remembered his father asleep under the fount of many hands. He remembered losing Bartonomous to Sidaxa. When they drew near to the swamp's border, Tristan was relieved when Halbert told them to head west instead.

They traced their way along the outskirts of the slough into rockier territory. The patchy grass interspersed with oleander triggered something else in Tristan's mind.

"Hey, Stilnife's home is near here. He might know something more about this garden. Let's pay him a visit," Tristan said.

"Is it far from our destination?" Okacheybay asked.

"Ask Halbert."

"If he doesn't live far, we can still make it before sundown," Halbert said.

The huntsmen headed off, now led by Tristan. Mikhelena hiked close by his side. Tristan's memory did not fail him. They reached the base of the rocky hill on which Stilnife built his home by early afternoon. The climb up was every bit as difficult as the last time. However, when they reached the top, the scene was very different from what he expected.

Stilnife's hovel lay in ruin, crushed from top to bottom.

Chapter 11:
THE HEDGE MAZE

The inside was devastated. Shards from the roof timbers littered the ground. The walls and floor bore deep gashes, and not a trace of human activity remained. Tristan rushed in, calling Stilnife's name. The frame of the cot where Mersha had slept contorted in "V" shape, its edges singed black with fire. The rock where they had eaten breakfast so many months ago was cracked down the middle; the stone stools tossed aside. Even the hearth was torn asunder.

Tristan searched the hovel, flinging the detritus out of his way. The air choked his throat with ash as he rummaged through the debris. Yet, not a single overturned stone or burnt rack of wood yielded any clue as to what happened nor where the silent huntsman might be.

"Looks like a giant attack," Analor offered, peering in.

"What are you looking for, my friend?" asked Okacheybay.

Tristan kicked a pile of ashes. "Bones, a body, anything. He's not here."

Mikhelena came by his side. "Maybe he got out alive."

"Maybe," Tristan said, putting his hands on his hips.

Halbert and the other huntsmen were waiting outside when Tristan emerged. One opened his mouth as if to ask a question, then cast his eyes to the ground and remained silent.

"There's nothing for us here. Time to go," Tristan said at last.

They descended the hill and headed east. After some time, Tristan looked to his right. He pointed to the north and said, "That's where Thaul's garden was. Way over there. I half expected you to take us there, Halbert."

Halbert nodded and said, "I just want to say I'm sorry again, Tristan."

"Your heart was in the right place, but you failed to use any wisdom. The Cause does not bless reckless fate. It never wants us to test our luck."

As they continued on their way, the images of Stilnife's decimated dwelling rolled in Tristan's imagination. It was almost hateful the way the humble hovel was ravaged. A place that had once been a refuge, a source of comfort was violated and destroyed.

"You seem quiet, Tristan," Okacheybay said, looking up at the sky.

Tristan glanced at his friend. "Sorry."

"What is on your mind, if I may ask?"

Tristan shrugged as they kept walking. "Just thinking about Stilnife's home."

"Ah, your thoughts are always drawn to one home or another. Did you know him well?" Okacheybay asked.

"Not too well," Tristan said with a wrinkled forehead.

"Still. It is a shame."

"Yeah. It just worries me. It's as if the Unhallowed are changing their tactics. Why come all the way out here to attack one huntsman? What's the point?" "To strike fear?" Okacheybay offered.

Tristan shook his head. "Few people knew Stilnife lived there. It's like they're trying to eliminate our presence here. Stilnife's home, Thaul's garden—both attacked. The slough isn't far, and I think I overheard several troupe leaders say they refuse to patrol the swamps anymore."

"Sidaxa's dogs have grown more vicious in the last year," Okacheybay said.

"Shhhhh," warned Tristan. "Not loud enough for Miki to hear. I know she still thinks about her sister."

"And your father. You last saw him in the slough, did you not?" Okacheybay asked.

Tristan cast down his eyes and nodded. "Yes, the swamps have grown more dangerous. But, why now?"

"Perhaps it's related to Halbert's discovery in the hedges?" Analor said.

"Perhaps. Aside from that, though, I think we're going to need more fortifications," Tristan said.

Okacheybay wagged his finger. "We are struggling to rebuild the stockade of the village. Could we start projects elsewhere as well?"

Tristan shrugged. "We might have to, Oak. We just added a bunch of huntsmen to our ranks last year. I'd hate to start losing them to ambushes if Unhallowed are the ones hunting *us* for a change."

Okacheybay grunted an assent as they reached the bottom of the hill. Halbert led on, passing through a scraggly forest of tamarisk trees. The path seemed interminable. Tristan wondered if Halbert hadn't gotten lost. At last, they came to the entrance of the hedges.

"I remember this spot," Tristan said.

"How?" Analor asked.

Tristan eyed the entrance as he slid off one of the straps of his pack. "I saw it when we were climbing up to Thaul's garden. It looked like the maze farmers build with their hay bales near the gardens at harvest time for the children."

"It is something like a maze," Halbert said, head hanging low.

"What's inside?" Mikhelena asked as she moved closer behind Tristan.

Halbert looked into the maze. "Inside the paths, it's different every time. The center is the same, though. There's the Master of Games in the middle with his magic boxes."

Tristan moved a few paces to the right where several filbert bushes were growing unusually close together. Their limbs were just now sprouting with pale green leaves. He brushed aside the interlacing branches and examined the ground beneath. The heavy smell of fresh growth nearly overpowered his senses.

"Pile your gear in this," he commanded. "I don't know what we might find in there, and I don't want us encumbered. The smell will hide it from animals and the branches and leaves should keep it hidden from Unhallowed passing by."

The others sauntered over and shoved their packs beneath the tangle of twigs, hidden from view. When all was in its place, they turned, drew their weapons, and entered the hedge maze. Immediately, the world grew silent. The sky turned dark. Stars peeked in and out of clouds, twinkling down on the huntsmen. Tristan had taken the lead but pushed his way back out again. The sky was lighter, the birds sang outside the maze. He tested the inside of the hedge again: dark, silent. He gave Okacheybay a grave stare.

"We're in an enchanted place. Be on your guard," Okacheybay said.

"But there's never been any danger here previously," said Halbert.

Emma took a step back. "I don't like the feel of it."

"Halbert, you lead the way," Tristan said, gesturing down the path.

"You're acting so paranoid, Tristan. There's nothing to worry about here. Parier has always welcomed me and any of the townsfolk I brought."

"You've brought townsfolk here, too?" Tristan asked.

"Y-yes. Why?" Halbert asked.

Tristan shook his head in disappointment. He took Halbert by the shoulder and gave him a shove down the path. They proceeded down the walkway. The corridors grew wide. The sides were adorned with a stone menagerie. Graven images of beasts, demons, and wild amalgamations of men and animals lined the way forward with menacing stares. They passed through them until they came to an intersection blocked by a winged sculpture.

"How do we get past it? Climb?" Tristan asked with a nod toward the statue.

"I don't know. This place is different every time," Halbert said.

"Anything we should worry about?" Tristan asked.

Halbert spun around with a smile and said, "There's nothing to fear. I've been here several times, and there's really not much going on—"

A bizarre series of cracking noises preceded a dark form dropping from the sky next to Halbert. Winged and demon-like, it swung a muscled arm against the unsuspecting huntsman, knocking him far down the path.

"The master told you never to bring huntsmen, Halbert," it growled.

The hunters' weapons instantly sprung to life with fires of gold, crimson, sapphire, topaz, and violet. Tristan lunged at the creature. The point of his burning blue broadsword struck between two of its ribs. The blade merely glanced off. Mikhelena whirled around, switching from Tristan's right to his left, slicing the beast on its back. Her strike, likewise, failed to break its stony skin.

The beast turned on Tristan and brought a massive, clawed hand down upon him. Tristan saw it coming and raised his shield; deflecting the monster's arm across its chest. He dodged out of the way and Emma thrust her short spear at the winged beast. Again, the fiery blade did no damage.

"It's a gargoyle! Blades are no use. Slam him with your shields!" Okacheybay called out.

Stanislav rushed past Emma and rammed the monster with his shield. The winged creature pounded its fists on the hunter's back, dropping him to a knee. Mikhelena, still in good position, smashed the edge of her shield against the monster's hip in three quick, piston-like blows. The creature bent, as if in pain, then twirled around and swept her legs with its serpentine tail. Halbert's shield came flying from afar. It caught the brute in the eye, shattering the left side of the its face. Reeling back, clutching its wound, the gargoyle howled in rage.

With a flap of its wings, the creature over-leaped the huntsmen and landed before Stanislav. The mutant grabbed the huntsman by the collar and threw him into Halbert. The two of them careened into the shrubs.

Tristan, seeing his chance, charged. He dove at its legs, remembering the lessons he learned fighting giants long ago. He tackled his enemy and knocked it to the ground. The attack fractured its legs with a radial pattern of cracks emanating in all directions from its stony knees.

A flaming arrow whizzed through the air, striking the bat-winged-goblin on the chest as it tried to pull itself up. The projectile splintered into a dozen white shards and ricocheted off into the darkness.

"Analor, arrows are useless against this creature! This beast requires heavy blows to kill," Tristan called.

Emma flipped her spear around and used the Eldanar bulge at the opposite end like a club. Her strike hit the creature in the thigh. It dropped to the ground again, using its wings to hold itself up in a half-inclined position. Chunks of green-grey stone scattered in all directions. Stanislav recovered and jumped high into the air, then brought his shield down upon the creature's back. A spider's web of cracks spread to one of the wings. Tristan attempted another shield strike to the monster's head, but it raised its arm and blocked his attack, losing two fingers in the process.

Mikhelena let loose a war cry and took her shield to the back of the creature's neck. The beast swiveled around and clutched the huntress by her throat. Stanislav and Tristan instantly attacked, shattering the gargoyle's arm in two places. Analor planted her mace between the abomination's shoulder blades. It reared back and roared in agony.

Emma put both hands on her spear and swung the heavy bulbous end down with all her might. The weapon caught the gargoyle and shattered its head, finishing the beast. The headless body slumped forward and fell flat to the ground. Tristan saw the monster's claw still clenching Mikhelena's neck. Her eyes were wide in panic; her skin took on a bluish tint.

He rushed over, dropping his weapons on the way. He wrapped his fingers around the thumb and forefinger of the stone fist. Tristan pulled with all his might. Mikhelena began to thrash, her legs and arms flailing helplessly. Tristan closed his eyes and focused all his energy into his fingers. His hands ached from the strain and, for a moment, the clenched fist seemed permanently locked around her throat. Suddenly, the stone cracked, and Tristan's arms flew apart. Mikhelena was free, gasping for air.

Tristan dove to her side. She rolled onto her back, the color returned to her cheeks. Her eyes, which had been rolled back in her head, came forward and refocused. Stanislav kicked the stone hand into the shrubbery.

"I'm fine," she rasped.

"Bless The Cause," Tristan said.

Tristan helped her to her feet. She wobbled for a moment, then dropped back to her knees. Tristan knelt next to her and tried to lift her once again, but she leaned over and scooped up some of the shards from the gargoyle.

"What are you doing?" Tristan asked.

Mikhelena did not look up. "These may be useful for something. I'll take them to Garrov to see what he can do with them."

"I've only just heard of these creatures. I had no idea that some of them were in the valley," Okacheybay said.

"Who told you about them?" Emma asked.

"Eldo, the Provisioner."

"The old gatekeeper?" she asked.

"Yes. He says they are guardians of pleasure, constructs made by the Unhallowed but not fully Unhallowed themselves," said Okacheybay.

"Makes sense," Stanislav said with a shrug.

Tristan grabbed Halbert and pulled him close. "Any more statues like that along the way?"

"N-Not that I remember," Halbert stammered.

"What did he mean about not bringing any of us here?" Analor asked.

Halbert shrugged. "The master of the garden doesn't want too many to come. He wants it kept secret."

"Why?" Tristan asked.

"I don't know," Halbert said with a shrug.

"I'm liking this mission less and less. Let's get going and be done with it," Tristan said, releasing Halbert from his grasp.

Mikhelena finished picking her specimens, and they moved on. Halbert led them, but rather than a relaxed walk through the verdant hedges, they stalked their way down the perplexing paths. After a few more twists and turns, they came to a bureau with a mirror blocking the way forward. The mirror was glowing with ghostly blue light and the image reflected in the glass was distorted and bizarre.

"My skin looks charred in this mirror," said Emma.

"Careful, this place is full of evil," Mikhelena said, moving toward the front.

As soon as those words left her mouth, the great looking glass broke from its frame, enlarging to enormous size. It crushed the bureau beneath with a thunderous blast and vibrated with radiant energy. Suddenly, the glass shattered into ten thousand tiny fragments. Jagged shards streaked the huntsmen with tiny lacerations. The ruined mirror left behind a thrumming portal. From within the swirling purple, green, and grey cloud, a man with white beard and green cloak stretched himself inside it, holding the edges of the portal open with his hands and feet.

"Drastist!" Tristan exclaimed.

From behind the warlock, a werewolf leaped onto the path. Dropping to its hands and raising its feet, it kicked Halbert into the bushes.

"Which one? Which one, my friend? Hahahaha! Which shall I grab?" Gibbous asked in his high pitched, lyrical voice.

"The girl, you fool," Drastist growled.

Tristan swung at the lycanthrope, but the mad werewolf dodged. Gibbous swept the leg of Stanislav with its foot, then leapt to the far side of the huntsmen. His massive fur-covered claws snatched Emma by the shoulders with inhuman strength and speed. In a single motion, it hauled her through the portal in a backflip. Drastist nodded his head and smiled at the huntsmen.

"Ta-ta! She'll be at Dreadstone Keep if you need her," the warlock said.

The ethereal doorway began to snap shut. Tristan dropped to a knee, drew an Eldanar dagger from his boot and flung it through the portal. The blade, tumbling end over end, buried itself in the gut of the warlock.

"Vicious fool," Drastist hissed as the portal constricted further.

"You hold on to that. Someday I'll take it off your corpse," Tristan called.

Drastist hissed as the portal condensed and disappeared out of sight. Tristan swung his sword where the portal used to be, but to no avail. All had vanished.

Tristan found Halbert and shoved him down the path. "First this was just about money. Now it cost a huntsman's life. Get us to the center now!"

Chapter 12:
THE HEDGE-MAGE

The evergreen corridors opened into a square with a garden at the center of the labyrinth. Heaps of gold nuggets, silver coins, gemstones, and all manner of wealth and opulence piled against the walls. An inner ring of cypress inlaid tables, stands, and intricate mechanical contraptions framed a well-manicured lawn.

At the head of the ring stood a hunched figure upon a red marble pedestal. His blue robes, fringed with gold and white animal fur, highlighted a pair of red-tinted spectacles resting on the tip of his up-turned nose. Upon his head sat the skull of a bull, completely out of proportion for the diminutive Unhallowed, almost comical. Gold and silver rings adorned the dwarf's chubby fingers which constantly fidgeted with the fur lining the chest of his robe. His pinkish skin bore many wrinkles, damaged by the bright summer sun.

"Not a warlock, but a dwarf," growled Mikhelena.

"Halbert. So, you *did* have dealings with a dwarf?" Tristan barked.

Halbert gave him a hurt look. "He seemed taller before."

Tristan shot him an angry glance then stepped closer to the grinning Unhallowed. The huntsmen, flaming weapons glowing with flickering light, spread out among the gold-laden contraptions. Tristan rose to his full stature and stared at the grinning dwarf, eye to eye.

"You are the one swindling my people of their coin?" the huntsman asked.

The dwarf bowed very low. "Nay, mighty hunter. I have done no such thing. I merely provided them the chance to increase their fortune. I am but a humble servant of Vitalba and Celandine."

"Kill him, Tristan. Don't let him beguile you with his words," Mikhelena said as she readied her weapons and moved behind him.

Tristan adjusted his grip on his sword and pointed it at Halbert. "This man says he brought you our treasury. You took it from him and gave nothing in return. Is this so?"

"Esteemed huntsman, I--of course--had no idea. As I said, I simply offer those in the valley a chance to increase their wealth. I am not to judge how they accumulate it in the first place. How can I know?" asked the dwarf while wringing his hands.

Tristan shook his head, lowering his sword to his side. "You will return all you have taken."

The dwarf bowed again. "Forgive me, great stalker of beasts. I cannot do that. We made a true bargain. The handsome Halbert had his opportunity, and what is chance without risk? Surely you recognize that all gain is based on taking some risks. Is that so wrong?"

"What's wrong is you took no care to ask the people that have come how they got their coin, whether they could withstand the loss of their coin, or if they understood the risk they were taking. How many have come to your maze?"

"Dozens! Many of them are happy and come back," answered the dwarf, again making a bow.

"And some have been ruined. You will return what you have taken. Now!" Tristan ordered.

The dwarf raised his hands. "Forgive me. I cannot. I do not have the power to restore what has been lost."

Tristan moved to the table before the dwarf. The dead sockets of the bovine skull stared at Tristan. The huntsman turned his eyes down upon the quivering gamemaster.

"Kill him, Tris. He can't be trusted," hissed Mikhelena.

"Who has the authority and power then?" Tristan asked as he shifted his feet into a fighting stance.

"I, uh, I cannot say!"

Tristan dropped his shield with his left hand and reached across the table, pulling the dwarf off his feet. Gold coins scattered in all directions, and the dwarf closed his eyes and pulled his knees to his chest. Tristan slammed the Unhallowed to the table inlaid. The crash resounded in the center of the maze.

"Tell me," Tristan demanded, his face red with rage.

The dwarf shook his head. "No!"

Tristan brought his blue flaming blade up to the dwarf's neck. "Last chance," he said.

The dwarf's face contorted with anger. "Dreadstone!" he chirped just as he brought his hands up to Tristan's chest.

A sudden burst of energy blasted Tristan's cuirass. The force launched the hunter backwards into the shrubbery. He scrambled to his feet and raised his sword.

"You are our enemy, and because you have refused to cooperate, you will die," Tristan rasped.

Halbert stepped between Tristan and the dwarf. "Maybe we can find a way to win back what was lost. Parier is reasonable. He—"

Tristan pointed at him. "Shut your mouth, Hal, and do not open it again until we leave. Everyone else. Attack!"

"Did a warlock teach you magic, dwarf?" growled Okacheybay as he advanced.

The half-size freak leapt upon the table, producing a bull-headed wand from inside his shirtsleeves.

"Oh yes, and so much more," it screeched.

The lifeless eyes of the skull upon the Unhallowed's head came to light. The dwarf flicked its wand at Mikhelena. She raised her shield and deflected the fiery bolt. Tristan and Okacheybay charged together, but the gamemaster blinked from the table to the back of the hedgerow. Analor launched an arrow blazing with purple fire from her bow. The dwarf dodged and waved his wand in response.

A gargoyle rose from the ground, its bat-like wings stretching to their fullest extent. Mikhelena swooped in from the right, slashing a deep wound in the membrane of the gargoyle's wing. It whirled around with razor claws and swiped at her head. She blocked and struck again on its outstretched arm.

"He's got another one!" shouted Analor.

Stanislav engaged the demonic form as well, thrusting quick strikes at its chest. The winged beast maneuvered away from each one, but failed to evade another of Mikhelena's shield strikes.

Tristan cornered the dwarf. His broadsword raged with blue flame. He feigned an attack to the monster's right, and when the dwarf darted left to escape, Tristan slammed him with his bejeweled shield. The red gem in the center of the shield glowed, and a flash of brilliant light knocked the swindler to the ground. The dwarf blinked from sight then appeared on the other side of the hedges.

Tristan raised his sword for a charge. Mikhelena came crashing into him. The two of them careened into the hedges, arms and legs flailing in all directions. They landed amongst the thorns while the sounds of battle bathed them in urgent fear.

"Sorry, he hurled me at you," Mikhelena said.

Tristan nodded and helped her to her feet. "We're going to need your leylines," he said.

"This room is much too large. Besides, I want to be the one to kill that dwarf," she replied.

Tristan gave her a quizzical look. "Try the lines anyway. We'll never trap him otherwise."

"Fine."

The lovers parted ways. Tristan chased down his prey who just finished ambushing Analor with a fiery dart from his wand. Tristan knocked Parier to the ground, and Analor opened up a crack on the bull skull with her purple flaming mace.

"Halbert, help me kill this dwarf!" Tristan yelled. All the while, Halbert had been cowering in the corner, his shield raised to protect him from danger.

"I—I can't. I made a promise I wouldn't hurt him," Halbert replied.

Tristan kicked the dwarf as it rose to its feet. The tiny gamelord rolled away with a grunt.

"Then kill the gargoyle. Help us!" Tristan answered.

The dwarf jumped back on his feet. He twirled his wand along the ground in front of him. Great tongues of fire leapt up, surrounding him. The huntsmen started back from the heat, but the anger inside Tristan burned hotter than the flames.

"Your tricks have no effect on me," he called.

Tristan crouched behind his heater shield and charged through the fire. The burst of heat lambasted his skin, curling the hair on his chin and eyebrows backwards.

In the center of the flaming ring, the dwarf leaned on his hip bearing a devilish grin. Tristan approached, holding his shield in front and allowing the blade of his broadsword to rest upon it. He hoped another of his huntsmen would follow him into the inferno, but no help was coming.

"You suffer unwarranted hatred, dear huntsman. What have I ever personally done to offend you?" the dwarf asked.

Tristan took another step closer, tensing his muscles for a strike. "You've swindled the townsfolk and left the Lodge almost penniless. You'll pay for your thievery."

"So, it is money that matters then, hm? Well, I have plenty here. What if I were to offer you a grand sum? Enough to make you comfortable, enough to buy a house, let's say? With a stable, too - or a shop of some kind, perhaps?" the dwarf said, inching to his left.

Tristan smiled and said, "Your charms may have worked in the past, but I know all too well the cost of parlaying with dwarves. My father roams loose in the swamps, driven mad by the deal he made with Dernigar. I'll not be moved by your treachery."

The dwarf gave a little bow. "Truly your wisdom is growing, young huntsman. Yes, all the gold and gems here are cursed. So, it would seem I'll just have to kill you."

Tristan launched forward and swung down at the dwarf. The impish creature dodged under the blade then lurched upward, catching Tristan in the chin with the butt of his wand. Tristan staggered back from the blow. Blood trickled from the corner of his mouth. Tristan smeared it away with the back of his gauntlet. The dwarf waved his arms and the surrounding fire condensed into a swirling vortex. The gamemaster thrust his hands forward and a stream of flame bolted at Tristan.

The hunter raised his shield to block it, but the assault was too large to stifle entirely. Tongues of fire licked the edges of his bulwark, and his armor became hotter and hotter. Suddenly, a second shield appeared to his right, then another to his left. Okacheybay and Stanislav lent their protection. Together, the three of them withstood the fiery onslaught until it finally abated.

"Dispatched my gargoyle so easily, did you? There's more where he came from," the dwarf hissed.

An arrow flew through the air, catching the dwarf's wrist. The wretched abomination dropped his wand, screaming in agony. Tristan saw Analor trying to notch another arrow, but she dropped it in her haste.

"Charge!" he called.

Tristan, Okacheybay, and Stanislav rushed toward the Unhallowed. They brandished their blades. The dwarf moved with blinding speed. In an instant, he recovered his wand and used it to block a strike from the trio. The dwarf backpedaled into the shrubbery. He vanished into the wood then reappeared behind them. Tristan whirled around in time to see it flick its wand with its good hand.

"Analor, again!" Tristan ordered.

By now the huntress recovered her arrow and let it fly. It caught Parier in the calf as he bolted for the far end of the enclave. The dwarf tumbled to the ground. Rolling to a shoulder, he flicked his wand at the archer. An orb of green light shot across the expanse at her. Analor flinched and brought her bow up to block the attack. She caught the orb with her weapon, but the bow dissolved in her hand, the taut string snapping in two, lashing against the skin on her neck.

Tristan closed on the dwarf now. He raced across the last few yards, but the twisted little man scrambled to the edge of the shrubs once again and disappeared into them.

"Watch him, he's coming back!" Tristan shouted.

A cry of agony erupted from Okacheybay. The dwarf had reappeared and drove a knife into his back. Stanislav darted behind his comrade and swiped at him with his burning blade. The dwarf released the knife and fell back into the bushes once more. Tristan raced to catch Okacheybay as he wobbled.

"You okay?" Tristan asked, sliding his shield arm under his friend to brace him.

Okacheybay grunted. "I am fine. Focus on our enemy."

The dwarf appeared next to Analor but, by now, she had her mace and buckler drawn. He flicked another green bolt at her, but she evaded. Tristan joined her and they drove the fallen creature back into the safety of the thickets.

"Where is he now?" Analor asked.

"Stay ready," Tristan answered.

"Over here," came the heavy voice of the dwarf.

Tristan looked to his left. There the dwarf stood, behind a kneeling Halbert holding a curved knife to the hunter's neck.

"Don't come closer or this will be the end of him," the dwarf threatened.

Tristan glanced at Analor, then relaxed his muscles. He stood erect, letting his armaments droop in his hands.

"If you kill him, what then?" Tristan asked, locking eyes with the Unhallowed.

The dwarf chuckled. "I know huntsmen. They do not sacrifice one of their own."

Tristan turned to Analor and gave her a smirk. She returned a worried glance.

"Is that so?" Tristan asked, returning his attention to the hostage taker.

"You are to leave at once. After you exit the maze, I'll let him go," it rasped.

Tristan shook his head and took a half step toward the dwarf. "I don't think that's going to happen."

The dwarf pulled the knife closer to Halbert's throat. "I'll stab him!"

Tristan shrugged. "I ask again. What advantage will that give you?"

"Tristan, no. Help me, please. Don't come closer," Halbert pleaded.

"You will not put his life in danger. He is one of yours," the dwarf growled.

Tristan took a full step toward them now, still holding his weapons at his side. "Is he? Is he really? He betrayed the Lodge. Stole from us. We have much to rebuild and no coin to pay the workmen, and it's all because of him. And because of you."

The dwarf shifted nervously. "I'll do it! You watch! I'll do it!"

Halbert squirmed in the dwarf's grip. "No Tristan! I'm sorry. Stay back, please. I don't want to die!"

"Be still, you," the dwarf ordered.

Tristan took two steps forward. "Puncture his neck and you lose all your leverage. All we lose is a traitor."

The dwarf began to breathe heavily. His eyes shifted from Tristan to Analor to Okacheybay, grunting with a trickle of blood staining the hem of his brigandine.

"You betray your Cause like this?" the dwarf screamed.

A few moments of silence passed as the adversaries stared each other down. Every sound hushed. Even the fire in the censers seemed to stand still.

Tristan brought his weapons up and smiled. "Now, Miki."

From behind the dwarf a flaming scimitar punctured through the gut of the dwarf. Tristan dropped his weapons and leaped forward. He grasped Halbert and flung him away. As he did, the knife snagged Halbert's armor but drew no blood.

As Halbert rolled away, Tristan snatched Halbert's sword from the sheath and brought it up with both hands. The dwarf screamed with blood gurgling from his throat as Tristan planted the sword deep inside the dwarf's skull, the blade slicing open the flesh and bone.

The little game-dealer crumpled to the ground in a heap. Mikhelena stepped back. Analor raised her mace.

"Any chance we get lucky and he returns to us?" asked Okacheybay under heavy breath.

"Doubt it," Tristan replied, backing off a bit.

The garden was quiet. Shadows danced among the huntsmen from the silent braziers guarding the entrance. Tristan relaxed his muscles for just a moment. In an instant, the dwarf leapt up with a wretched growl. He flung a clod of dirt in the eyes of Tristan and rolled away from Mikhelena's attack. He dashed for the edge of the shrubbery but as soon as he drew close to it, he bounced back into the enclave as if he hit a wall.

"Leylines," Tristan said, wiping the mud from his face.

"Humph. We'll see," said the dwarf. The creature staggered, then laughed. He pulled the cow skull from his head and let his blood pour into it. Tears streaked down his face as he reached down with his other hand and placed his wand inside the bones.

Mikhelena darted over to him and delivered the final shot, slicing open the dwarf's throat to the sounds of gurgle and foam. The Unhallowed crumpled over the skull and collapsed to the ground. She thrust her scimitar into Parier's corpse until it went all the way through.

Okacheybay dropped to a knee behind Tristan, grasping the wound on his back. Tristan knelt next to his friend and placed his hand over the wound.

"Miki, help!" Tristan shouted. "He's dying!"

Chapter 13:

THE UNSACRED COW

Thick, warm blood oozed between Tristan's fingers. Okacheybay's breathing was heavy yet strong. Beads of sweat raced down the side of the fallen huntsman's face and his eyes stared straight up to the heavens. Mikhelena gave her blade a twist and withdrew it from the fallen dwarf. She slid next to Okacheybay, pulling open her satchel of healing herbs.

"Will he be okay?" Tristan asked.

The huntress examined Okacheybay's wound. With a fresh cloth, she wiped away the crimson blood from his sable skin.

"It's hard to tell. The wound doesn't look deep, but dwarves are treacherous. There could be something I can't see," she said as she helped Okacheybay remove his armor.

Tristan re-applied pressure while Mikhelena found the vial she was looking for. She flicked the small cork from the top and poured out a thin, cloudy liquid onto a new silk cloth.

"Press this up against him for a moment," she said, handing it to Tristan.

Tristan pushed it up against the wound. Okacheybay jerked and grimaced as soon as it touched his flesh.

"Hold still, Oak," Mikhelena said.

She opened a small leather satchel and retrieved her hooked needle and silk thread from inside. She threaded it through the eye then rolled the end in her fingers to tie it in a knot.

"She's sewn me up a dozen times, Oak. Don't worry," Tristan said.

"I am never worried," Okacheybay answered.

Mikhelena nodded for Tristan to remove the cloth, and she set about closing the wound. Each time the needle punctured the skin, Tristan glanced at his friend's face, but Okacheybay's stern expression never changed. Mikhelena sat back after a few moments, tied a knot against the hunter's closed wound, and cut the thread.

"Finished. You should lie still for a while," she said.

She began putting away her implements, and Tristan stood to full height, surveying the remnants of the battlefield.

"So, what do we do with all this treasure?" Analor asked.

The commotion of combat overturned the tables and machines. Gold coins, gold bars, gems of all colors and cuts lay strewn about glittering in the flickering torchlight. A breeze rustled through the hedges, overturning their dark green leaves onto their lighter underbellies. Tristan kicked at a pile of treasure. The precious items jangled as they scattered in a fan of prismatic wealth.

"It's cursed. All of it," Mikhelena said.

Analor leaned over a wooden treasure chest. "How can you tell?" she asked.

"Dwarves are wretched, cursed creatures. Anything they touch is corrupted," Mikhelena answered.

Tristan joined Analor at the chest and said, "I've learned never to doubt Miki's intuition. If she senses that it's cursed, then it is. The dwarf's treasure isn't important at the moment. Maybe someday we'll figure out how to lift the curse, but right now getting everyone back safe and sound is our goal."

"Safe and sound? You were going to let him kill me!" exclaimed Halbert as he charged up to Tristan.

Tristan put his hands up. "Halbert, I was playing for time. Miki hadn't finished the leylines yet. I needed him to keep his eyes on me so he wouldn't notice her. I had to be threatening, a distraction."

"Still. You gambled my life, put me in danger when you didn't have to."

"Do not lecture me on the perils of gambling. We were all in danger, and it was because of you," Tristan growled, poking his finger into Halbert's chest. "Now go, find what you took from the Lodge and let's see if Parier had a chance to lay a curse on it yet."

Halbert slinked away to a corner of the hedge to begin his search while the others gathered around the corpse of the dwarf. Mikhelena kicked it with the toe of her boot.

"Where do you suppose a dwarf learned magic like that?" Mikhelena asked.

Tristan stared at Parier, lying lifeless upon a heap of golden coins. His blood bubbled up through its skin as if it were boiling from the inside out. Tristan jabbed at him with his weapon and said, "I think it's time we stop looking at the Unhallowed as separate tribes. It's clear they have coalesced into one force."

"But why?" Analor asked.

Stanislav moved next to her. "He wants the valley."

Tristan nodded. "He'll put an end to humanity in this valley once and for all. Dreadstone's plan must be to comingle his servants of evil together until he finds one that can overcome us."

"Can he overcome The Cause itself?" Analor asked.

Okacheybay rose to his feet. "The Cause? No. Never. Selfish, ignorant, indulgent, hateful humanity? Oh yes. Most certainly."

A jingling sound from the opposite side of the yard caught Tristan's attention. Halbert squatted on the ground, scooping a mound of coins into a soiled bag. Tristan marched over to him and knelt down to examine the loot.

"Here, Tristan. I found it," Halbert said.

A sack bearing the marks of the Huntsmen's Lodge laid open, spilling its silvery guts onto the grassy floor. He knelt down and picked up the bottom of the bag, dumping the rest of the contents into view.

"Miki, has this stuff been cursed, too?" Tristan asked, looking over his shoulder.

Mikhelena approached the spilled silver coins. She stretched a tremulous hand in their direction.

"No, they're clean," she said after a moment.

"Alright, this is it. Stanislav, separate the silver from the other stuff, then place it in the bag," Tristan said.

"I'll do it," Halbert offered.

Tristan turned on him. "No, you guard the entrance. Don't move from that spot."

"Yessir," Halbert sneered.

Tristan and Mikhelena left Stanislav to his work and moved to the center of the alcove. All around them the gold glistened, weighing on Tristan's mind more and more.

"What now?" Okacheybay asked, joining them.

"If we leave all this here, the villagers will just come looking for it, or another Unhallowed will just take up the games to start anew. We need to destroy it," Tristan said.

"How do you want to do that?" Mikhelena asked.

"Burn it," Okacheybay replied. "Gather all the tables, all the carts, everything that can burn and pile it up on Parier's corpse. Shove all the gold and gems there too, but keep your hands covered. We do not know what kind of curse may be on it. Best not to let it touch your skin. After that, we'll light it. The flames from his body will drag everything touching down into the depths of the world. No one will ever find it."

Tristan nodded. "Excellent. Keep Hal away from it. Treasure fever has him, I think."

The huntsmen set about the work as Tristan commanded. Stanislav finished collecting the silver. "I bet the bag weighs a good bit more than it did when he first brought it to Parier's wagering tables," he said.

Stanislav offered it to Tristan who took it with a slow, satisfied sigh. They helped Mikhelena and Analor pile the detritus on the dwarf. By now, the heap had grown as tall as a man.

Tristan cut down branches from the hedge on the opposite end of the maze. They withered in his hand. He nodded with approval then heaped as much as he could in the space of half an hour. When they finished, Parier's body could hardly be seen under the heaps of gold, gems, wood, and silk.

"Light it," he said at last.

Stanislav took the censors and torches from around the enclave and tossed them on the pile. The dry branches crackled as they ignited. The huntsmen stood watching it for a moment, the flames casting intermittent orange and yellow light on their faces.

"Tristan, I just want to say I'm sorry. I didn't mean for it to come to this." Halbert began.

Tristan turned on him in anger. "Oh, I'm sure you didn't. Just thought you'd turn a quick profit, no doubt. We lost Emma. Who knows if we'll ever see her again? Oak's wounded. And this could have ended in disaster for the village. What if we couldn't rebuild the stockade?"

"I'm sorry. What more do you want me to say?"

Tristan gave him a shove. "Swear off wealth. Swear that you'll give up on being a rich man. Swear you hate the Unhallowed and will never have dealings with them again."

Tristan was saying this to himself as much as to Halbert, for he too felt the temptation of wealth ever-present in his mind.

Halbert backed away, his face pale. "I swear it! I swear it!"

Tristan turned his back and motioned the others towards the exit of the alcove. "It's time for us to go, before the fire gets too dangerous," he said.

Just then, something popped inside the burning debris sending a shower of sparks in all directions. The leaves of the hedge maze sizzled then turned brown and fell to the floor. Night turned to day as the enchantment of the place shattered into its nethereal essence.

The huntsmen broke and ran, crashing through the dried branches of the desiccated maze. They left behind a fire that grew quickly amongst the shrubs lacking their moisture. They never looked behind as they made their way out, but if they had, they would have witnessed a scene most miraculous and terrifying.

The boiling, bloody body of Parier was undergoing a transformation. Muscle, sinew, flesh, and gore wrapped itself around the bovine skull that once adorned the dwarf's head. As the fire raged on, the corpse swelled and disgorged its vital fluids. The head developed eyes, tissue, teeth, and tongue. The dwarven ichor sprung a spine, ribs, and hooves. In a moment, the red-drenched beast rose from the flames. Its stripped body grew skin, then fur, and it let out a deep bellow as its form took final shape. Amidst the conflagration, a bull--larger than any ox roaming Celandine--pawed at the ground, then charged through the blaze in a direction opposite the huntsmen. Amongst the burning clamor of the maze and the blood pumping in his ears, Tristan never heard the beast's cry.

The huntsmen grabbed their gear from under the bushes outside the maze and put significant distance between themselves and the conflagration. Their quick march was aided by cool breeze and damp spring air. It wasn't until the third hour of their trek that Okacheybay collapsed on the rough path.

"Oak!" Mikhelena called as he crumpled to the ground.

Tristan rushed to his friend, Mikhelena by his side.

"What's wrong with him?" Tristan asked.

"He's bleeding," she answered, pointing to his bloodstained belt.

"Why didn't he mention this?" Tristan wondered aloud.

"Doesn't matter. Help me," Mikhelena said.

Okacheybay opened his eyes. "Sorry, my friend. I was trying to ignore the pain."

Tristan helped her unfasten Okacheybay's armor and remove his shirt. A stream of blood trickled down his back from a reopened wound that gaped and closed like a little mouth. Mikhelena immediately pulled out a cloth and pressed it to the little opening.

"The world grows dark," Okacheybay said as his eyes rolled back, and he slumped in Tristan's arms.

"He's lost consciousness," Tristan said.

"It's worse. I must have missed a stitch somehow. Hold this here," she said, handing Tristan the cloth.

Tristan pressed it against the wound while the other huntsmen gathered around.

"How can we help?" Analor asked.

"See if you can find some fresh water nearby," Tristan said, tossing his waterskin to her. "Miki, what else do you need?"

"I should have what I need," she said as she rummaged in her pack.

The others quickly left and Tristan held the cloth against his friend. Slowly, inky red blood changed the cloth from white to crimson. Miki pulled out a bottle of distilled spirits from her satchel and poured some out on a cloth. She wiped Okacheybay's wound with it. The tincture made the blood runny, and the full depth of the cut could be seen.

"It's deep but not fatal. He's lucky," she said. Tristan thought he heard a slight tremble in her voice. He moved closer, staring intently at his friend.

Mikhelena set about her work. Her needle glinted in the clear light of the sun as it poked in and out of Okacheybay's bloodstained skin. Tristan dabbed away the blood to keep the pinkish wound clear. Soon, it was sewed tight. Mikhelena made a bandage and spread a small dab of honey on it. Then she placed several Calendula petals on the honey.

"Hold him up," she said.

While Tristan cradled Okacheybay by the chest, his wife placed the bandage over the sutures then wrapped up his trunk with a long strip of cloth. She tied it off in a knot and motioned Tristan to lay him back down.

"That should take care of it," she said at last, resting on her heels.

"You saved his life then," he said.

"I should have noticed it earlier. I lost my focus. It's that dwarf. He's still on my mind."

Tristan stared at Mikhelena. "Mik, I um, I noticed that while we were fighting the dwarf you seemed kind of—"

"Anxious?"

"Overzealous, I was going to say. Almost like you hated him, hated him more than just the general feelings we have toward Unhallowed. Is there something you want me to know?" Tristan asked.

"I've never told you what happened to my family."

"No, you've always kept it a secret. I figured you had your reasons."

"I appreciate you not asking about it all these years, but I suppose there's no reason for secrets between us anymore. All of my family belongs to the Unhallowed because of me. My father, both sisters, and my mother."

"I'm sure it couldn't be because of something you've done, Miki. You're the last person I could imagine leading someone to that twisted life," Tristan said.

"Thank you, but I know my own sins."

"How could you be at fault?"

"I sold them."

"Sold them?"

She pulled her knees up to her chest and looked off into the distance. "Yes. We were traveling here from Swetland, north of the great desert outside the valley. We didn't know the way. A huntsman told us about the valley, how we could find safety and a new life here. So, my father packed us in a wagon, hitched up the oxen, and we started. We lost nearly everything in the Merchants' City. Those swindlers robbed my father with their endless hoaxes and false promises. As we traveled the side road--not Everpass Way, the side road--a storm came up. Lightning struck the mountainside and sent an avalanche down on top of us."

Tristan rubbed her back. Electricity. "It must have been harrowing for you."

"Worse. The wagon was smashed, the oxen killed. The whole left side of my body was broken. While I was lying there, in a puddle of blood and rain, a man came up. A short man, I thought it was a child my age at first."

"How old were you when this happened?"

Mikhelena began rocking back and forth. "Eleven. I remember it well. Anyway, he promised to save my life and heal my family if I let him take them away. I didn't understand what he meant. I looked around. I thought they were dead, Tristan. You should have seen the blood. There was so much. I asked how he could. He said he knew a man with magic. I agreed. I didn't know what to do, but I wanted to live. After that, things get fuzzy. I think I was coming in and out of consciousness. Eventually another man came. It was Jaconius."

"The warlock Thaul killed six years ago?" Tristan asked.

"Yes, him. I hoped when he died it would break the curse on my family, but no, it didn't. Anyway, the dwarf took my family away in a cart. Jaconius healed my body. Then, they left me there on the mountainside. I begged them to take me, but they said the deal was only for my family, not myself. They disappeared out of sight. Then, not a minute later, huntsmen showed up. They were on patrol, looking for the very dwarf I made a deal with."

"Good thing they found you," Tristan offered, giving her a gentle squeeze.

Mikhelena shook her head. "Not that good. I wish they'd been there sooner. If I had said no to the dwarf, if I had refused the deal, the hunters would have found us before any of my family died. They never would have been Unhallowed. You see, it's all my fault and the fault of that cursed race of dwarves."

"You can't hold yourself accountable for that," he said, taking her in his arms. "You were just a child."

She pushed herself away. "Yes, I can. It's my fault. I'm responsible. The worst part is, every time I see a dwarf, I feel tempted. I want to make another deal. Maybe a deal to get my family back or a deal to never be bothered by them again; a deal to protect my husband."

"I-I didn't know," he said, looking away.

Tristan could feel her emerald eyes staring at him. "I didn't want you to. We all live with secrets. We all live with weakness. Mine is with the dwarves. Your father and I have that in common."

Chapter 14:
A FAMILIAR FACE RETURNS TO VITALBA

The huntsmen made their camp for the evening. Analor snared a couple hares for dinner and Tristan roasted them on a makeshift spit. Night swallowed day, and the stars spread out among the heavens in their cold and distant glory.

Despite the heavy fighting and hurried hike from the maze, Tristan couldn't sleep. He turned over and over in his bedroll until an interminable time passed. Gazing off toward the horizon, he could make out the lonely silhouette of Halbert taking his watch. Tristan could see himself there. He thought back to all the times he put treasure over mission, and how Mersha scolded him for it. In those moments, he wanted nothing more than to quit the huntsmen and maybe even flee the valley. However, each day with Mersha was a new day. She never made Tristan feel like he wasn't wanted or wasn't valuable to her troupe.

Halbert would be punished by the council back in Vitalba, that much was certain. *But do I also have to punish him the whole way there?* Tristan's conscience picked at him and, as much as he wanted to shut it out, he knew what he had to do.

He joined Halbert on the bluff and stared out on the moonlit valley.

"It's not time for a shift change yet. I'll take your watch, too, if you want," Halbert said in a raspy voice.

Tristan examined his companion. Halbert's hair was wild and unkept, his nails long and dirty. He sat there, unmoving, with his body hunched over like a wolf humbled by a pack leader.

Tristan pat Halbert on the back. "Nah, not necessary. In fact, I should probably take yours. I owe you an apology, Hal."

"Me?"

Tristan nodded. "A couple years ago, I might have been right there with you, bringing a bag of coins--mine or not--to that dwarf to try to get more. I've craved wealth ever since my father left, and I'm not sure I'll ever fully get past it. Even now, I think about getting my own home and living a peaceful life of prosperity. I fight those feelings every day. What you did was wrong but, browbeating you the whole way home won't make it any better. For that, I'm sorry."

Halbert's body untensed and he sat up straighter. The wild look in his eyes went away. "Thank you, Tristan."

Silence lingered for a time. "What will we do about Emma?" Halbert finally asked.

Tristan folded his hands and rested his chin upon his knuckles. "Right now, I don't know. I never believe anything Drastist says, but he mentioned taking her to Dreadstone Keep. If she's there..."

"I'd trade places with her if I could. I know it's my fault."

Tristan shrugged. "It almost sounded like they were looking for her specifically. If so, it might not matter what we did. Get to bed. I'll stay up. I can't sleep anyway."

Halbert rose to his full height and let out a relieved sigh. "Until morning," he said, his voice returning to normal.

"Until morning," Tristan replied.

The next morning, the huntsmen loaded Okacheybay onto Halbert's stretcher. The fallen huntsman still had not regained consciousness. Mikhelena examined the bandages and found them secure. The slow trek home began.

In the low places of the valley, fog still lingered like skulking ghosts watching the hunters' movements. Low places made Tristan nervous. A pack of dire wolves or giant spiders could easily conceal itself in the lingering vapors. As a child, how many times did he pass such places, blissfully unaware of the dangers lurking in them? Traveling to the streambeds to dig clay or glaze minerals seemed such a simple life compared to that of a huntsman.

Progress came with great difficulty. Tristan gave Halbert scouting duties, but he only led them off course. It took Analor three hours to discover a path that would take them back toward Vitalba.

By the next day, Okacheybay was able to walk under his own power again. He ate well and recouped his strength. Upon reaching the village that afternoon, they took him to the infirmary to be checked. A dreadful sight greeted them when they arrived.

"Mikhelena, we have needed you," Darian shouted as she walked in.

As she dropped her gear and walked over to where he was tending a slick-skinned villager, she asked, "What's happened?"

"The disease worsened in your absence. Six villagers died," he said, not even looking at her.

Mikhelena tied her hair behind her head. "Oak, find an empty cot. I want to check your wound later. "Where's Nicole?"

Darian shrugged. "Out looking for a cure."

Mikhelena knelt down and took the pulse of the man on the cot. "I guess there was no right choice after all," Tristan heard her mutter.

"You've been here alone?" Tristan asked.

Darian just nodded, then got up to check on another wheezing woman.

A tired-looking Deveraux sauntered over to Tristan. "Your trip was successful, I take it?" he asked, eyeing the sack Tristan carried.

Tristan moved it away from him. "None of your concern."

"Tell me, though. How did the dwarf die?" Devereaux asked.

"How'd you know it was a dwarf?" Tristan said, casting a sideways glance.

"Tristan!" a voice called from behind.

Tristan turned to see his cousin, Michael, running up to him.

"What's wrong?" Tristan asked.

"You gotta come to the Oak Sprig," Michael said, brushing his long hair from his face.

Tristan, tired from his journey, closed his eyes and shook his head. "I just got back. What is it?"

"I don't know the right way to tell you this, but your father, he's at the inn, and he wants to talk to you."

Tristan's eyes sprung wide. He handed the bag of coins to Analor. "Take this to the library and tell Aranka. Don't let anyone stop you until it's deposited."

Analor nodded and left the room.

Tristan's gaze fell on Mikhelena. She busied her hands on unconscious villagers. Turning to his cousin, he drew in a breath and said, "Lead the way,"

On the way to the inn, Michael explained that Tristan's father was no longer an ogre. He arrived in the village just that morning and came to the Oak Sprig looking for Gideon.

"Of course, I had to tell him my dad went to the mountains last fall. He grimaced, then asked for you," Michael said.

Tristan rubbed his goatee. "How'd he look?

Michael shrugged. "Fine. Normal. I haven't seen him in years, but he seemed in control of himself."

Tristan paused outside the inn. His cousin waited next to him. *Inhale. Exhale. He's come to get our house back and make things right between us. I know he has.* Tristan broke through the door of the inn and scanned the common room. All the patrons hunched over tables furthest from the northwest corner. Tristan turned his eyes in that direction to see the sweaty back of a man spooning up mouthfuls of some type of stew.

"He's over there," whispered Michael as he pointed to the solitary individual.

Tristan swallowed hard. His heart beat faster and he could feel adrenaline pumping in his veins. In the years since Father left, he'd become a man. He was a leader, a husband, a warrior. In an instant, he reverted to a child and son.

Tristan stepped over to the table, inching up on the hungry man a little at a time, trying to verify for himself that his face aligned with the last image of his dad. The hair matched. The build matched. Even his heavy breathing remained just as Tristan remembered.

The huntsman placed his hand on the back of the chair opposite the man. He gave it a tug and the resulting screech on the hard wooden floor seemed loud enough to wake the dead. The eyes of all in the inn were affixed on Tristan. He gave them a hard stare, and they returned to their own matters. Tristan sunk into his seat and, for the first time in over two years, looked upon the face of his father.

"Dad?" Tristan began.

The man pushed his bowl to the side but kept his gaze upon the table. "I wasn't sure you'd come," he said in a low voice.

"Of course, I'd come. How'd you get here?" Tristan knew the answer but couldn't think of what else to say.

His father didn't look up. "How are you, my son?"

"Um, I'm—I'm fine."

There was silence for a moment.

"Why did you come, Dad? What's happened?" Tristan asked.

"I finally woke up, woke up from my stupor and realized I'd done something horrible."

Tristan placed his arms on the table and folded his hands together. "Were you still in the slough?"

The man nodded.

"Are—are you alright?"

Father rubbed the table with his index finger. "I'm getting better. I gave up the fountain, cursed it. But the thought of it still has a hold on me."

Father's voice trailed off and the old, muscled man stared out the latticed windows of the dining room.

"I understand," Tristan didn't, but the only thing he wanted was to continue the conversation. "Is that all?"

Never taking his eyes from the window, the man said in his gravelly voice, "It's a hard thing, Tristan, to get what you thought you wanted all your life, only to realize it cost you everything you had. And then to learn everything you had was what you wanted, really deep down, in the first place."

Tristan's face brightened, and his pulse steadied. "I've missed you, too, Father. I wish we still had our shop together."

"Oh, it's not the shop I really wanted," he said, still avoiding eye contact with Tristan.

"How can that be? What was it?" Tristan asked, leaning in.

"I started giving up everything I wanted long before I became a potter," Father explained.

"Like what?"

Father shook his head. "Bah, everything important: the parish, the Lodge, the townhall, all of it. No one understood that I wanted stability. I needed it. As the years went on, I just turned toward my craft more and more until that obsession broke me. I gave in to the worst parts of greed and addiction. But I don't want to talk about me anymore. Tell me about you."

Tristan leaned back against the chair. "Well, I'm a huntsman now, and I'm on the Sun's Council."

For the first time, Tristan's father looked up at him. "The council, eh? They haven't had one of those in ages. Things are amiss, I take it?"

Tristan moved his hands to his lap. "I suppose you wouldn't know. A year and a half ago our leader, Thaul, was captured by the bloodborn. Tatterdemalion holds him in Greyfell Tower. Since there's no White Rose in the Lodge to lead us, the elders decided to bring back the council."

Father's face shifted with anger that made Tristan tense up and shift in his seat. "Thaul was never a good warrior and a bit of a coward, I always thought. Well, who am I to talk?" Father remarked.

Tristan relaxed his shoulders. "What do you mean?"

Tristan's father again turned his eyes to the latticed window nearby and looked out into the village. "Tristan, I'm sure Gideon must have explained it."

Tristan leaned in again and shook his head. "No. Explained what? How do you even know anything about Thaul?"

Father cleared his throat and returned his gaze to Tristan. "He and I went to school together. We knew each other since childhood and, for a while, we were good friends. He had courage when he started in the huntsmen, but his heart was never truly in it. He wanted to find a way to live by himself, out away from the village—to find some perfect garden where he could live off the land and never have to work."

"I've seen his garden. It's a ruined mess," Tristan said.

Father grunted. "A fitting end to his dream, then."

Tristan narrowed his eyes. "What was your dream?"

"Well, it changed over time. I wanted to make a name for myself, I guess. To be known for something. At first, I thought it would be killing. But, after you were born, I quit the huntsmen and took up pottery."

Tristan was not sure he heard his father correctly. "What did you just say?"

"I had to provide for my family. The Unhallowed weren't as active back then, so filling my trunk was hard. I'd always want to spend what I got, too. Your uncle indulged me with discounts since he knew I'd pound him if he didn't. He thought he was helping, but it just made things worse. Anyway, my dream changed from being a renowned hunter to being a renowned potter once I realized there was more stability and security in artisan work."

"You—you were a huntsman?" Tristan asked as he leaned in even closer.

Father shifted in his chair and scrunched his eyes together. "Yeeesss. Didn't Gideon ever tell you that? Once I was gone, that is?"

"No. He said you had secrets, but he never told me what."

A half smile worked its way across Father's face. "Yes, I was a huntsman for many years as a young man. I was uncommonly strong and good in battle but, like I said, I couldn't keep my coin. I couldn't raise a son in the chaos of the Lodge."

Tristan crossed his arms, his face perplexed.

The father waved off his son. "There're so many dangers. I mean, just look at what happened to your mother as a result."

Tristan narrowed his eyes; his voice became gruff. "What about Mom, Dad? How many secrets did you keep?"

Tristan's father cocked his head to the side. "No one told you after all this time? Shame on them. Your mother died because she thought she could save the world. The town put ideas in her head that made her feel obligated to rescue everyone in danger."

"What's wrong with that?" Tristan asked, cocking an eye.

"Fah, it's foolishness, reckless. You have to count the costs. I mean, to get to her, the Unhallowed took you into the dwarf caves in the north. She died rescuing you. The little scrunts collapsed a tunnel on her as she was getting you kids out."

Tristan was on the edge of his seat. His knuckles were white as he grasped the table hard. "Kids? Rescuing me?"

Father shook his head. "Yeah, um, you and that fair haired kid, can't remember his name, got yourselves kidnapped one day when you were playing outside the village gate. Your mother and another huntress went to save you. They didn't wait for anyone else, just left. I should have gone with them, but I was out of the Lodge, so I didn't. Eventually, they tracked the dwarves down to their hole east of the Everpass Range. I always blamed you for her death, and I hated you for it. I want to apologize for that. I shouldn't have."

Tristan's eyes widened. "You hated me?"

"It's like this," Father said, leaning forward and folding his hands together. "I have a hard time expressing myself. I really only know two emotions: contentment and rage. I've never been able to manage how I feel. You know that. When your mother died, I needed to channel my anger, or it would kill me. I couldn't blame myself, so it had to be you. You're the reason she had to go, the reason she put herself in danger. You didn't know any better, but I couldn't see that. So, I always blamed you for it. That's wrong, I know, and I'm sorry. So very sorry. I told her to quit the Lodge, give up being a huntsman. I said it would get her killed, and there's more stability in pottery. I wanted you to follow in my footsteps. We'd have a house, a family, be safe, and—"

Tristan stood up. "You were BOTH huntsmen?! I was supposed to be a hunter all along? You kept me from school, from friends, from the truth about Mom, and—"

Father put his hands up. "It's all in the past now."

Tristan turned his back and glared over his shoulder. "Not for me. It's my present! I'm just now learning this."

Father stood up. "No, Tristan. Wait. You saved me. You're why I came back. I just…"

Tristan waved him off and stormed out of the inn. He could hear his father's voice calling for him to come back. The voice got deeper and raspier the further Tristan went. *I can't believe he hated me. All the years I wasted, trying to please him… Worthless.*

Eldo

Chapter 15:

AND A CIRCUS CAME TO TOWN

Tristan found himself outside the heavy wooden gate of Vitalba. His body vibrated and the muscles in his face worked back and forth as his teeth ground against one another. One of the guards started toward him, but the expression Tristan shot in his direction chased him away. Several times, Tristan pounded his fist into his palm. Other times, he placed his hands on his hips, turned his eyes up to the grey, overcast sky, and shook his head.

Amidst his doubts and questions, the tell-tale sound of footsteps on the dry road to Vitalba brought his attention to the little hill up ahead. Four men were carrying a stretcher to the village. They were huntsmen but were not adorned in the hodge-podge armor common to Vitalba hunters. They wore the servant-warrior uniforms of Everpass Hold. Tristan narrowed his eyes at them as they approached. *Everpass guards are never found in this part of the valley.*

He strode over to them as they kept their steady march. A man lay on a stretcher covered with a sheet from the waist down. His face was so haggard, so pale and sweat covered that Tristan didn't recognize him at first. It was only upon a second glance he realized it was Eldo, former gate captain of Vitalba.

"What happened to him?" Tristan asked as he pressed his finger against Eldo's wrist to check for a pulse.

The hunters continued their march. "He crawled his way to Everpass Hold. He said he found some new keep up in the Everpass mountains, northeast of The Hold. Inside were pleasures for every sense and desire, he said, but it was guarded by gargoyles. They shredded his legs. I honestly don't know how he made it back to us."

Tristan lifted the sheet as he walked with them. Eldo's legs were bandaged, but it was plain to see misshapen forms and chunks missing from his thighs and calves.

"You couldn't treat him at Everpass?"

"We have no healer," the soldier answered.

Tristan took the lead, calling out for villagers to clear the road. The streets had become unusually busy. The merchants must have set up their temporary shops. Tristan pushed the experience with his father out of his mind and, for the moment, concentrated on a sudden new duty.

They arrived at the Lodge and Tristan ushered the Everpass guards to the infirmary. Darian, Devereaux, and Mikhelena rushed over. Mikhelena's careworn face betrayed her exhaustion. Almost a dozen villagers lay in their cots struggling with varying degrees of consciousness.

Another huntsman ran in. "Tristan," he called.

Tristan whirled around and with an aggravated tone answered, "What now?"

The young huntsman stopped on his heels. "An ogre! An ogre was seen in town! It came from the Oak Sprig inn and ran out the gate just seconds ago. Shall we pursue it?"

Tristan knew immediately who it was. *I must have just missed him.* "No. No, don't. Just let him go. Don't send anyone after him."

Mikhelena's voice brought his attention back to Eldo. "I think we'll have to amputate," she said.

Darian grimaced, then nodded. "I don't think we'll have much choice."

"And so it goes," added Devereaux.

"We have the powders and spirits to make a sleeping potion for him but, Tristan, we'll need your strength to hold him down if he wakes up," Mikhelena said.

"Anything to keep me busy," he said.

Mikhelena gave him a strange look, then rushed to another room to grab the supplies.

"Help me get him to the cutting room," Darian said, taking one side of the stretcher.

"I'll stay with these sick ones for a bit longer if you don't mind," Devereaux said, backing away.

Darian nodded. Tristan helped Darian move Eldo to a small adjoining room. Mikhelena entered with a white cloth and small canteen. She handed them to Tristan and demonstrated how he was to pour modest amounts of the liquid onto the handkerchief and occasionally cover Eldo's mouth and nose with it.

"If he wakes while we're doing this, he won't be able to control himself," Mikhelena warned.

Tristan poured some of the mixture on the cloth. A dull, heavy aroma assaulted his senses, and he instinctively turned his head away. "I'm ready to hold him. He won't escape my grip," he said.

"Just don't break any more of his bones," Darian said.

"I'm not very experienced at these, but I'll be as quick as I can," Mikhelena said, taking up a scalloped blade in her hand.

The surgery was a gruesome thing to witness. In the wilds, Tristan had carved up wolves and vampires with ease, but seeing a friend's body sawn apart by people he knew and loved struck him in a far more visceral way than any battlefield combat. Mikhelena's calm, emotionless disposition as she carved into Eldo's bones, flayed his muscle, and sewed his skin was so discordant with the bloody work being done. At the same time, Tristan was thankful for the gore of it. The revelations his father dropped on him were instantly put in perspective as Eldo's disfigured legs were removed and set aside like a pair of broken candlesticks.

With great precision Mikhelena sewed the remaining flaps of skin shut while Darian dabbed copious amounts of distilled spirits to clean the area. Then, they watched to make sure her work had sealed his veins and arteries completely. Afternoon slipped into evening, and Tristan was famished.

Once they finished laying a still unconscious Eldo back in the infirmary to recover, Tristan looked at Mikhelena and saw that she, too, was weak from hunger and work.

"You look like you need a break. The merchants have set up their shops. Let's go find something to eat there," he said.

"I should stay. With Lise out traveling in the mountains with Mersha, there's so much left for the healers to do in the infirmary," she replied, scanning the room full of invalids.

Tristan took her into his arms. "They're stable. They can do without you for a few hours."

"Juanitos just showed up. We should be fine for a while. I'll watch them," Darian said, taking a seat on the west wall.

Mikhelena turned her eyes up to Tristan. "Ok. Let's go. Just for a little bit."

They left the Lodge through the front double doors and descended the steps onto the village street. The cool spring breeze and the warm spring sun were instantly refreshing. The dark clouds from earlier that day had dispersed, revealing the pleasant hues of Vitalba's post-winter season.

"I didn't expect to see you back at the Lodge so soon. Your father, what happened?" Mikhelena asked as they strolled toward the village green.

Tristan nodded. "I think he left again."

Mikhelena bit her upper lip. "Why?" she asked after a moment.

Tristan cast his gaze to the damp earth of Vitalba's main thoroughfare. "We talked for a bit. He seemed happy to see me, but it turns out that everything I believed about my family was a lie. Did you know my mother was a huntress?"

She shrugged. "I wondered about it. Phen thought she might have been the one who used to supply the Lodge with all the roses given to new hunters. I didn't know if she was actually a hunter herself. It would have been long before my time here."

Tristan's face scrunched up with irritation. "My father kept it from me. He was a huntsman, too, it turns out. Never told me."

"Is that what you talked about? Huntsmen?"

Tristan nodded again.

"Do you think he'll be back?"

Tristan shrugged. "If you don't have a house, you don't have a family. That's what he said to me before he left the first time."

Mikhelena grabbed his hand. Electricity. "Did you argue?"

"I guess. I mean, I don't know. I got mad. I was more shocked, really. Not angry, just shocked. I left without saying anything else, and I think he ran off again. As an ogre."

"Ogre…" she said, then hugged his arm. "If I had any potion or herb that would have kept him here, I would have used it. I wish I could fix it for you, where he could always be here."

He returned her affection. "I don't know if he'll ever be fixed. I'm not even sure what I think of him right now."

"Well, right now you have the Lodge to worry about. And Eldo."

Tristan turned his eyes up to the clouds. "True. I imagine Aranka will call a council meeting soon."

They found a merchant selling roasted nuts at an exorbitant price, but the deep, smoky aroma wafting from the cart deepened the pangs of hunger in the two huntsmen. Tristan begrudgingly paid the man and handed one of the two paper cones to Mikhelena. They began munching greedily on their snack.

Just then, a roar erupted from a nearby congregation followed by laughter and jeering. Tristan and Mikhelena spied the crowd gathered surrounding the village green.

When they made their way through the throng of villagers, they found a man in a tall, black top hat dressed in a blue coat and red vest holding a whip in a white-gloved hand. Next to him sat a grizzly bear licking his claws, while one of the young men of the village dusted himself off.

"Is this the circus?" Tristan asked.

"Not the one that usually comes, and it's two weeks early," Mikhelena said.

"Same outfits. Different people," Tristan remarked, glancing around from performer to performer.

"Tristan," said Devereaux, who was standing nearby, "come, watch this with me."

The two hunters moved over next to him. "Good evening, Devereaux," Mikhelena said coldly.

"I think it will be," he answered, drawing in a satisfied breath.

"Shouldn't you be helping in the infirmary?" Tristan asked him, leaning on one foot.

Devereaux bowed his head for a moment and said, "I was until the priest showed up. I heard the circus arrive, and who could pass up an opportunity to see something like this? It's been ages since I saw such a performance."

"Performance?" Tristan echoed.

"Anyone else?" cried the ringmaster in the blue coat. "Ten gold pieces to any man who can pin my bear!"

"What is this?" Tristan whispered down to Mikhelena.

She shook her head. "No idea." "Step right up, folks. What could be easier to earn a fortune? Your Cause may be with you, after all. There's no danger from this beast. He'll be gentle," the man continued.

Someone in the crowd yelled, "Tristan!" Another agreed. "Yeah, Tristan!" Soon, three dozen voices were all calling his name.

Tristan looked up in surprise, his cheek bulging with chestnuts. He pointed to himself with his eyes wide.

The ringmaster walked over Tristan. "You, young man? Are you Tristan?"

"Yes, sir," Tristan said in a muffled voice while trying to swallow his treat.

The man in the blue coat put a hand on Tristan's shoulder and said, "These fine people would like to see you wrestle my bear. Are you up for it?"

Tristan put up his hands. "I—I don't think I should. I—"

Devereux spoke up, "I think you should. Never know what might happen."

"Are you scared?" the ringmaster asked.

"No, no, not at all," Tristan said with a half-hearted laugh.

"Well, then, what is it?" the man asked with a large grin and his arms spread wide.

"I just don't know if it would be fair," Tristan explained.

The man in the blue coat nodded as if he understood. "He is a large bear, I know. But you look quick and spry. Perhaps you can outthink him and pin him when he's off balance. Try to use his size and strength against him. That's honest advice. I'm no conman."

"No, no, that's not what I'm saying. I'm saying, I could easily beat—"

Tristan was cut off by the villagers calling his name over and over. "They want you to do it," the ringmaster said with a reassuring grin.

"Ten gold?" Tristan asked.

"Ten gold," he answered.

Tristan shrugged. "Alright. It's your money to lose, I guess."

"And so it goes," Devereaux added.

Tristan handed Mikhelena his food and stepped onto the green. The bear rose and glowered at Tristan. Tristan glowered back. The claws would be dangerous. He'd have to avoid those.

The bear circled to the left; Tristan went right. With a sudden ferocity the bear rushed toward the huntsman, paws outstretched. Tristan ducked and slithered out of the bear's way. It charged past him, then skidded to a stop and spun around. The crowd cheered.

Circling again, Tristan sized up his opponent. The bear moved with more deliberation and care than an ordinary animal. Even its facial expressions connoted a level of understanding Tristan did not associate with a common beast.

The animal charged once more, this time with more determination. They locked arms and Tristan dug his fingers into the beast's fur. They sank in deep. He could feel the flesh and muscle and bone underneath. It was a new sensation, different from the werewolves and giants he had wrestled in the past.

Tristan shoved the animal backward, and it went tumbling head over heels. The crowd gasped and the huntsman gave the ringmaster a sly grin. The ringmaster's face betrayed his surprise at Tristan's strength.

Hunter and prey again engaged in their duel. This time, Tristan caught its paws and squeezed them in his hands. If he wanted, he could have broken every bone. The bear frantically tried to pull itself free from Tristan's mighty grip, but the huntsman had no intention of simply letting go. Tristan yanked the bear to the side and flung him off into the dirt.

The crowd increased in size. At least fifty villagers--men, women, and children--were now whooping and hollering. The bear galloped back at Tristan with an angry roar. Tristan took a quick step forward and caught the bear in the chest and gut. The mighty huntsman lifted the beast above his head, then gently dropped him to the ground. He had no intention of hurting the brute; indeed, he felt sorry the animal was put in this position in the first place.

The crowd cheered, and Tristan's face beamed with a smile. The ringmaster adjusted his collar as the two opponents in the round grappled with each other once more. Tristan grew weary with embarrassing the beast and decided to end it there by pinning him. Just as he was about to make his move, the bear put its snout next to his ear.

"Save me. Get me out of this suit," the bear whispered.

Tristan forgot what he was doing, shocked the bear could speak. The momentary lapse of concentration allowed the bear to trip Tristan and drive the hunter's shoulders backwards into the ground. Tristan hit the earth at full force with the entire weight of the bear coming down on him.

"Pinned!" shouted the ringmaster.

"Find my cage. Save me!" whispered the bear a second time.

Chapter 16:

THE REVOLUTION OF RESPONSIBILITIES

The crowd cheered and laughed. Men and women with painted faces circulated among the villagers with hats held out. The people dropped coins and small tokens of appreciation inside. The ringmaster walked over to Tristan and helped him up.

"Fine work! That's the closest anyone has ever gotten to pinning Brutus," he said.

Tristan steadied himself and looked around. The bear sat cleaning its claws with its flicking pink tongue, never taking its eyes off Tristan. "Can that thing talk? Where did you find this animal?" Tristan asked.

"Talk?" exclaimed the ringmaster. "I think you might have hit your head, young sir. Tell you what folks, this fine young man did very well against my bear. How about I give him half the prize?"

The crowd roared with approval and tossed even more coins at the ringmaster's feet. The blue-coat man reached into his pocket and counted out five gold disks marked with the face of the king.

"My name's Alexandre de Mensonge. Thank you for putting on such a fine show," the ringmaster said as he pressed the coins into Tristan's hand.

"He's not like other creatures, is he?" Tristan pressed.

The ringmaster clapped him on the back. "You have me worried, my young friend. People would find you very strange if you said you were talking to a circus animal, wouldn't they? Go home and take a rest. I have to get this beast back in his pen now and feed him. Too dangerous if I don't. Good day, sir."

The ringmaster whirled around before the huntsman could say another word. Tristan scowled, then returned to Mikhelena. As he passed Devereaux, the old hunter said, "Wonder what you might be able to turn that gold into if you had the chance?"

Tristan shot him a bewildered look.

"What happened?" Mikhelena asked.

"Come with me, away from here," he whispered, leading her away. He took one last glance back at the ringmaster who was leading the bear by a chain. The creature stared back at Tristan; eyes fixed on his.

Tristan and Mikhelena ducked around the corner of the nearby church while the ringmaster declared that he and his carnival would stay in Vitalba the next two weeks to delight and entertain the people. Once they were behind the chapel, Tristan scanned the roads in all directions to make sure they were alone.

"What is it?" Mikhelena said in a worried tone.

Tristan kept his eyes on the village streets and said, "The bear talked to me."

She smiled and said, half-jokingly, "You can talk to animals now?"

"No, no," Tristan said, raising up his hands and scrunching up his face.

Mikhelena looked back around the corner toward the green, then turned back to Tristan. "Then, what are you talking about?" she asked.

"It asked me to save him, to get him out of a 'suit' as he put it," Tristan answered.

"A suit?"

He nodded. "Yes, a suit. I'm not sure that's a real bear."

"Strange," she said, biting her upper lip. "It could just be a hoax of some kind. I don't recognize these people."

"I know. I wonder what's going on," he said, casting his eyes back toward the beast.

She leaned against the aging boards of the church and looked in the direction of the great stained-glass window on its west side. "Things have gotten so bizarre lately," she sighed.

Tristan placed his hands on his hips. "I know. The maze, Gibbous, the sickness, even Devereaux makes me unsettled. And where did these gargoyles come from all of a sudden? I thought they were just fairytales. Now they're slaves to dwarves. One almost killed Eldo."

She took his hand. "The last few years have been trying. Dreadstone is clearly on the move."

"He should be ripped out of this valley once and for all," Tristan declared.

"Not an easy thing," she said, looking away.

He dug the toe of his boot in the ground. "I know. It's just how I feel."

There was a pause between them. "Five gold pieces, then?" she finally asked.

Tristan fished them out of his pocket and held them out to her. "Yeah. Not a bad start on a house and shop. Just need, well, a bunch more."

She closed his fingers around the coins with her hand. "We'll work on it together," she said with a warm smile.

"Now, let's get back to the Lodge. I need to check on the patients. I hope Nicole will be here soon. I want her to inspect the job we did on Eldo's legs. I haven't performed an amputation without her before."

They started back for the Lodge. "It seemed like everything went smoothly," Tristan said.

She shrugged. "The proof will be in whether he dies from infection or if gangrene takes him. What will you do about the bear?"

"I'm not sure yet."

"They'll be in town for a while, no doubt," Mikhelena said as she scuffed toward the Lodge.

Tristan nodded and remained silent the rest of the way back. That night, Aranka called a meeting for the Sun Council. Tristan was the last to arrive, which annoyed him.

Patric, Aranka, Valere, and Halbert were seated around the center table. Devereaux was reclining in a chair by the large window that overlooked the north of the village. He held a scroll, dingy with age, in his hand.

"What's he doing here?" Tristan asked as he took a seat.

"Who?" Aranka replied.

Tristan shrugged. "Devereaux. Isn't this a private meeting?"

Patric leaned in and pointed his thumb at his chest. "I invited him. Is there a problem with that?"

Tristan scoffed. "It was a simple question, Patric."

Patric flicked his hair over his shoulder. "We can invite anyone we like for any reason we like. You don't get to decide everything, Tristan."

"I wasn't trying to, you—"

"Gentlemen, let's get to the task at hand," said Valere, holding his arms out between the men.

Aranka set down her papers. "The reason we are here tonight is gravely serious. One of the council has betrayed the Lodge and put the village in mortal danger. Our stockade is weakened from the blood snow, and the woodsmen deserve their rightful wages for the timber they bring and the work they do. With our treasury stolen, we might—"

"But we got the money back," Halbert started, rising from his seat.

"I was not finished," Aranka snapped back. She leaned back in her chair and folded her arms. "Halbert is no longer worthy to sit on the council nor carry the rose of a huntsman. I move that we expel him immediately."

Silence lingered in the air for a time. Halbert's expression changed from concern to panic. Tristan could feel his eyes burning a hole in him, desperately searching for any sign someone would speak up for his honor. No one did.

Patric cleared his throat. "I have to agree."

"Same," said Valere.

Tristan shifted in his seat, then looked over at Halbert. "Sorry, Hal. They're right. I don't think we can trust you anymore."

Aranka slammed her gavel onto the table and said, "The motion is carried."

"Wait. Let me have another chance," Halbert pleaded.

Aranka turned her face from him. "You are dismissed. Do not return."

"But—"

"Go," Aranka ordered.

He stood up, fidgeting, almost frantic with his hands and speech, "I need this. I need all of you. Don't expel me."

"I will personally find you some other line of work, Halbert. You needn't fear for yourself, but the Lodge would never be able to trust you again. How could we let someone who robbed the treasury stay among us?" Valere confirmed, placing his hands on the table.

"You gave me no indication that I'd be expelled when I came before you last time," Halbert countered.

"We needed your cooperation. There was nothing to be gained from expelling you at that time," Aranka said.

"Tristan?" Halbert said plaintively, but Tristan turned his face aside.

Valere shook his head. "Time for you to go. You're still a villager. Be glad for that."

Halbert's eyes darted from face to face, but not a word escaped anyone's lips. Eventually, his shoulders slumped and he trudged his way out of the library. Aranka strained her neck to see down the corridor.

"And so it goes," said Devereaux.

"Now we have to decide what to do about the empty roles on the council," she said.

Tristan leaned on the table. "It's been a hard week," he said.

"I, for one, have no desire to fill any of the missing roles nor add their responsibilities to mine," declared Patric.

Aranka narrowed her eyes. "Someone will have to take over the treasurer position."

Tristan started to speak, but he was interrupted by Valere saying, "I'll do it. Though it would be difficult for me to take charge of the warriors and treasury. The first requires me to be in the field. The second requires me to stay near the village to pay the woodsmen and laborers as they work."

Aranka leaned back for a moment, folding her hands under her chin.

"That is quite a conundrum," chimed Devereaux from the back.

They all turned to stare at him, but he never lifted his eyes from his book and scroll. Aranka slowly turned around and said, "Tristan, we need you to take both the provisioner and commander positions. Valere shall be our treasurer and guardian. He'll see that the stockade is finished. Once some time passes, and we can evaluate some of the other potential leaders in the Lodge, we'll reconvene to add new council members and reassign roles. Are we in agreement?"

"Aye," said Valere.

"Acceptable to me," added Patric.

Tristan's heart leapt. As commander and provisioner, he could get back hunting on a regular basis for the first time in two years.

"Tristan?" Aranka prompted.

"Oh. Yes, that's just fine with me," he replied.

"And so it goes," said Devereaux, closing his tome.

The meeting adjourned, and Tristan hurried from the library. He searched the Lodge for Okacheybay to tell him the good news. He eventually found his friend, standing at the top of the clock tower with Janelle. They were holding each other in their arms, staring out into the starlit night.

"Oak, I've got great news," Tristan said as he dashed onto the balcony.

Okacheybay's face did not display pleasure at seeing Tristan. Instead, he turned and slowly released Janelle from his embrace.

"I am sure it could wait. Janelle and I have not seen each other in some time, and I have been in the infirmary healing. We would appreciate some time alone together. I am sure you understand."

Tristan's eyebrows raised and he smiled back at his friend. "Oh, uh, of course. Sorry. I'll be off now." He left the lovers in the tower and found Mikhelena in the infirmary. She was tending an extraordinary number of sick villagers. Their grey, slick skin glistened in the lamplight. Tristan knelt down next to her as she examined one of her patients.

"Are they getting any better?" he whispered.

She shook her head no.

"Any idea when Nicole will be back?"

Again, she indicated no.

"I have some news for you, but it can wait," he said and started to get up.

"No, you can tell me. I'm just watching, trying to understand what afflicts them," she said.

Tristan knelt back down. "Since Eldo is… Since Eldo can't be the provisioner anymore and Halbert was expelled as treasurer, Valere is taking over the stuff in the village for right now. The council put me in charge of the warriors and provisioning. We can leave the village again, any time we want."

She shook her head. "I can't leave these people right now. Not until Nicole gets back anyway, and even then, she might need me to stay."

"Well, we'll figure it out somehow," he said.

"What are you going to do about the bear?" she asked as she began dabbing the patient's forehead.

"Still on your mind, is it? I'll try to find him when he's alone. There's always a guard. Maybe when they've locked him up at night, around suppertime even, I'll get a chance. We'll see."

She nodded, stood, and moved to the next villager. She took a long, hollow wooden tube that flared at the end and placed it on the patient's chest. Then she tilted her head to the side and placed her ear against the other end.

"I'll leave you to your work," Tristan said with a smile and a bow.

"Congratulations," she whispered. "I know it's what you wanted."

Garrov

Chapter 17:

PEOPLE START DISAPPEARING

Each night, over the next week, Tristan attempted to visit the talking bear. Each time, a member of the carnival sat on a three-legged stool guarding the cage. One evening, as he was on his way to check the cage, Tristan stepped out onto the main thoroughfare in Vitalba and was totally alone. No villagers roamed about, running their final errands for the day. No merchants hollered their wares for any to come and buy. The street was left deserted for the first time in Tristan's memory.

He went to the Oak Sprig Inn wondering if, perhaps, Bindle was putting on a special show that night. The inn was nearly empty, as well.

"A light crowd tonight?" Tristan asked his cousin.

Michael was leaning against the bar counter, a dry dishrag next to him. He grabbed a tankard from a nearby stack, put it in front of Tristan, and poured him a generous amount of some potent spiced cider. "Been light the last few nights, Tris."

"What's going on?"

Michael shrugged. "No idea. The carnival has been hosting events outside the stockade, but they're usually long over by now. The people should be back."

Tristan rubbed his chin. "Outside the village? That's new. Maybe the shows have run long. Where're all the merchants?"

"Word has gotten out about the disease. Most of the merchants left. If they don't come back, people will start to get desperate. You want any supper?"

Tristan smiled. "Nah, just ate in the Lodge. Maybe tomorrow?"

"Bring Miki," Michael said with a tip of his tricorn hat.

Tristan laughed as he drank from the tankard. "I'll try, but I doubt I can pry her from the infirmary."

Michael shrugged. "I'm sure whatever it is will pass soon. Disease never lingers long in Vitalba."

Tristan cocked his head to the side. "Perhaps. Anyway, I have to get going. See you soon."

"Hope so," Michael said with a smile.

Tristan turned right and headed for the bear cage. As he went, he noticed few villagers in their homes or in their shops. Even the artisans' workshops were deserted. He shivered even though no breeze was blowing. From a distance, Tristan spied Eldo sitting in a wheeled chair near the gardens. The old gatekeeper rested his hoary head upon his hand, motionless. Tristan wasn't sure if he was awake or asleep. He approached carefully and quietly tapped Eldo on the shoulder.

Eldo jumped and twisted his head around. "Oh, Tristan, didn't see you."

"Sorry about that," Tristan said, taking a seat on a nearby bench.

"What brings you here?" Eldo asked in his gravelly voice.

Tristan stretched. "Came to check on the dancing bear. I—I'm intrigued by the creature. His cage is always guarded, though, by one of the carnivalmen."

Eldo looked in the direction of the cage. "Yeah, I've gotten to know a couple of the men who sit there. Not the brightest."

Tristan nodded. "Glad to see you about town."

"Garrov made me this chair. It lets me get out a bit, at least when the roads aren't too muddy," he said, patting one of the wheels.

"You like the gardens?"

Eldo adjusted himself in his seat and scratched the end of one of his bandaged leg stumps. "Never spent much time here as a gateguard. I suppose I just came here to see something different. The laughter is nice, too."

Eight or nine children frolicked among the shrubs and lattices. They were mere shadows against the orange and red backdrop of the evening sky. Tristan gazed at them for a moment, looked back at Eldo, then once again turned his eyes to the playful silhouettes.

"You know," Tristan began, "You can still be a guard."

"I have no legs, Tristan," Eldo scoffed.

"You don't need legs to protect someone. The town's kids always come to this place to play, yet no huntsman guards them. No one's watching them. They are entirely unprotected. What if the Unhallowed ever infiltrated the village. Who would help them here?"

"Bah, they'd just run to the church for protection," Eldo replied.

"True, but what if they can't make it? What if Unhallowed stand between them and the church doors?"

Eldo looked away. "I'm not a guard. I'm only half a man now."

"Half a huntsman is better than no huntsman," Tristan offered.

Eldo folded his arms on his chest and grunted, "Hmph."

Tristan rose and patted Eldo on the shoulder again. "Just something to think about."

"Indeed."

"Well, it looks like I'll not get a chance to see the bear again tonight. The guard is still leaning on the bars," Tristan said.

Eldo scratched his head and his expression turned mischievous. "How long you need?"

"Not long," Tristan said with a shrug.

"I can give you that," Eldo replied. "Hey you. You over there by the cage! C'mere. You tired? I got something you're gonna want."

The carnivalman at the cage lifted his hands to his mouth to amplify his voice. "Cain't. Gotta stay 'ere and watch the cage. This bear tries to 'scape!"

"Won't take long. We're right here. You can still see him!" Eldo shouted back.

"What you want me to see?" the man called back.

"I bet you'd like a break. There's berries in this garden that'll make that bear sleep for hours. You can pick some, then hit the inn for some drink and friendship!"

"That's never going to work," Tristan said.

"It'll work. Like I said, he's not very bright," Eldo replied.

The guard took a few furtive steps towards Eldo.

"Now's your chance, Tristan," Eldo said.

"Thanks," Tristan replied, darting off in a different direction.

The carnival man scuffed his way to Eldo, while Tristan stalked around some nearby houses to make his way to the cage. He could see Eldo point to various places in the garden and the carnivalman standing close by, his hand on top of his head.

When, at last, the cage guard made his way into the bushes, Tristan scuttered over to the cage. The bear was lying on the ground, curled into a giant ball of black fur.

"Hey, you wanted to talk to me. I'm here," Tristan said.

The bear opened its eyelids, then scrambled up on its paws. "Get me out of here," it whispered.

Tristan took hold of the lock on the door, then dropped it. "I have no key," he said, playing for more information.

"Not the cage," the bear said, shaking its head. "This skin!"

Tristan leaned in closer. "Skin?"

"Yes. Bartram Fauxcroix, the ringmaster's ward, trapped me in this bear hide. I gotta get out. Help me!"

Tristan shook his head. "How?"

"When he cursed me, he said the only cure would be a bone blade, an 'ancient bone' blade he said. Find one and cut me loose."

Tristan squinted at the talking animal. "How do I know this isn't some sort of trick?"

The bear began to pant. "I'll give you something. Information. If it's true, will you trust me then?"

"What's your name? Your real name," Tristan said.

"Maynard Kwan."

Tristan nodded. "Tell me your information."

"Have you noticed since the carnival arrived, your people dwindling? Are your shops empty? Is your tavern bare?" Tristan took a step back. "Yes…"

"It happens to every town we take this carnival to. Only this time, it isn't some sleight of hand. Someone in your village has conspired to bring a great plague to your people. It is a magical cow that can grant wishes!"

"Wishes?" Tristan asked with a half laugh.

"Yes," the bear hissed, "but it's evil. Normally, it's just a tree and only small gifts can be exchanged. But this beast, it's something the shadowmasters have been searching for a long, long time."

Tristan drew close to the cage again. "Who are the shadowmasters?"

"People outside your valley who understand what's in it. They look for Unhallowed in the old places of the world: in heathen texts, in ancient ruins, in bygone legends and scrolls."

"I don't understand."

The bear pressed its snout through the bars of the cage. "One of them, I don't know his name, discovered a ritual where he could fuse a human with an Unhallowed."

Tristan stepped back a bit and looked sideways at the beast. "It's not hard for a human to become an Unhallowed."

The bear raised his whisper to a low voice "Ah, but this creature would be different. The resulting abomination could appear as human whenever it wished or as Unhallowed whenever it wished. It would be killable only with an ancient bone blade. I was their first experiment. They fused me with an animal. I'm not beyond hope, though. I can be rescued with such a blade. But the magic cow and the fused abomination can only be killed and only by an ancient bone blade. Do you have one?"

Tristan backed away again. "I've never heard of one."

"Find one. And find your villagers. There, you'll see the wishbeast of which I speak."

"Hope it works for ya!" came Eldo's call from the gardens.

Tristan's eyes bolted up toward the garden. The cage guard was emerging from the garden with an arm full of sky-colored berries.

"I have to go," Tristan said, crouching down.

The bear pulled itself tight against the cage. "Don't forget me. Come back for me. Please."

"I have to go," Tristan repeated, then dashed behind the nearest structure, out of sight.

He circled back to Eldo and thanked him for the help then made for the Lodge. If anyone would know about ancient bones and magic animals, it would be Aranka.

Tristan hurried to the Lodge along the empty dirt streets, snagging a glance at his old home on the way. He could make out a dim, flickering candle behind a pulled down shade. The potter was back from the Merchants' City. Lingering smoke from a dead fire danced around the kiln outside. Tristan shook his head and pushed the envious desires for his home out of his mind.

As he entered the library, he spied Aranka at her desk. Her customary oil lamp burned brightly as she dipped her quill into a pitch-black inkwell. With her right hand she followed along the lines of a decaying manuscript. With her left, she transcribed the words into a fresh-bound tome. He waited for her to finish the sentence before speaking.

"Ranka?" he said, clearing his throat.

"Tristan? I would have thought you would have been off on a hunt somewhere by now," she said without looking up.

Tristan looked out one of the huge windows of the library. "Miki can't leave right now, and there's something in the village that's caught my attention."

"Oh?" Aranka replied, sounding half interested.

Tristan grabbed a nearby chair and dragged it to the front of Aranka's desk. While taking his seat, he said, "Have you ever heard of a weapon called an ancient bone blade?"

Aranka scrunched up her face without looking at him and paused for a moment. "No, not that I recall," she said after a time.

"A talking bear just asked me to save him by using one," Tristan said, crossing his legs.

Aranka sat up straight and placed her quill in the inkwell. "Excuse me?"

Tristan nodded. "Yep, a talking bear. He also mentioned wishing trees and a magic cow that can give you anything you want."

"Is your cousin experimenting with the distiller again? The last time you tried some of that stuff, it took Miki hours to get you down from the clock tower."

Tristan smirked and leaned back. "Nah, I'm being serious. Have you heard about any of this before?"

"Is the creature a heifer or a bull?"

Tristan's eyes brightened. "Ah, you do know something, then? I'm not sure. I can find out, though."

Aranka grabbed her pen and returned to work. "Do that. I'll see what I can find."

Tristan nodded, returned the chair to its place, and exited the library. Passing one of the leaded windows, he could see that the sun would set soon. *Too late to go outside the stockade now. Better check on Miki.*

He entered the infirmary. Villagers and huntsmen lay quietly on the cots. Mikhelena swayed back and forth on a wooden stool next to one of the patients, her eyes closed. Tristan approached her, one quiet step after another. When he was just inches away, he extended his hand and brushed her left shoulder.

Her eyelids fluttered open and as the rheum of half-sleep faded from her eyes, she smiled at Tristan.

"You look tired," he said, getting into a squatting position before her.

She nodded. "I am."

"Did you get any food?"

"It didn't smell good to me for some reason."

He placed a hand on her knee. "I know it's early yet but come upstairs. You need a rest."

"The patients…"

Tristan looked around. Nicole was tending to a teenage girl who was trying to choke down some broth from a bowl.

"I bet Darian will be back soon. Nicole is finally here. You can take a break."

Her shoulders slumped, and she exhaled sharply. "I suppose."

Tristan took her by the hand. Electricity. They trudged their way through the corridors and up the quiet stairs to the council members' bedroom.

"They finished moving all our things into the equine room on the council floor. I've added a few decorations and found a nice rug for the floor," Mikhelena said.

Tristan opened the door and helped her in. She collapsed on the bed and grabbed onto the pillows, pulling it tight against her chest. Tristan unlaced her boots and pulled them off, one by one.

"Aaron takes his final test with Nicole tomorrow. If he passes, he'll be an apprentice healer. He'll be able to take some of the load in the infirmary. It'll be good practice for him," Mikhelena said with obvious effort.

Tristan removed his boots as well and placed them near the door. "Have you discovered the cause of all the illness?" he asked. "No, not yet. The only thing they have in common is that all of them have been outside the village recently," she answered. Mikhelena rolled over and began to worm her way under the covers.

Tristan went to the bureau. A half dozen playful ornaments in the shapes of smiling woodland creatures were arranged neatly in a half circle. "Where'd these come from?"

"Oh, one of the villagers gave them to me, just as a thank you item. I thought they'd make the room look nice."

He set his things down and turned to her. "Hm. Where did the villagers all go?"

She pulled the quilt over her shoulder. "All over, I guess. Some said the river. Others said the North Wood. Some couldn't remember."

"The North Wood? Seems a bit risky for them to go without hunters along," he said, coming back to the bed.

"Yeah, now you mention it."

Tristan sat down on the edge of the mattress. He mulled over the events of the day in his mind. At last, he said, "There's something going on. I think the villagers are being led into this sickness somehow. Tomorrow I'm going to check it out. Something dark is working in the village, and I mean to stamp it out."

Chapter 18:

A BEAST THAT CAN'T BE KILLED

Tristan awoke the next morning, finding himself alone in bed. *Slept longer than I thought.* He dressed and searched out Mikhelena. Entering the infirmary, he found his wife tending to her duties, in her customary way.

Mikhelena worked at a long oak table, biting her upper lip while folding freshly washed cloths. Tristan watched her delicate hand bring the fabric over itself, rotate it, then fold it three times. Over and over, she performed the same ritual with quiet precision. He stepped up to the other side of the table and began helping.

"Get any sleep last night?" he asked.

"Not enough. I've been tired lately. Knocked these towels over a minute ago because I wasn't paying attention, I guess," she replied, eyes fixed on her work.

"I'm still thinking about what you said last night, about how the villagers are traveling to the river or the North Wood," Tristan said.

Mikhelena shrugged. "Yeah, so?"

"I'm going there now, to investigate something."

"Is something troubling your mind?" She took the towel he just folded and redid it properly.

He took a new one and followed her pattern more closely. "I got to the bear last night. He told me about something going on with a magic cow north of the village."

"The talking bear told you about a magic cow?" she asked with raised eyebrows.

Tristan placed his towel on the pile and chuckled. "Well, when you put it that way…"

Mikhelena chuckled. "So, what did he mean by that?"

"I don't know what it meant, but I'm going to see. Just wanted you to know I was heading to the North Wood."

"I'll come with you. The sick are doing much better today. Some were well enough to go home, and I haven't seen the North Wood since before you joined the Lodge. It's so beautiful this time of year."

"The patients don't need you?"

"The priest visited this morning and lifted their spirits. As I said, they're doing better."

"Juanitos is always good at that," he said.

"He is," she said without making eye contact. "I'll send a paige to tell Juanitos to come back this afternoon. His presence worked wonders."

She folded the last cloth and whispered something to one of the young men working in the room. Snatching her healing satchel from a nearby hook, she followed Tristan as he left the room.

"I just need to find Oak, and then we can be off," he said.

"I am here," came the rich voice of his friend. Okacheybay reclined in a chair, rocking back and forth, waiting for them outside the infirmary.

Tristan turned to see Okacheybay fully dressed and armed. "It's uncanny how you just show up like that sometimes," Tristan said.

"It is the will of The Cause, my friend," he replied.

"You're wound doing better?" Tristan asked.

"Much," Okacheybay replied.

"Take it easy anyway. I don't expect any fighting, but there's no need to reactivate your cut. If something does come up, let Miki and me handle it."

Okacheybay smiled and wagged his finger at Tristan. "Haha! You worry too much about me, but I will abide by your command just the same."

Tristan nodded, then retrieved his armaments. The three of them left the Lodge, then passed through the village gate. Workmen labored nearby fixing a section of the wall, while others carved runes into the newest post. Some were using axes to sharpen the end of a log about to be installed on the stockade. Another pair trimmed branches from a newly felled cedar.

As they left the gate behind, Halbert came running up to Tristan.

"Tristan, help me," he said; sliding to a halt, then tumbling to the ground.

Tristan recoiled from him. Looking down on the plaintive man, Tristan winced and turned away.

"What can *I* do?" Tristan asked.

Halbert eased up to his knees and folded his hands. In a trembling voice he said, "I-I'm afraid. I'm losing everything. My friends, my courage, my life, it's all gone. I'm so sorry for what I did, but I'm afraid I might—I might turn into something wicked."

Tristan closed his eyes and let out an audible breath through his nose. "Halbert. You've been given work on walls, yes?"

"Yes," his feeble voice answered.

He clapped Halbert on the shoulders, then lifted him to his feet. "It is good work; noble work. The stockade is almost finished, and the dedication will be soon. All who worked on it will be celebrated. You have nothing to fear. Just trust The Cause."

"How can The Cause bless me when I've been so unfaithful?" Halbert demanded.

Tristan shrugged. "You must trust in it. We have to get going."

He motioned to Mikhelena and Okacheybay, and they sauntered off north into the forest ahead. The final vestiges of winter had been fully wiped away, and the woods were bedecked in bright greens. Crab blossoms peeked out of their buds from among the thin, brown branches and displayed their deep pinks and whites for the world to see. Starlings chirped as they built their nests high above in the branches, preparing their homes for the next generation. All around the smell of dampness signaled new life and new beginnings.

"There! A wild turkey. Fifteen spotted to your twelve," Okacheybay said.

Tristan shook his head. "You win again."

"How is it someone blessed with farsight like you cannot see something so close?" Okacheybay asked with a chuckle.

"The Cause only knows," Tristan replied, giving his friend an elbow to the side.

"Play again?" Okacheybay asked.

Tristan shook his head.

"How is Janelle doing?" Mikhelena asked.

Okacheybay let out such a sigh of happiness and fulfillment Tristan wondered if he even heard Mikhelena's question.

"She is happy which makes me happy," Okacheybay answered, finally.

"Among all of Garrov's contraptions?" Mikhelena asked.

"She has found her calling, she tells me," Okacheybay said.

"She's one of the few who's been able to put up with all of Garrov's personal quirks," Mikhelena said with a laugh.

Okacheybay did a little skip. "Yes, she loves working in the steamworks. She is such a marvelous woman. Every minute I spend with her is better than the last. I have never felt more at peace than when she talks to me, and it does not matter what she says. It could be the most common, ordinary thing, yet her voice is like music."

Tristan chuckled. "I'm happy for you."

"Yes, well, my friend, I think you have a good match, as well."

Tristan looked over his shoulder at Mikhelena. "Yes. Very much so."

"The jobs in the steamworks can be dangerous," Mikhelena said. "How does she manage that?"

"With the nimbleness of a deer. Her body is so slender yet so long, she can maneuver herself in places Garrov can never go. She has saved him many hours of disassembling and reassembling; he gave her the day off just last week in gratitude."

"I'm glad she's so happy, Oak," Mikhelena said.

After less than forty minutes of walking, Okacheybay spotted a path newly trampled. Tristan was sure it was one he'd never used before. They followed it north and, before long, they emerged in a clearing. Woodsmen had recently felled trees here, for several axes were still implanted in the hewed stumps. At the edge of the clearing, twenty villagers were waiting in a line. At the head of the line stood Devereaux looking off into the distance. With him was the Alexandre de Mensonge, the Ringmaster, barking orders at his monkey to collect donations from the villagers.

Tristan and his companions waited behind a holly bush to see what happened next. Before long, a succession of snapping sticks announced the entrance of a giant bull, just as the talking bear had foretold. Its back was reddish-brown, its chest and belly brilliant white. There was a wound on its side, healed and scarred. The beast sauntered up to Devereaux who caressed its head with tender care. The Ringmaster bowed to the crowd of villagers and ushered them toward it.

"What in The Cause's grace are they doing?" whispered Okacheybay.

The first villager stepped up to the animal. Kneeling before it, he placed a basket on the ground and unfurled the cheesecloth that covered it. One by one he set out a half-dozen jars and bowls adorned with intricate blue patterns.

"Porcelain. Very beautiful," Tristan whispered, looking at Mikhelena.

The great bovine sniffed at the items, then lurched slightly forward and took one of the taller jars in its mouth. The sound of cracking pottery echoed in the air as it devoured the porcelain. Again, it dipped its head and took one of the items and consumed each until they were gone. The villager stood up and went to a nearby tree where the trunk was rotted and hollowed out at the bottom. He reached into the hollowed part and pulled out a large wooden tray. On the tray was a pheasant; dressed and ready to be roasted. Oranges, grapes, pineapples, and truffles were also piled in great heaps. The man struggled with the load but marched away whistling a festive tune.

The next villager knelt before the bull. She opened a leather bag and reached inside. Gold and silver coins dripped from her fingers as she removed her hand. The beast hunched over and devoured the coins; bag and all. The woman rose, went to the tree and removed two large clay jars. Ropes were attached to their handles and tied to a wooden shoulder harness. The woman positioned herself underneath it and stood to her full height. Uneasily, she began making her way back to the village.

"What is this sorcery? What could those jars be?" Okacheybay asked.

"Terracotta. I bet there's wine inside those. See how the tops are sealed with wax?" Tristan said.

A third villager came. He placed several farm implements before the cow. It ate them with relish. From the tree, the farmer pulled a large, feathered cap.

"Kinda looks like Bartonomous's," Mikhelena remarked.

Tristan nodded in agreement.

Each of the villagers presented their gifts to the mystic beast. Some brought weapons, precious stones, jewelry, even hens and goats. The bull gobbled them all up. In return, they received perfumes, flowering wreaths, exquisite foods, strong drink, and fine clothing.

The line was two-thirds through when a young widow came forward. She carried with her a large package wrapped in brown paper.

"That's Elayna," Mikhelena said.

"You know her?" Tristan asked.

She nodded.

Elayna pulled the paper from the package, strip by strip. The paper revealed a magnificent oil painting. A man, woman, and two young children sat in a formal pose upon pink granite stone.

"She can't!" Mikhelena gasped.

Tristan leaned closer to get a better look. "I don't get it. What is it?"

"Her family."

Elayna dropped to one knee, then to both. She held the picture in her hands for a moment, staring at it in silence. Then, she turned the frame around and presented it to the animal. The beast, as it had done before, ingested the thing bite by bite.

When it finished, Elayna sat for a moment. She appeared like a painted statue, unmoving. An interminable time passed before she rose and advanced toward the hollow tree. Kneeling before it, she slid a hand inside. There, she waited. Then, with sudden energy she yanked out her arm revealing a sheer cape in all the colors of the world. She twirled and danced with it in her hands; the shimmering crimsons, sapphires, golds, aquamarines, and corals fluttered in the sumptuous rays of the sun. She twirled and twirled closer and closer to the forest edge when the cape snagged the branches of a black thorn bush. She yanked at the delicate cloth. A shredding sound ripped through the air.

A wretched, "Nooooo!" burst through the young woman's lips.

"Take her away! Take her away!" shouted Alexandre.

The woman rushed to the bull screaming, "Give it back! I want it back!"

The bovine turned away from her and the ringmaster's chimpanzee took her hand. The small creature started to lead her away when Devereaux came and took her into his arms. Holding her up, he walked her back past the line of villagers toward Vitalba.

"This is enough," Tristan declared.

He stood to his feet and marched toward the ringmaster, Okacheybay, and Mikhelena following close behind. The crowd turned their faces toward them as Tristan met the red-clad entertainer chest to chest.

"What's happening here?" Tristan demanded.

Alexandre smiled, removed his top hat, and bowed. "Ah, the young lad with unusual strength. Good to see you again."

"I'm no lad. I'm a huntsman, and there is an air of Unhallowed magic about this creature. Where did it come from?" Tristan asked, jabbing a finger into the man's left lapel.

The ringmaster backed off. "I know not. We were simply entertaining the woodsmen working this place when it showed up. One of the woodsmen tossed his axe at its feet hoping to scare it away. The creature ate the axe then pointed at yonder tree with its great horns. Inside, the man found a goose stuffed with almonds, walnuts, and berries. He rushed it home to his family. The villagers came on their own accord. I am simply a witness."

Tristan looked over at the docile bull. It patted the ground with a hoof and breathed softly.

"I do not like this creature," Okacheybay broke in.

"Me, neither," Mikhelena added.

Tristan nodded and turned to the remaining crowd saying, "This is over. The beast is evil and is swindling you from your possessions. This kind of magic does not come from The Cause. It is the work of Lord Dreadstone. Leave this place."

The crowd stood silent for a moment, then began to grumble. "We're not leaving," some said.

"I'll prove it to you!" Tristan shouted. "If my blade cannot cut its skin, then it may be The Cause. But if my edge pierces it, you will know that this thing is altogether evil."

The ringmaster took a step toward him. "I don't think that will be necessary. The people are happy. They get what they want. Why are you interfering?"

Tristan glared at the red-coated entertainer, then marched to the bull. He drew his broadsword, already flaming brightly with blue fire. Seeing the blaze upon the blade only confirmed Tristan's suspicions.

He grasped his weapon with both hands and raised his sword high above his head. With all his power he brought it crashing down on the spine of the monster. The searing blade cut through, splitting the creature wide open halfway down its ribs. The flesh, bone, and muscle pulled away to reveal its bloody innards.

Tristan lifted his head in satisfaction and withdrew his blade from the flesh of the still standing beast and presented the wound to the villagers. They stood aghast for a moment, then began to murmur among themselves. Tristan's sword strike was true, yet there was no blood. As soon as he withdrew his blade, the gaping wound closed itself and healed entirely. Tristan struck it again. And, again, it healed. He slashed, hacked, and thrusted his broadsword into the mighty creature, all to no avail.

"Is it of The Cause, huntsman?" one of the villagers asked.

Panting, looking at his friends, Tristan gasped under his breath, "It can't be killed!"

Chapter 19:

THE CONTROVERSY OF THE RUNES

The three huntsmen raced to Vitalba. Tristan replayed the images in his mind: the blade blazed with fire, the edge sliced through flesh and bone, yet the creature did not die. Questions about the bull's origin and what its indestructibility might mean for all Unhallowed swirled inside his head as the village gate came into view.

They reached the village barely keeping their breath. Tristan pushed himself on toward the Lodge and then through the halls until he burst through the wide doors of the library. Expecting to see Aranka alone, he was astonished to see Valere, Garrov, Patric, and Nicole sitting around the great oak table along with two workers from the wall.

"Ah Tristan, good, I'm glad the messenger found you. Please join us," Aranka said.

Tristan approached the table and said, "I think we might have a situation. The villagers—"

"Yes, yes," Aranka waved him off. "That's why the workers are here. We're going to sort this out now."

"I couldn't kill it," Tristan protested.

Valere raised his shoulders. "Who said anything about killing? This is about the wall."

"Please take a seat, Tristan," Aranka repeated.

"You're not listening to me," Tristan said, pounding the table.

Aranka held up a finger. "It can wait."

"Have you ever heard of a creature we can't slay? This cannot wait!"

"Oh, but It can," she insisted with stern eyes. Then, turning to the laborers, she said, "Start over so he can hear."

Tristan sunk down into his seat with his arms folded. He leaned back and made no attempt to hide his contempt.

The woodsman cleared his throat and began, "The repairs to the stockade are finished. All of the bloodrot is removed and there is no danger from that, at least not until winter comes again."

"There is some contention between the workers and some of the villagers concerning what to do next," added the other.

"This is what we were in the middle of deciding," Aranka said, looking at Tristan.

The older worker continued, "Some of the laborers want to be done and move on to felling timber for other projects. Some of the villagers are demanding we cover the timbers in Eldanar to protect them from more bloodsnow and from attacks by the Unhallowed. Bindle and Juanitos want us to let them carve runes in them, ancient runes from the holy books to protect the village."

"The question is: what's best for the village. What do you think, sir?" Valere asked.

The woodsman looked down and shuffled his feet. "Honestly, sir, my men have other enterprises they wish to begin. Homes need repairs, animals need pens, the winter cords of wood are almost exhausted, the carpenters have their projects, and—"

"We get the idea," Tristan interrupted.

Aranka looked over at Garrov. "Morritz, do we even have enough Eldanar for that sort of thing?"

The white-haired inventor leaned forward and twitched his mustache. "Ze miners in ze mines located a streak of Eldanar amongst ze coal and brought it to ze village. I have processed it and added it to ze stockpile Thaul left us, but even with ziss, zere's not enough to cover all ze timbers."

"That settles it, then, the villagers will just have to be disappointed," Aranka said.

Just then, Devereaux entered the library. He bowed to the members of the council and said, "I just heard about the controversy as I was escorting Ms. Revellere home. May I ask what you've decided?"

"Why's he here? Did you invite him, Patric?" Tristan asked.

Patric flicked his golden hair to the side, "Not today, but I will extend that invitation now. Come, my dear friend, you may sit next to me."

Devereaux bowed again and took an empty seat a little behind Patric.

Aranka shook her head and returned her gaze back to the woodsmen. "I think your work is done, gentlemen. We don't have enough of the metal to please the villagers."

"And so it goes," Devereaux said.

A silence hung in the room for a moment. The old woodsman nodded and said, "And what about the runes?"

"What runes?" asked Devereaux.

"Juanitos and Bindle wish to carve holy runes into the posts of the stockade to ward off the Unhallowed," answered the younger woodsman.

"This is a bad idea," Devereaux whispered in Patric's ear.

"This is a bad idea," Patric said.

Nicole squinted at Patric then leaned over to get a clear look at Devereaux. "Why do you think that?" she asked.

"May I address the council?" Deveraux asked, flashing a broad smile.

"If you are just going to speak through Patric, save us the trouble and say what you have to say," Aranka answered.

Devereaux pushed his seat back and stood. Maintaining a deferential tone, he said, "Well, if I may speak freely, the customs of this village are quaint and very traditional. I enjoy them a great deal, myself. The festival, the carnival, all these bring so much meaning to our little town. To the outside world, though, they do not. Merchants come to us from the city and from places beyond the wilderlands. They do not share our holy rituals or our archaic languages. They are strangers, and we would be such rude hosts--I think--as to subject them unwillingly to the runes and dictates of holy books from a bygone era. Consider that they very likely will be confused or, perhaps worse, offended. Can we, in good conscience, subject the livelihoods of so many craftsmen in this village to a risk like that? What if, upon seeing the holy script so pridefully displayed, they choose never to return? Such a thing would reflect poorly on Vitalba's reputation, would it not? Not to mention throw our craftsmen into poverty."

Devereaux took his seat but kept his head bowed low.

Tristan squinted at him. His blood rushed in his veins. A sense of violation overtook his senses, and he blurted out, "I don't think their sensibilities are really a concern of ours."

"Agreed," Valere said.

"Your opinion carries great weight, no doubt. Though, I have a congregation of many villagers who would agree with me, I think," Devereaux responded.

Tristan ignored him and looked at his fellow council members. "Well, *I think* I have an idea that I think will please everyone. For those who want Bindle and Juanitos to carve the runes, I say we give them what they want. Same for those who want Eldanar on the walls. But since we do not have enough to cover every timber, let the pastor and the scribe inlay the runes the workers make with Eldanar. I know Bindle's craft, he will make them very pleasing to the eye, even the eyes of merchants who come here. This way the walls are protected, the woodsmen can get to their work, and our village is beautified."

There was a general nodding of heads. A nearly inaudible whisper broke the assent and Patric blurted out, "I object!"

"I don't. I think it's a fine idea," said Nicole.

"Seconded," said Valere, looking over at Aranka.

"I, as well," added Aranka.

"Garrov, do we have enough metal for that?" Tristan asked.

"If zey are economical with it and leave enough for my own projects and weapon crafting, I should say yes," the inventor answered.

"Motion carried," Aranka declared.

"And so it goes," Devereaux said.

"And so it goes," Patric echoed.

Everyone stared at them for a moment, then Tristan relaxed and sat back in his chair. "So now can we talk about the beast in the woods?"

"What beast?" Devereaux demanded.

All turned their eyes to the black plumed huntsman.

"The magic bull in the north forest. You know of it," Tristan said, pointing at Devereaux.

"That thing is real? I have only found myths and fairy tales about such a creature," Aranka said, turning her attention back to Tristan.

Tristan nodded and turned to her. "It's real, and it's Unhallowed. My sword flamed around it, but I couldn't kill it. Aranka, did you find anything about the ancient bone blade?"

"About the sword, just mentions, so far," she said.

Garrov interjected. "I may have come across such a zing. I believe zere is an entry in my weapons book back at ze steamworks."

"It might be the only thing that can kill this beast," Tristan said. "Garrov, can you show me the entry in your book?"

"Yes, of course, but it may take me time to find it in my laboratory. Come see me in the morning" Garrov said.

Aranka hit the table with a gavel and said, "Meeting adjourned. I'll continue my research, Tristan. Garrov, report what you find."

Chapter 20:
ON WINGS OF METAL

As Tristan left the library, he put an arm around Garrov and spoke quietly in his ear.

"I'm wondering if you might help me with a project," Tristan said.

The inventor looked surprised. "What is it?"

"Eldo has lost his legs. I'm sure you've heard. Could you rig up some kind of weapon or shield he could use? I'm going to ask that he be stationed near the gardens. The children playing bring him joy. Think you could make something?"

"It may be possible. Let me zink on it for a while."

"Of course," Tristan said, letting the grey-haired man go.

He continued on in search of Mikhelena. He entered the infirmary. Among the cots, he found Mikhelena tending a crowd of villagers who had just come in. Darian and Okacheybay were there also, helping as they could.

"Tristan, help these people find a bed," Mikhelena ordered.

Tristan nodded and began ushering the feeble villagers to clean cots scattered throughout the room. Other hunters were busy pulling the dirty canvass off and replacing them with new ones.

Once all the villagers were resting, Tristan brought in fresh towels, hot water from the kitchen, and dried herbs from the apothecary. Darian, Mikhelena, and Nicole (who had also joined them at this point), along with the freshly certified Aaron all tended to them. When there was a lull in the commotion, Tristan leaned on the ledge near one of the iron latticed windows of the infirmary.

Okacheybay approached him and asked, "Do any of these people look familiar to you, my friend?"

Tristan put his hands on his hips and scanned the room. He nodded. "Yes. They were all in the forest this morning with the bull. That's the farmer, the widow Revellere..."

"That was my suspicion, as well, except... Devereaux was there, and he's fine. If anyone has been exposed to it, besides healers, it is him. His study group, the people at the river, many of them have shown up at the infirmary."

Tristan stared at the floor. "I hope Garrov can find something about that ancient blade. We were just starting to clear out this infirmary. It seemed like things were getting better."

Okacheybay wagged a finger in Tristan's face and said, "Ah, it is in those moments we must be extra vigilant against evil, for it is then we start to trust in ourselves and not The Cause."

"Indeed," Tristan said, then left to retire to his chamber on the top floor.

Upon sitting on his bed, he snatched his weapons and armor along with Mikhelena's. He went through every inch of her brigandine and then his cuirass, making sure each aspect of it was repaired and secure. He grabbed a wet stone and linseed oil, then began sharpening the edges of his broadsword, doing the same for Mikhelena's scimitar. The repetitive kthink-kthink-kthink of stone on metal focused his mind.

His memories traced back over the last few months from his interrupted honeymoon to the infirmary that day. A gloom had stuck its icy fingers in his mind ever since his shield was destroyed by the Vekkenwulf. The ragged gouges left by the wolf's fangs still marred the remnants of his family heirloom. Tristan could almost smell its foul breath upon it. Yet, it wasn't the loss of the shield that was so troubling. A shadow leached upon his back like an imp draining him ever since that day: a dark presence whispering doubts and confusion in his mind.

"I'm missing something," Tristan said aloud.

"What?" Mikhelena asked as she closed the door to their room.

He looked up at her with a start.

"Sorry," she said as she began changing out of her work clothes. "What do you mean?"

Tristan finished his work and began putting away his things. "I dunno. I feel like there is a presence in the village--something dark and hidden."

"The sickness?"

Tristan shook his head. "No, the sickness is just a symptom. There's something else out there; something we haven't uncovered."

"The wishing bull?" she asked, taking a seat next to him.

"Another symptom, I think," he said.

"I just hope Garrov can find something about the ancient bone blade in his lab. I don't think it will solve the mystery, but it will help treat the symptoms. Sometimes, that's all you can do, right?"

Mikhelena nodded. "Sometimes."

Tristan got up and went to the window. The setting sun cast crisscross patterns on his face and chest. The windows were grimy, and he could barely see the village below. Aaron passed his test, didn't he?" he asked.

She hunched over and turned her face to the floor, her long golden locks--somewhat darker than in the past--hung over her face. "Yes, he did," she said.

"Good. I'll need you to come with me. You, and Oak, and who knows who else. I'll need all of you to make sure we get this right," Tristan said, pounding his fist on the windowsill.

"I'll come," she said in a weak voice.

Tristan nodded and leaned against the window.

Morning came, and the roosters crowed, waking the sleepy village. Tristan's eyes sprung open, releasing a flood of dread and excitement.

"Morning already?" she mumbled.

Tristan rose and went to his bureau. "Yes. Already."

She leaned up against the headboard, amid the carvings of men at arms fighting horrific beasts. "There's something you need to know," she whispered in a hoarse tone.

"Garrov is an early riser. I know he'll already be at the steamworks. Let's try to get ready as quickly as we can. Sorry, what did you say?" he asked.

"Nothing. I'll get dressed."

Tristan dressed himself, fitted his sword to his belt, and slung his shield on his back. Mikhelena finished putting on her clothes, then grabbed her medical kit and draped it over her shoulder.

As they trod along the uneven dirt street Tristan's senses picked up something in the air. The heavy scent of burning coal, like that of singed oatmeal, lingered among the houses and shops of Vitalba.

"Garrov has the steamworks working hard this morning," Tristan remarked.

"He must have found something," Mikhelena replied.

Okacheybay was waiting for them at the boiler works. It was a massive structure. The great steel boilers hummed as their contents turned to vapor. The pipes rattled and shook, diving into the ground below the village. Bulky bolts protruded from all directions with soot-covered steel intermingling with tarnished brass. The entrance looked more like a cave than a doorway carved out of metal rock.

Upon entering, they spotted Garrov hurrying across one of the dark, twisted corridors carrying an armful of leather, wood, and metal sheeting.

"Garrov," Tristan shouted, bringing his hands up to his mouth.

Garrov vanished into a doorway. "I do not think he heard you," Okacheybay said.

Tristan led them to the tunnel where they last saw Garrov. It opened up into a huge, domed atrium with pipes and vents crisscrossing in every direction. The white-haired inventor had three large leather packs with cedar frames mounted on the stout stands. In Garrov's hand was a massive key, so large in fact, that it would take two hands to turn it. Janelle worked behind one of the stands, making final adjustments to the packs.

"Garrov," Tristan repeated. "We're here. Did you find anything about the sword?"

Garrov jumped at the sound of his name and whirled around to face Tristan and his companions.

"Ah, yes. I have discovered ze secret to making ze blade."

Tristan clapped his hands together. "Good. Let's get to it."

Garrov went to a nearby table and laid the key down with a thud. He proceeded to a nearby stand; upon which rested a massive open tome six feet wide, three feet long, and half a foot thick on each side.

"Not so easy. Come look," he said to Tristan, motioning with his hand.

Tristan and Okacheybay drew near to the massive book while Mikhelena joined Janelle at the packs. The pages of the book were not paper nor parchment; they were engraved in thin sheets of silver bound by seven bronze rings. Upon each page there was a diagram and many words written in the runes of the huntsmen.

"I can't read these," Tristan said, passing a hand over the bottom edge of one page.

"Zat's a shame," Garrov said, shaking his head.

Okacheybay stepped up to the book and said, "I can."

"Good. Tell me what it says about making ze ancient bone blade. I do not want you to zink I am deceiving you when I tell you ze plan to get one."

The hunter leaned his lanky frame over the massive page and scanned it for the information Garrov desired. After a moment, he stood straight.

Okacheybay pointed to a section of tiny runes and said, "It says here that the bone for the blade must come from one of the Goliaths."

Tristan looked up from the tome and stared at Garrov. "What's a Goliath?"

"A giant of ze ancient world: an extinct race of violent brutes zat ravaged ze valley during my grandfazer's grandfazer's time."

"Extinct?" Tristan repeated.

"Yes, all dead. Thavide the Great slew them all, as the stories go," Okacheybay added.

Tristan turned back to the tome and placed his hands on either side. He strained his eyes to make sense of anything on the page that might provide some hope.

At last, Tristan said with a twinge of frustration in his voice, "Is there no way to kill this wishing beast, then?"

"Of course zere is," Garrov said.

Tristan slumped. "How? You just said they're all gone."

"Dead, yes. Gone? No. Zere is one place zey can be found."

Tristan looked over his shoulder. "Where?"

"Ah-ha! Come see," Garrov unfurled a map of the valley on his table. He pointed to the furthest south-west corner of Celandine Valley where the Betherian and Razorspine Mountains met.

"That's days away. We should get started," Tristan said, standing erect.

"Show me again where that is," Okacheybay said.

"Zey are here. I have heard many confirmed reports from ze huntsmen zat patrol ze west zat remains of giants are still in ze caves of zose mountains. Except zey are not living giants, of course, but ze skeletons of the ancient ones. Buried, but not forgotten. We shall go and find one zere and take what we need," Garrov explained as he pointed to the place a second time.

Okacheybay studied where Garrov pointed, then grabbed Tristan by the shoulders and looked at him with stern eyes. "While I was in Infuria's pack she spoke to us of those mountains, my friend. She told us of ancient times when creatures far stranger and more vicious than any Unhallowed walked the world. She warned us never to go there, for some of the ancients still dwell in those places. Take extra care, Tris. There are older and more perilous creatures than dead giants lurking in those peaks."

Tristan turned to Garrov with a skeptical look.

"Zis is ze only way," he said, shrugging his shoulders.

Tristan leaned back against the book. "It's still a long journey. The villagers will give up half the town before we get back, and the illness will only get worse."

Garrov pointed his finger to his head. "Ah, but see. I have zought of zis. Come, let me show you."

He led Tristan and Okacheybay to where Janelle and Mikhelena were talking.

"Are zey ready?" Garrov asked.

Janelle smiled. "Yes, just like you wanted."

Mikhelena stepped from behind one of the large packs. "He won't believe what you're going to tell him," she said.

"Ah, zen perhaps I must show him," Garrov replied. "Janelle, help fit zis one to my back please."

As Janelle hefted one of the packs off the stand, Garrov began putting on a heavy, fur-lined coat and gloves. His face he covered with a padded mask and pulled a pair of glass goggles over his eyes. Janelle helped Garrov strap the pack to his back. He then took the massive key from the experiment table and handed it to her. She inserted the key into the pack.

Garrov motioned Tristan toward him. "Young man, I know zat you are blessed with great strength. I have twisted the key as much as I could. Would you mind twisting it as far as you can? Let me brace myself as you do."

Tristan took the key and began to turn it. It felt heavy and primitive in his hand, but it moved counterclockwise easily enough. Each turn caused Garrov to almost lose his balance. Slowly, the mechanism grew tighter and tighter.

"Am I going to break it?" Tristan asked.

"Not possible. Ze springs are made of Eldanar. Crank away, my son. We will need all ze torque we can get for such a long journey," Garrov replied.

Tristan shrugged and continued to turn. At last, the key felt like it hit something inside the mechanism, and it could turn no more. Tristan gave it one last shove and nearly flipped Garrov on his head.

"Ok, ok! Zat shall do," the inventor said with a laugh.

"What now?" Tristan asked.

"Take ze key out and do ze same for ze other two. Now we may have to fend off a stray Unhallowed or two, so I must ask: who shall be coming?" Garrov asked.

Tristan looked around. "All three of us, I guess."

Garrov made a clicking sound with his mouth. "Alas, no. I have made only zree packs, and I must come."

Tristan furrowed his eyebrows, giving the inventor a quizzical look. "Why? What do these packs have to do with getting to the mountains?"

"Heh. These machines will help us travel far faster zan you can imagine. I have to come in case zey break down. Do you have any experience with zese machines? Could you so easily navigate your way to one of ze most remote places of ze valley? Would you recognize a Goliath skeleton if you saw one?"

Tristan just stared at him.

"Zat's what I zought," Garrov said from behind his mask.

Tristan looked at his friends. Okacheybay was the best warrior, but Mikhelena's skills would be most needed.

Tristan put his hand on Okacheybay's shoulder. "Oak, my friend, I want you to come, but if Garrov or I get hurt, we'll need Miki to patch us back up."

"Understood," the grim huntsman said.

"Talk to the townsfolk. Find out from them where the wishing beast is located and be ready to help us track it down when we return."

"With all pleasure," Okacheybay said with a slight bow.

"Make sure to turn ze key in those packs before putting zem on. Oak, you and ze ladies may want to brace the frame so Tristan can turn ze key all ze way," Garrov said.

Tristan went to the next pack and began cranking the key. "How much faster will these get us there?"

A maniacal laugh escaped Garrov's throat. "Much faster than any horse can sprint! If they can hold together, that is. You may take your weapons but leave any gear you don't think you will need. We must travel light, so we can return with as much bone as possible. Meet me at ze scaffold on ze chimney when you're fitted and ready to go."

Garrov exited the room as Tristan finished his work on the second pack.

"Hold together? What do you think he means?" Tristan asked Janelle.

She shrugged. "With him, I never ask how his inventions work. I just trust that they do."

The last pack was wound as tightly as it could go then Okacheybay and Janelle helped Tristan and Mikhelena into fur-lined outfits that covered over their regular clothes. Janelle strapped a mask and pair of goggles to each of their heads and then she directed Okacheybay on how to attach the packs to their coats.

When all was finished, Garrov reappeared in the doorway and clapped his hands saying, "All is prepared above. Please follow me."

Tristan and Mikhelena struggled up the winding staircase. The heavy packs and thick clothing made it difficult to move. They exited the stairs and found themselves on the roof of the steamworks.

"Up here," Garrov yelled from the top of the smokestack.

Another spiral staircase confronted the two huntsmen. Tristan exhaled and began the ascent. Up and up and up the rickety stairs they went until finally the three of them stood looking out over the village. The wind beat their faces, but the chilly spring breeze could not penetrate the warm outerwear. "Now, a quick crash course on how to operate ze system," Garrov said.

"What exactly are we doing up here?" Tristan asked out of growing suspicion.

"It is simple. Here, on ze left strap, zere are zree knobs. Ze first adjusts your speed. Ze second toggles between glide and flapping. And ze zird begins ze landing sequence."

"I don't understand," Tristan said looking down at all the switches and wiring of his harness.

"Now, watch me. Do exactly as I do, and you will be fine," Garrov said, patting him on the back.

Mikhelena and Tristan stepped back, and Garrov clambered to the top of the railing. Yanking a cord on his right shoulder, the leather pack convulsed. Two enormous metallic wings made from beaten Eldanar with bamboo supports sprung out from either side.

Garrov looked back over his shoulder and said, "Go one at a time. Ze span is more zan twenty feet, so you don't want to hit each other."

With that, the mad inventor leaped from the railing and dove headfirst toward the ground. The wings began to flap feverishly, and Garrov rocketed up into the sky. He began circling the chimney far above. The hunters could just barely hear him call out, "Hurry! Ze mechanism will not last forever! Full speed!"

"This is inconceivable," Tristan said.

Mikhelena made no answer but made her way to the railing. She yanked the cord and released her wings. Without any hesitation, she jumped. Tristan rushed to the side to see her rise up just before him.

Shrugging his shoulders, he followed their motion. When the wings shot out from the pack, it suddenly felt light and more comfortable somehow. Holding tightly to the straps on his chest, he let his balance fall forward. As soon as his descent began, he twisted the knob on the top left and arched his back upward. The wings caught the air and began to flap like a giant bat. Instantly, he gained altitude and joined the others above the village. *This must be the giant birds the villagers have seen. Garrov should have known better than to develop his inventions in secret.*

Garrov motioned them with his hand, and they flew to the south-west. Garrov increased his speed. Tristan and Mikhelena followed suit. In an hour, they were above the prairies. In another, they passed The Furrows. The goats and sheep below dotted the rolling hills like so many white dandelions in a field. In the third hour, they were in the mountains.

The winds grew more erratic as the peaks grew taller. Several times, Tristan suddenly lost altitude only to be thrust upward again. Mikhelena likewise struggled while Garrov seemed to pass serenely through the sky. The currents became ever more violent. The wings vibrated as they oscillated back and forth. Soon, his whole body shook. Tristan thought for sure they'd crash. Mikhelena struggled to keep herself level as the howling gales increased in ferocity. He was suddenly thrust upward while Mikhelena was forced down. Tristan called out to Garrov, but the wicked air whipping past them drowned his voice.

Chapter 21:
BONES THAT MOVE

Tristan strained against the force of his wings. To his relief, Garrov began his descent. Tristan followed him down, as best he could, easing back on the speed of the contraption. He stayed far enough behind Garrov to watch him begin the landing sequence. The Inventor slapped his left shoulder and suddenly the wings rotated forward. Garrov dangled from them like a rat caught in the talons of an owl, but the tinker huntsman settled down on a flat cliff as lightly as a feather. Tristan followed him down, and Mikhelena landed last of all.

After she touched down, she scrambled out of her harness and raced ahead of the men. She wretched onto the ground.

"Well done, I wasn't certain we'd all survive," the inventor applauded. "Just a little motion sickness, my huntress. All will be well."

Tristan went to Mikhelena and rubbed between her shoulder blades. Electricity.

"Don't forget to retract ze wings. The leather packs will keep ze inner workings safe from ze elements," Garrov warned.

As Tristan followed his directions, he looked at the inventor and said, "Your skill in inventions has reached a new peak, Garrov."

The inventor laughed aloud. "Oh, I'm working on something much larger zan zis, lad. Give me a few more months and I'll put zese trinkets to shame!"

"I think you've been scaring the townsfolk, though. We've gotten reports of a giant bird or bat stalking the village for the past few months. Have you been testing these near Vitalba?"

"Of course," replied the inventor.

Tristan nodded. "Well, just let us know next time."

"My apologies. I had no wish to alarm anyone. Now, zere must be a cave entrance near here somewhere. I'm sure of it. Ze Goliaths made zis range zere home for centuries. We just need to find ze remains of one of zem, preferably a femur, and we'll be able to make ze sword."

The three of them hefted their equipment onto their backs and trekked down the gentle side of the grey cliffs. On several occasions, they thought they may have found an entrance but, the false leads turned out to only be shallow crags and crevasses.

Evening was coming, and the explorers sat huddled together eating their jerky and hardtack. Tristan pulverized the tasteless biscuit in his hand and shoveled the dry powder into his mouth. Mikhelena poured something from her satchel onto her biscuit. The dry wafer grew three times in size, becoming moist and chewable.

Tristan hunched against the back of a cliff, figuring that their search for the day was done, when a haunting moan rose up among the mountains. Garrov and the hunters perked up at the sound. They scanned the rough paths and empty peaks for any sign of movement.

"See anything?" Mikhelena asked.

Tristan shaded his eyes, but nothing appeared among the lifeless grey stones. "Nothing," he replied.

The moan rose again as the wind lashed their faces. Garrov implored them to be silent and not move. The gales picked up once more, stronger now, and with them, the moaning sound reached a crescendo. It was like the sound of a ghost or lost soul clamoring for relief from penance.

"We must find ze source of zese wild sounds," Garrov declared.

"The sun is fading. It's not safe to hunt so late in the day," Mikhelena said.

"We must," Garrov repeated and stood to his feet.

The wailing continued as they began their search. Tristan's eyes watered from the constant assault of the air currents. As they groped along, they drew nearer and nearer to the source of the frightful howls.

At last, coming over a ridge, they beheld the great mouth that lamented so pitifully. It was the opening of a massive cave. The moaning picked up every time the wind blew.

"We found one!" Garrov exclaimed. "Ze stones must vibrate just enough to make ze wailing sound. Let's go inside."

Garrov strode toward the entrance, but Tristan and Mikhelena waited. "Tristan doesn't like caves," Mikhelena said.

Garrov paused and stared back at them.

"I used to fear going underground. Entering the mines to fight Infuria took every ounce of courage I had. I thought I was going to die in the prisoner's tunnel under the stockade back when Patric thought I was in league with the vampires. But thanks to my father's recent visit, I now know why

I've always felt that way. I no longer fear the darkness and cramped spaces. Let's go," Tristan said in a dead voice.

Garrov smiled approvingly and turned back toward the cave. They crept closer to the mouth. It wailed once again, but upon passing through the entrance, the noise was dampened.

"Not so loud now," Garrov said.

"Let's make camp here," Tristan said in the dying daylight.

The huntsmen arranged their packs and trifling amount of gear inside the cave entrance. It would be a comfortless night with no bedroll and few provisions. With that task completed, Garrov pulled three small spheres from a satchel and passed one to Tristan and another to Mikhelena. Then, he produced a small tuning fork from his pocket and struck the spheres upon their crowns. Instantly, they began to glow with warm yellow light.

"Let's see if we're lucky enough to find some remains here," Garrov said, his face beaming with satisfaction.

The walls bore the marks of tools and the egg-shaped roof was designed in such a way as to prevent cave-ins. It was obvious the cave was worked by hand. It wasn't long before a fork in the passage presented them with a choice.

"Anyone have a sense of which way we should go?" Garrov asked, holding his light sphere above his head.

They stood for a moment without speaking. "The left seems more unsettling to me," Mikhelena said.

"Then, that's the way we go," Tristan said, taking the lead.

They continued on forty yards when a glint of blue light on his left caught his eye. He looked down at his side. The broadsword clinging to his belt glowed inside its sheath. Tristan drew it and slung his shield from around his back.

"We're not alone," he said as he crouched into fighting position.

Mikhelena did the same, while Garrov moved behind her and fished something from behind his back. Tristan tossed his glowing sphere to the side; his sword provided all the light he needed now.

They crept forward and the cave opened up into a huge atrium. The arching roof spanned a space large enough for sixty men to sit at a table and feast. Tristan raised his sword above and behind his head to get a better look.

The room was empty, but the walls were not smooth like the tunnels. Instead, they were rough and disheveled. Nature carved out this rock. One particularly unusual formation caught Tristan's gaze. He moved closer to inspect it. The rocks looked like brine-colored pillars. The stones took on a more organic look. The streams that poured through this room in ancient times cut strange channels that looked like ribs coming together. Two other stone pillars had fallen against the ribs in a symmetrical a-frame.

He was about to move away when a crunching, crumbling sound held his senses a moment longer. The stones began to vibrate, then move, then erect themselves into the form of a man but not a man, a beast of a creature twice the size of Tristan.

"Garrov, I found one!" he yelled.

"Don't destroy its femurs," the inventor yelled back.

"These things are alive?" Mikhelena shouted.

"Garrov. The legs are the weakest part. You sure I can't attack them?" Tristan asked as he backed away from the advancing monstrosity.

"Save ze legs!"

"Alright. The hard way, then," Tristan muttered as he raised his shield.

"Garrov, did you know these were alive?" he heard Mikhelena ask.

"No," the inventor said. "Someone is controlling it. We must find him."

The bone-giant brought a hulking fist down at Tristan. The huntsman dodged and rolled to the right. A second massive fist charged him from the left, but he caught it with his heater shield, deflecting it away from his body. The colossus radiated an otherworldly green-blue that illuminated the cave with flickering light. Tristan dashed under its attempt to stomp him and waited for the creature's next attack. It came from the right. Tristan dodged and struck at the monster's wrist with his sword as it flew by. The burning blue blade bit deep into the monster's bone, yet the cut did not sever hand from arm.

A second swipe came from the opposite direction. Again, Tristan dodged, struck with all his might, and barely gouged a quarter of the way through its hardened bones.

"I'm hitting him, but I can't break through," he yelled to Mikhelena and Garrov.

"Zere must be a necromancer nearby controlling it. Come, huntress, we find him!" the tinker yelled.

Tristan dodged another stomp while the other two darted into a smaller tunnel just behind the beast.

"Just you and me now," Tristan said, adjusting his grip on his broadsword.

The monstrosity brought another foot down to crush the hunter, but Tristan knocked it to the side with his shield as hard as he could. The resulting blow caused the ungainly giant to lose its balance and come crashing to the hard stone floor.

Tristan seized the opportunity and savaged the chalky left arm of the creature, chopping a "V" into its forearm as one might chop a log of wood with an axe. Bits of luminescent bone sprayed in all directions, but a flinch of the creature's arm knocked Tristan back ten feet onto his stomach.

The creature's jaw opened, as if it wanted to roar in pain. Tristan scrambled to his feet, noting that his strategy was sound, he just needed more time to break through.

The mammoth skeleton moved slowly. Tristan sized him up, hoping for another stomp so he could knock the creature down once again. Instead, the beast shuffled closer and reached down with both hands to grasp at Tristan. The hunter leaped forward and turned around, intent on striking the damaged arm of his foe.

His sword struck true, and the crackling of blanched bone encouraged Tristan. The monster, though, did not retract its appendage. Instead, it swiped again, barely catching the leg of Tristan's trousers. It began to lift the huntsman from the ground, but Tristan wrenched himself free and fell to the floor.

Instantly, the monster brought down his uninjured fist to crush him. Tristan rolled right to avoid it. The fist came again. He rolled back the way he came. The piston-like punches of the giant came furiously now, and Tristan only narrowly dodged each blow. One hit would be enough to stun him. A second would crush him utterly.

The rolling about on the floor and the fear caused by the near-misses took a toll on Tristan's energy. The bulky coat and pants he wore to keep him warm during the flight slowed him down and made each evading move increasingly difficult to execute. The driving attacks from the giant came closer and closer.

At last, Tristan rolled behind the heel of the giant, forcing the brute to maneuver awkwardly for his next strike. This bit of fortune gave Tristan just enough time to stand but not enough to dodge. The creature's hand flew at Tristan and shoved him back against the wall of the cave. Tristan wormed his shield in front of him, allowing himself to breath, but the glowing behemoth pressed harder.

Tristan's weapon hand was somehow free and, with all his might, he brought his sword down on the enemy's elephantine hand. Bone splinters exploded in all directions, and Tristan swung down as rapidly as he could; desperate to chip his way free.

"Find that spell caster!" he shouted with all his might.

The fingertips of the giant scraped against the dark cave wall, leaving green-white lines in the stone. Tristan hacked away, fully aware that, in a moment, he'd be within the monster's grasp and unable to escape. The flames of his sword leapt up in new ferocity, and he was sure he had never struck anything so hard in all his life. While the ghostly hand showed cracks in all directions and a great channel had been cut between the thumb and forefinger of the leviathan, the clutching fingers were almost upon him.

Chapter 22:
THE GOLIATH SWORD

Tristan slammed his sword into his foe again and again. The great hand closed tightly around him, ready to squeeze his life into the ether. Through his grimace and rage, he cried aloud, "The Cause help me."

In that moment, purple and red flames assailed the creature. It reeled back in surprise, dropping Tristan to the ground. Two new huntsmen joined the fray and pressed their advantage.

"Lise? Yanis? Where's Mersha?" Tristan shouted.

"Right here," came a voice from behind.

A bright, yellow-flamed mace came sailing through the air, smashing into the ribs of the bone-giant. The three huntsmen below were showered in pale blue-green fragments.

"Do not strike the legs! We need them," Tristan shouted to the others.

He regained his strength and readied himself for combat.

"You here by yourself?" Mersha called while stalking to the monster's left.

"Miki and Garrov are in the next tunnel over, looking for the necromancer controlling this thing," Tristan replied.

"Filippos, you're with me," Mersha said, diving to retrieve her weapon.

The yellow and orange flames of Mersha and Filippos disappeared into the adjoining tunnel. The bone-giant resumed his advance on the three remaining hunters. It raised its foot to crush them below.

"Lise, Tanis, be ready," Tristan commanded. "I'll knock him to the ground, and we must sever his hands from his arms."

Hoping they understood, Tristan readied his shield. When the lumbering foot of the bone giant came, Tristan braced against his shield and knocked it aside with all his strength. The monstrous skeleton kicked its own leg out from under itself and fell to the ground, sprawling out in all directions. The huntsmen beset the damaged wrist of the bone-giant, and as it began to raise itself, they finished hacking through.

The giant drew itself up to a knee, then grasped for Lise with its other hand. She tumbled away, but the lightning quick claws of the undead creature snatched her cloak and yanked her back to the floor. The impact knocked her weapon from her hand. It skittered across the cold, stone floor. Tristan and Yanis savaged the monster's grip. Showers of bone scattered in all directions. Lise slithered out of her garment and scrambled for her lost sword.

"A sling would come in handy right now," Tristan muttered as the three hunters aligned in a fighting formation.

Yanis shrugged. "Sorry, we just have arrows." Erecting itself to full height, the giant examined the stump of its arm. It shook its cracked and crumbling fist at the hunters in apparent anger as its radius bone dropped to the floor.

"Eet cannot take too much more puneeshment. We've almost got eet," Lise said.

The bone giant charged. The three huntsmen scattered. It went after Yanis. Tristan clipped its foot with his broadsword as it lurched by. The fiery blade hit true and dissevered several toes from the creature.

Tristan dodged a backswipe from the giant and rolled to the right, behind a small boulder. Lise and Yanis each struck the other foot of the beast; trying to mimic Tristan's attack. Without warning, the bones disconnected themselves and fell into a massive heap amid a thunderous clamor. Lise and Yanis sheltered under their shields as the falling debris pelted them from above. The bones lost their glow and the flames of the hunters' swords diminished, then snuffed out altogether. The room was dark.

"They found the necromancer," Tristan said, hopping to his feet.

"I've got torches, hang on," Yanis said in the blackness.

In a moment, the room was lit with a blazing brand. Yanis ignited two more and handed them to Lise and Tristan.

"We'd better go check the others and see if they need any help," Tristan said. "How did you find us?"

"We were tracking some dwarves that stole some of Lise's equipment, including the acid she uses to refine the moonberry root that grows in the ruins. We saw your packs inside the cave and decided to see who might be here. The glowing sphere you dropped back in the tunnel told us there must be huntsmen nearby."

"Zat's when we heard you fightink," Lise added.

Yanis kicked one of the nearby bone fragments. "Why would you take on something like this by yourself?" he asked.

Tristan shrugged. "There weren't supposed to be any alive. We're just here to collect some remains and leave. None of us had any idea there'd be a necromancer in this cave."

A few minutes later, as they were about to enter the side tunnel, Garrov emerged, carrying one of his light spheres, followed by Mikhelena, Mersha, and Filippos.

"Was he alone?" Tristan asked.

"He was blinkin' all over the cave, but we got 'im," Mersha said as she pushed her elbow across her neck until her shoulder popped.

"Who was eet?" Lise asked.

"Atratheries," Mikhelena answered.

Yanis nodded with a half-smile. "Wondered what happened to him after the incident in the Golden Fells three years ago. Anyone hurt?"

"We're fine. What are you doin' here? Come lookin' for us? We're not goin' back," Mersha said.

Garrov busied himself about the heap of bones, and Tristan found a place to lodge his torch in the wall.

"Nah, we're here to get these bones for a weapon we need," Tristan said.

Mersha looked over the bones Garrov arranged. "Something new attacking the village?" she asked.

Lise and Mikhelena found a place to sit in the light. They began trading herbs and healing reagents back and forth like two antique dealers meeting for the first time.

Tristan knelt down next to Garrov. "Some kind of magical beast has come to the village. It's Unhallowed. My sword glows whenever I get close, but I can't kill it. It heals whenever it's cut. Ranka says the only kind of weapon that can kill it comes from the bones of a Goliath."

"Garrov, could you make me an axe out of the scapula?" Mersha asked, crouching down next to him.

"I zink zat would be possible. Tristan, you're a strong lad. Help an old man carry zese bones to ze entrance. Mikhelena, my dear, I'm afraid we will have to tie ze femur to your pack to even ze weight. Do you zink you can handle it."

She shrugged. "I'll try."

Just then the moaning of the cave rose up again. Tristan scooped the bones Garrov had chosen into his arms and the group of hunters returned to the entrance. Upon reaching the winged packs, a terrible sight greeted them. The leather casing had deep cuts gashed into them. Parts of the wings and apparatus were sizzling and melting. An acrid smell permeated the air, making the huntsmen's lungs burn.

"Our acid," Lise said in a defeated tone.

"What happened here?" Tristan demanded.

Mersha walked closer to the packs and bent down. "I'd wager the dwarves we were trackin' found these. They laid their axes into them pretty good here, here, and here. Then, dumped their stolen acid on the wings. Sorry, Garrov. They looked difficult to make."

"Not so difficult as time consuming," the inventor replied.

Tristan dropped the bones to the ground. "Great. Now it'll take a week to get back. Maybe longer."

Garrov knelt down and examined the damaged contraptions closer. "Zey did a poor job of sabotaging zem. I may be able to cobble together one or two from ze spare parts. Zen you could fly back yourself, Tristan."

"And who would make the sword?" Tristan asked.

Garrov stood up and yanked at some of the wispy white hair on his head. "Janelle is learning. She doesn't yet have ze skill Syra did but, she could perhaps form ze blade. Oak can read ze runes in the silver tome for her, I think."

"That's not good enough, Garrov. The people are blindly giving that creature their treasures and taking trash in return. It must be stopped. Can you form the blade here?"

The inventor laughed. "No. Impossible. I have no Eldanar."

Mersha set down her pack. "How much you need?"

"You have extra?" Garrov asked, surprised.

"Mersha never goes on a mission underprepared," Tristan added.

"What have you got?" Garrov inquired, peering into her backpack.

"Short swords, daggers," Mersha said.

Garrov erected himself. "Hm. Zat would be enough to inlay the edge and runes, but how would I melt it?"

Mikhelena stepped forward. "I have a crucible. It's not very large, but you could use it if you want."

"We use coal for our fires," added Yanis. "There's no wood in the mountains, but we worked out a deal with the miners to supply us with what we need."

Garrov put up his hands. "Eldanar does have a low melting point. All very well and goot, but how would I shape the blade and carve the runes?"

"I carry tools for carving stone and wood," said Filippos. "It's come in handy where we've been—"

"Don't. Don't say. Not yet," interrupted Mersha, holding out a hand.

Slowly, Garrov said, "If-if I could borrow zose tools, it just might work. We would have to break down ze blades into pieces. Melt zem, and zen carefully pour ze liquid metal into ze carvings."

"How long?" Tristan asked.

"A day, at most, perhaps," Garrov replied.

"And to fix the wings?"

Garrov leaned against the cave wall. "Zat might take longer. Ze locks and springs are very delicate. Zey have to be synchronized perfectly. Who knows what is damaged in zere to begin with. Ze acid has to finish its work unless we can wash it off. Any springs in zis area, Mersha?"

"Not that I know of," she replied.

"Well, we can't waste our waterskins on zat. I'll begin. Tristan, would you mind breaking ze blades into smaller pieces?"

Mersha handed Tristan a short sword, knife, and dagger. He took them, grabbed a nearby stone, and began hammering at them. After a few blows, the rock disintegrated in his fist. He then slid one of the blades in a narrow crack in the wall and jerked back with all his might. The blade shattered. Over and over, he did this until each weapon had been broken down as much as he could.

The other huntsmen began setting up a camp just inside the cave while Garrov set about his work. Mersha and Filippos mended their gear while Lise and Yanis whispered to each other in a nearby alcove. Tristan paced back and forth. Sat for a moment. Jumped back up. Examined the walls of the cave and sighed in defeat.

"Something wrong?" Mikhelena asked, taking his hand.

He squeezed back and faked a smile. "I can't just sit here. We were supposed to be getting back. I feel like I'm letting the village down."

"You shouldn't. There's nothing you can do," she said.

He nodded. "I know. I'm just… I feel like I'm wasting my time."

"What else is there to do?"

Tristan peered deep into the blackness of the cave. The night draped the sky outside, and the only light came from the coal fire and Garrov's light spheres.

"I'm going to check out what else is in the cave. Who knows. Maybe I'll find something worth taking," he said.

"Want me to come?" Mikhelena asked.

He gave her a quick kiss. "Nah, I probably won't be good company right now."

Tristan grabbed one of the light spheres and headed into the blackness. When he came to the fork in the cave, he chose right. The left led to the bone-giant, and his curiosity drove him to explore the new.

The tunnel went on for a hundred yards or more, then changed. Up until that point, it was clearly worked by hand. But, here, the walls became rougher, more natural. This part of the cave was much older and probably existed long before the entrance.

Tristan stopped at the threshold for a moment. Something in the air was different. A sense of foreboding permeated the air. Even the temperature changed. Heat emanated from some unseen source deep within the tunnel. Tristan turned to head back, but a sound caught his ear. It was gruff, like a bear or wild boar grunting in the distance.

He drew his sword. No flame. Endeavoring to pierce the darkness with the light of the sphere, he looked as far down the tunnel as he could. Darkness there was and only mystery waited below.

With his sword still in his hand, he stepped into the natural cave, which began a slow descent. After a time, he stopped. *How long have I been walking? How far have I gone?*

Time seemed to be rushing by or maybe standing still. Tristan couldn't tell which. He stared back in the direction from whence he came. It was impossible to see how far the shaft went back. A force he did not understand pushed him onward. *I've come this far. No sense in turning back now.*

Chapter 23:
A FACE IN THE DARK

Tristan continued ever forward. The corridors led in tighter and tighter spirals until Tristan thought he was in the very heart of the mountain. The walls grew jagged and glass-like. The smooth stone glistened, reflecting the incandescence of his light sphere in all directions. As Tristan trekked on, the glass became crystal, black and hard-edged. Great and natural pillars shot at crisscross angles like arrows; molding the passage into a flattened diamond shape. The air grew hot, and beads of sweat trickled down his face.

The tunnel twisted further and further in on itself until it arrested at a dead end. The crystals formed a peaked roof far above him, then came down at sharp angles on either side of the cave floor. The geometry shaped this terminus into a great, unblinking eye. Tristan stood before the wall, stupefied. He placed his hand upon the perfectly smooth purple stone. *All this way for nothing? How can that be?*

He pressed against it with his fingers. The wall did not budge, nor gave any sign that it could. Tristan let his hand drop to his side. *Nothing.*

He started back toward his friends when he gave the wall a kick out of spite. The toe of his boot crashed through the wall with the sound of terracotta smashing to the floor. He paused, then kicked it again, next to the original puncture. Once more, the stone shattered to the floor. He vigorously attacked the wall. Kicking, pounding, bashing his shoulder against it until, at last, he had destroyed enough to allow passage.

The tunnel beyond the wall was exceedingly dark and full of ancient, musty air. The light sphere failed to penetrate the blackness; as if there were nothing from which its feeble rays could reflect. No roof. No walls. No floor. Tristan gingerly put one foot before the other, tapping against the ground to ensure there actually was any. Each furtive step became more cautious than the previous, for soon there was nothing around the hunter except the abyssal void.

At some point, with his poking about and groping the air, Tristan got the sense he was not alone. He paused, remaining motionless, to listen. Just above the rhythmic pulsing of the blood in his ears, he swore he heard the shallow sounds of breath. Inhalation, exhalation: smooth and shallow, like a newborn animal.

"Hello?" Tristan said to the shadows.

Tristan waited for an answer. The breathing grew heavier.

"I hear you. Who's there?" Tristan asked, slowly and silently drawing his weapon from its sheath. The sword did not flame.

Tristan's eyes went from the ineffectual light sphere to the place in the dark where his sword should be and back again. He endeavored to pierce the darkness with his sight but could only register the interminable obscurity of a lightless cave.

"I said, who is—"

Then, something like two voices answering in unison echoed and re-echoed, "[[I heard you the first time, hunter.]]"

Tristan took a step back and held his light high above his head. "Who are you?" he asked.

"[[I am the curse of the world, sewn into its final destiny from the moment of its fall from grace. I am a slave to destruction and misery,]]" the voices said.

Tristan stepped back further. The smell of ash and sulfur filled the room. "Why can I not see your face? Why are you hiding from me?" he demanded.

"[[To look upon my true nature would shudder you and The Cause would not allow me to destroy one of its agents before fulfilling his destiny.]]"

The obfuscating language of the voices irked Tristan. He suspected some foul trick or illusion was at play. "I don't understand. Why do you speak in riddles?" he growled.

"[[Mortal-kind is not yet ready to look up my species in all our terror and preeminence,]]" the voices replied.

"Show yourself," Tristan shouted.

"[[In a form your mind can understand.]]"

Mere inches from Tristan's face a pair of eyes began to glow with a pale blue light. Then, a second pair just above them and another just above those. The mane of a lion then sparked to life with the same phosphorescent glow. Then came a nose and cheeks. Just below them a wide mouth with three dozen jagged and razor-sharp teeth flourished. A second mouth, greater than the first, gaped below that one.

Tristan's skin went cold, his body trembled, but he held his nerve. Stepping back again, he raised his sword across his chest. The creature moved with him, and the muscled body of a lion came into view. Upon its chest was a mighty breastplate made from a red metal. Rising from its back came four great wings. Its feet were like the hooves of horses. Tristan shuffled back further, his eyes wide and darting from form to form of the creature. At last, coming from its haunches, a segmented tail rose high into the air. At the end of the tail protruded a barbed stinger that glistened with tiny droplets.

Tristan checked his sword to see if the Eldanar runes upon it flamed, but they did not. His sword felt cold and unperturbed.

He turned up his face again to the creature. "What are you? Where did you come from?"

"[[I have already answered you.]]"

"Are you a friend or foe?"

"[[Power has not been given to me to harm your kind, but I am no friend to humanity,]]" the creature answered.

Tristan lowered his guard. Somehow, he knew the monster's voice could only speak the truth. "What constrains you?" he asked.

"[[I am subject to The Cause, just as all things in this valley must be. You would do well to remember that, huntsman,]]" the voices answered.

Tristan nodded. "I will, but… Why are you here?"

The creature stepped forward once again. "[[I am here to take you back.]]"

"Back where?"

"[[To your village, so you may face your current foe. Have not the dwarves clipped your wings?]]"

Tristan's shoulders slumped. "How did you know?"

"[[It is my purpose. For now,]]" it answered.

Tristan waited in silence, unable to decide a next course of action. The vision of this conglomeration stole his sense of reason.

"[[Your friends should have your weapon finished soon. I will follow you to them, only do not look back. If you do, I shall disappear forever, and so shall the one chance you have to save your village from its self-destruction.]]"

Slowly the creature's instructions made sense to the hunter. "You'll follow?"

"[[Do not look back,]]" its voices said.

Tristan wrenched his eyes from the gigantic creature and turned his back. The light sphere now illuminated the path forward. He could see that this part of the cave was a perfectly square tunnel made from translucent blue stone.

He proceeded forward until he came to the black, diamond shaped branch of the cave. He paused at the transition, wondering how a creature so large could fit itself through the tiny man-sized hole he'd made. Tristan took a breath and went onward. A dozen steps later, he paused and listened, expecting to hear the sounds of shattering pottery or at the very least, the sound of hooves on stone. Yet, only silence followed him.

Lowering his right shoulder, he made a move to turn back but, his conscience caught him. He straightened his face and stepped boldly on. Past the jagged glass and into the spiral, unwinding the course he had taken earlier. He left the natural cave and entered the hand-carved tunnel. Soon, light from a mid-day sun reflected on all the walls.

"Tristan!" came a voice from ahead.

"Where have you been?" he heard Mersha call.

"I wasn't gone that long," he said as he continued toward the entrance of the cave.

"It's been two days!" Mersha responded as she joined him.

Tristan reached the mouth of the entrance and removed the cuirass he was wearing.

"Where were you?" Mikhelena asked, coming up behind him.

Tristan dumped his armor to the ground and felt around in his pocket. He pulled out a whistle, a bit of parchment, and a small bit of charcoal.

"I was with him," Tristan said, pointing over his shoulder.

They all turned their heads toward the back of the cave.

"With whom?" asked Yanis, rising to his feet.

Tristan put the whistle in his mouth and played a few high-pitched notes. "With that," he said again, not turning his head back.

The sound of hooves, faint at first, began echoing from back within the cave. Their rough clacking against the hard stone grew louder and louder. Tristan never turned around, but he knew when the creature came into view.

Yanis dropped to the ground next to him. Mersha drew her weapon. Lise gasped in shock. Tristan heard Garrov whisper, "A manticore…"

All remained still in reverent silence. A dove fluttered down upon a rock next to Tristan who had busied himself with parchment and charcoal. He attached his inscription to the bird and instructed it to go to Aranka in the village.

The dove cooed and then took flight into the east.

"Tristan, what is happening?" came Mikhelena's breathless voice.

"He is going to take me back to the village," Tristan said.

"How?" Mersha rasped.

"[[He shall ride upon my back,]]" the voices said.

"Garrov, get that sword finished," Tristan said.

Chapter 24:
A FLIGHT, FAR AWAY

The sun peeked above the eastern horizon the next morning just before Garrov finished the ancient bone blade. He formed it in the shape of a formidable cusped falchion. It was broad and powerful, with holy runes inlaid on each side and a razored edge of Eldanar along the bottom.

Tristan took the weapon and gave it a few practice swings. The handle and guard held solid. The edge sliced easily through the air. It was a lighter weapon than he was used to, despite its size. He held the flat of the blade to his face and nodded approvingly.

"I had only makeshift tools, but I zink it will still be as strong as any steel forged weapon," Garrov said.

"[[The time for you to leave has come,]]" came the voices of the manticore.

Tristan tucked the falchion in his belt and went to Mikhelena. They embraced and kissed one another. Electricity.

"He seems like a fell beast, Tristan. Something from a nightmare," she whispered in his ear.

"I don't know for sure whether I can trust this creature or not, but I feel I must. My love will always be with you," Tristan whispered back.

She held him tighter. "When we meet again… *when*, I'll have something wonderful to tell you about."

He pulled back from her. "I look forward to it."

The winged creature sauntered next to them and hunkered down against the floor of the cave. Tristan left Mikhelena, their hands holding each other until the last, and clambered onto the manticore's back. He grasped its thick crimson mane and wrapped the cord-like hair around his fists.

"Ready," the huntsman said.

"[[No, you're not, but we leave just the same.]]"

Tristan swallowed hard and crouched down lower in the beast's rough coat. With a low growl, the creature exited the cave and beat its wings against the air. The sound of a multitude of wasps or dragonflies filled the air, and the two of them took flight with the rising red sun gleaming against their faces.

Into the cold and misty air, they climbed. Tristan pulled himself low to the creature, using its thick fur for warmth. Higher and higher they ascended until the world dropped far beneath the clouds and the valley transformed into a patchwork quilt rather than hills, pastures, and forests.

Tristan stole a glance over the manticore's shoulder. The vale appeared so small and fragile from that vantage. *How insignificant we all must be. If creatures like this roam the world, what is mankind in comparison?*

The ancient being beneath him cruised along, silent and unphased by the whipping currents and gales. Tristan struggled to breathe in the thinner air. Hours passed and the sun chased them higher in the sky. At last, they passed over

Vitalba village--a small speck of brown--amongst a carpet of bright green. Yet, the monster did not descend. They turned north and crossed the river that sliced the valley in twain, separating the tamed forests from the dark and enchanted woods dominated by the servants of Lord Dreadstone.

The descent began, swift and sudden. Tristan's ears filled and ached with the drastic change in atmosphere. The manticore circled then landed in a clearing two leagues north of the river. Tristan's head pounded as he slid off the back of his carrier. He stared up at the creature once more, looking into its three sets of pitiless eyes.

"Could you not destroy the bull?" the huntsman asked.

"[[It would be trivial for me, but it is not my purpose to do for mankind what it is meant to do for itself. What would your world be like if all the creatures of the hidden world, the seraphs and cherubs, stedes and griffons, nightmares and behemoths suddenly entered your farms and cities?]]"

Tristan was at a loss. He turned his eyes to the ground and said, "I-I don't know."

"[[Then you are in no position to ask for such a thing.]]"

He put his hand on the creature's mane and looked up. "Will I see you again?"

"[[None shall see my kind again until the ending of the world, and our coming will be hailed by cries of anguish and groans begging for death.]]"

With those words, the manticore backed up, beat its wings, and took flight once again. Tristan stood alone in the clearing, watching the creature go until it could be seen no more. He shook it from his head; taking a moment to bask in the knowledge he had experienced something transcendent and primal.

Turning his attention to the clearing, he moved to the edge of the wood and began stalking his prey. Up ahead, a starcrest marked a tree. Tristan nodded in satisfaction and trekked directly for it. It wasn't long until he found Okacheybay waiting amongst a clutch of a dark green holly bush.

"You got my message then," Tristan said as he crouched next to his friend.

"Aranka relayed it immediately after the bird arrived. I tracked the bovine here, and I was about to send Devereaux to fetch you from the village," Okacheybay said.

"Devereaux?" Tristan asked, searching around them.

As they spoke, the long-haired huntsmen joined them in the blind. "I believe the beast is on the opposite side," he said.

"Why did you bring him?" Tristan asked.

Okacheybay shrugged. "He insisted he come."

"Why were you with the ringmaster and this thing anyway?" Tristan asked Devereaux.

"Oh, I heard of this creature before, many years ago. Rumors hit the town that it was in the North Forest, and I went to see for myself, naturally. Mensonge was already there with his performers, so I merely offered my services to protect the villagers and escort them as needed."

"How did you learn about this bull in the first place," Okacheybay asked in a deep voice.

"Shall we not focus on slaying it first? There will be time enough for old tales once it's dead," Devereaux replied.

"True," Tristan said, then turned his attention back to the clearing.

Devereaux stared at Tristan for a moment. "Do you have the sword?" he asked.

Tristan removed the ancient bone blade from his belt and held it up for his companions to see.

Devereaux held it up to his eyes and examined the edge. "Just as I imagined," he said.

"You imagined?" Okacheybay echoed.

"I-I did my own research in Vitalba. May I examine it?" Devereaux asked, holding out his hand.

Tristan shook his head 'no' and resheathed the weapon. He scanned the field ahead. There was no sign of their quarry.

A moment later, the rough grunting sound of a bull broke the placid peace of the clearing. Its hulking brown shape appeared fifty yards away, munching on the tender shoots of the field. Tristan noted that it had grown much larger since he last saw it.

"Time to go," Tristan stated as he rose to his feet.

Okacheybay rose with him and Devereaux scooped up a pile of kindling, then followed. Tristan stalked the beast, trying to stay downwind for as long as possible. The spring breeze whipped his face. The grass bent softly beneath his boots without making any sound.

When he was less than ten yards away, the creature looked up and grunted. It took a few furtive steps in the huntsmen's direction with its head bowed low. Tristan removed the falchion, now wreathed in blue flame, and readied his shield.

Upon seeing the ancient bone blade, the bull's eyes widened. It roared and raced forward. Tristan braced himself. When the beast was mere feet away, it tucked its head low between its legs and leapt forward, whipping its long horns up at Tristan as it crashed into his shield.

The force of the brute knocked Tristan up into the air. The bull circled, and the huntsman scrambled to his feet.

Again, the monster charged. Tristan sought an opening from which to strike at the creature, but the attack was so violent, all he could do was hunker behind his heater shield to absorb the blow.

He lost his footing again, having to scramble up to avoid the stomping feet of the beast. It closed on him now, jabbing at him with its horns. But, when Tristan tried to swing, it dodged and galloped away.

"This isn't going to work," Tristan grumbled.

Okacheybay stood nearby in fighting stance. "I suppose a hunter would not have experience fighting a bull, eh?"

Tristan's ears perked up upon hearing this. "Actually, I do," he said.

The bovine monstrosity charged again before Tristan could say more. This time, he was able to spin aside and take only a glancing blow.

"Oak, take this, and be ready to kill it," he shouted as he tossed the ancient bone blade to his friend.

The fire surrounding the falchion switched from blue to gold in Okacheybay's hand. "What shall I do?" he asked.

"Just be ready."

Tristan prepared himself for the next attack. He pushed his hand through the strap of his shield, keeping it on his arm but freeing up his fingers. Next, he pulled his gauntlets on tightly and relaxed every muscle in his body.

The abomination charged once more but, when it tucked its head this time, Tristan backpedaled. The leaping horns of the beast struck only empty air. For a moment, it stumbled when it landed. That fleeting loss of balance was all Tristan needed. He grabbed the monster by its horns and drove its head into the ground. The horns pierced deep into the soil, and he heard an audible grunt as the creature's skull hit the earth with full force.

"NOW, OAK! NOW!" Tristan shouted, hugging the creature's head as tightly as he could.

Okacheybay already slid to the beast's side and was swinging the sword. The blade came down with such speed and strength that it sliced cleanly through the spine and ribs of the creature, spilling blood and entrails upon the green.

The monster convulsed in pain and jerked its head aside, tossing Tristan ten feet in the air. A second slice from Okacheybay worsened the wound, and the third finally severed the rough beast in twain.

The two halves twitched on the tufts of grass for a moment and then became still. Tristan joined his friend who was hunched over, looking at the bloody mess.

"Well done. We got him," Tristan said with a pat on his back.

"Quickly, sever its head," Devereaux said. "I'm making a fire!" Tristan and Okacheybay turned in unison to see Devereaux striking a flint and steel onto a piece of tinder atop a small pile of sticks and arm-size logs.

"What are you doing?" Tristan said.

"We have to cut off the head and burn it, or it will return to life," Deveraux answered.

Tristan shrugged at Okacheybay who dutifully went to the corpse and severed its head from the remnants of its body. Tristan reached down and grabbed the gory thing by a horn and took it over to Deveraux.

"Perfect," he said, blowing into the fire until a flame took hold.

Tristan dropped the head at Devereaux's feet. "Aranka and Garrov never mentioned anything about this."

"Heh, you left before the research was complete," he answered as he removed his black plumed cap.

"I see," Tristan replied.

"And so it goes," said Devereaux.

The flames kicked up, and Okacheybay added some nearby dropwood. Devereaux showered him with thanks. When the flames were roaring, the long-haired huntsman hefted the bullhead up by both horns and dropped it in the fire. He then grabbed his cudgel from his side and removed the Eldanar lace that was wrapped around it, tossing that in as well followed by the dry rose upon his chest.

"To complete the process," Devereaux said when Tristan gave him a quizzical look.

Tristan went over to the carcass of the bull and squatted down to inspect it more closely as the heavy foul smell of burning flesh saturated the air. Okacheybay's cuts were clean and true. The innards were still oozing out onto the ground, but the blood had mostly drained. None of the severed pieces showed any signs of healing or regeneration.

"The beast is dead. Now, you want to tell the tale of how you learned of this creature and this ritual you're performing, Devereaux?" Tristan asked as he looked back over his shoulder.

Devereaux held his cudgel up to his eyes and examined it closely. "It is time, indeed," he replied. "The outside world has books on the legends of Celandine. Few believe they're true, or at the least, still true. There are those of us, though, from the outside who still recognize the power that the stories and the rituals and the magic of this valley can give."

"What do you mean?" Okacheybay asked, wagging a finger in Devereaux's face.

Devereaux cleared his throat. "Well, you see, the uncanny power contained in this valley is known to us. We recognize its effect on the world but will not bow to it. Instead, we wish to use it for our own ends. I, for example, wish to become a powerful leader of men. I found ancient scraps of half-remembered legends and pieced them together. They told me to bring a sacrifice to the steps of Dreadstone Keep, and I did. As a result, Lord Dreadstone sent the dwarf Parier to build the magic maze you visited. His death would begin the ritual that made this creature we now burn. It is Dreadstone's will we are carrying out."

"Dreadstone himself?" gasped Okacheybay.

Tristan drew his sword.

"Who else? I needed the help of you huntsmen to complete the ritual, though. Patric and Halbert were easy enough to manipulate. They're both so desperate for esteem in your village. You two, however, were more difficult. Chalk it up to your strong minds, I suppose. The dwarf had to be sacrificed and the bull slaughtered to bring it all about. I lacked the power to do so, but you did not. I had to be more careful in positioning you where I wanted. I think you'll see; it was worth it. The skull is almost finished, and I am ready to ascend into power."

"What can you mean?" asked Okacheybay who came closer to the fire.

The fire popped and crackled then the flames turned green and extinguished.

"And so it goes," Devereaux said.

Chapter 25:
THE TRANSFORMATION

Devereaux reached down into the ashes and pulled the blackened bull skull from the burned heap. He raised it above his head and pulled it down over his face. His body convulsed, and he cried out in agony. He writhed on the ground begging for help, begging for mercy, but the huntsmen stood back, shielding their noses from the piercing smell of charred human flesh. Eventually, Tristan and Okacheybay had to cover their ears from the terrible cries of pain that followed.

But soon, the plaintive cries grew quiet, and the pungent odors subsided. All was still. A cloud of smoke covered whatever remained of Devereaux, obscuring him entirely.

"What new sorcery is this?" Okacheybay called out to Tristan.

Tristan, waiting two dozen feet away, said, "I have no idea. I've never heard of any such thing—"

Before he could finish, a creature leaped out of the smoke and landed in a crouch. A low grunt announced its intentions. Drawing itself to full height, it revealed the feet of a cow, the legs and torso of a man, arms of an ogre, and the head of a bull. The huntsmen's swords sprung to life with raging fire.

"A minotaur," Okacheybay said, drawing back from it.

But before Okacheybay had a chance to raise a defense, the minotaur grabbed the cudgel at its side and clubbed him on the side of his helmet. The lanky huntsman crumpled to the ground.

Tristan charged the beast, jumping over the dead fire. The minotaur whirled around and swung its primitive weapon. Tristan blocked it aside with his broadsword and slammed into the beast with his shield. The minotaur stumbled back but retained its footing.

It charged; head down low with ivory horns glistening in the sun. Tristan dodged aside and brought his sword down on its back. The beast roared and turned on him. With both hands it swung the great cudgel down at Tristan. The hunter raised his shield to block it. The attack bounced off ineffectually.

He had to stifle a laugh. "That all?" the huntsman asked.

The creature roared and swiped at him again. Tristan dodged and jabbed. The beast evaded. The hunter angled his sword above his head and darted forward with his shield. He blocked the cudgel again. This time the swing was a bit harder. Then, he slashed the monster across his enemy's bare chest. The beast took no note. The wound healed immediately.

A third time the cudgel slammed into his shield. Tristan had to hold his shield a little tighter. The strike almost knocked it away from his body. He feigned a sword strike to the monster's left, then brought the blade back to the right. The tip of the broadsword grazed the creature's belly, opening up a small red slit.

The towering monster brought its horns down on Tristan, forcing him to raise his shield to deflect them. This opened his midsection to attack, which the minotaur took full advantage of. The cudgel slammed hard into Tristan's cuirass, knocking the wind out of him.

The huntsman retreated into a defensive posture, trying to relax the muscles in his stomach. His heaving encouraged the foul brute to attack harder. He ran towards him; head low for another charge. Tristan stepped away to evade it but lacked the wherewithal to riposte so soon.

Each combatant sized the other up for a moment. Tristan's wheezing subsided, and his breath returned to normal. The minotaur snorted at him. Tristan adjusted the grip on his sword and took a step back, hoping to goad the creature into charging.

The beast obliged and raced toward Tristan. The huntsman crouched low behind his shield. The minotaur tucked in its head, ready for a strike. Tristan waited, waited longer than usual to make his dodge. When the beast's horns were almost upon him, he jerked his body to the right, dropped to a knee, and drove his broadsword up through the monster's gut.

The minotaur's momentum yanked the sword from Tristan's grip. The beast skidded to a halt and turned around. The fiery broadsword protruded front and back from the Unhallowed abomination, but the creature stood tall; entirely unphased.

Tristan's eyes widened. *What manner of creature can withstand such a blow? How does the fire not burn it?*

Unarmed, Tristan backed away. The beast raised its cudgel and jogged toward the hunter. Tristan's mind raced for a solution. *How can I defeat something immune to Eldanar?*

The creature attacked Tristan savagely. The huntsman blocked each swing of the cudgel with his shield, but each time the impact hurt more and more. *He's getting stronger.*

The last blow struck so hard that it ripped the shield half off his arm. It dangled by a strap from his wrist. Tristan scrambled back and put the unconscious Okacheybay and the dead fire between him and his enemy.

The horned beast, with the sword still protruding from its gut, slowly closed the distance. Tristan searched every corner of the clearing, hoping some miracle from The Cause would save him. But, there would be no Bartonomous in the swamp, no Mathias in the tower, no Mersha in the cave this time.

As the Unhallowed stepped closer, its hoof kicked something on the ground and it jerked back in pain. Tristan's eyes focused on the high grass just before it. There, something glowed amongst a patch of camelia.

The march of the minotaur continued toward him. Tristan crouched low, almost kneeling, readying himself for the end of the battle. As soon as the beast started to raise the cudgel up for the killing blow, Tristan rolled forward past it, but the creature's aim would not be denied. The weapon came down on his shoulder and helmet as Tristan tried to stand to his feet. The huntsman's body dove to the ground in a crumpled heap.

The shock of the heavy blow reverberated in Tristan's bones. The world around him became blurry, and the air grew thick and sweet. His mind wanted to sleep. Blackness closed in around him and the thick grass, wet with morning dew, embraced him.

"No," he said aloud, and his eyes sprung open.

Next to him, hidden among the new spring flowers, rested the glowing bone blade the minotaur had kicked only a moment ago. Tristan's hand dove into the nest of unopened buds snatching a handle. The wind from the cudgel passing by his head grazed against the skin of his neck. Tristan whirled around and hacked the minotaur ribs with the edge of the ancient bone falchion. The flaming sword dug deep into Tristan's enemy, peeling back flesh and fur and bone. The bull-headed beast roared back in pain; kicking Tristan in his chestplate as it jerked backwards.

Tristan rolled away, favoring a cracked rib on his left side. A river of blood hemorrhaged from the minotaur who continued backing away from the huntsman. Tristan steadied himself and advanced.

"Mercy, mercy," the creature cried.

Tristan continued forward.

"I was one of you!" it said.

"You were never one of us, Devereaux. You have been filled with nothing but deceit since we first met."

Tristan increased his pace while the minotaur stumbled backward, clutching its gaping wound. The beast swung at Tristan, but the hunter flashed his sword, cutting the monster's hand off at the wrist. The cudgel dropped to the ground with a lifeless thud.

"Help me. I don't want to die!" it cried as it fell to its knees.

Tristan raised his falchion, then paused. "If you wish to live, reject the Unhallowed and come out of that form."

Tristan whipped his blade to the side, cutting open Devereaux's throat. The beast gurgled and slumped to the ground. Tristan rolled him over and pulled out his broadsword, tossing it aside. His ribs burned with pain, but he kept his guard up.

Moments passed. He thought he heard breathing return to the monster, but it did not stir. He tilted his head to the side to listen more intently. Nothing happened. He took half a step closer when the horns of the beast launched themselves at him. He barely caught them with his shield and deflected them away.

Thunderbolts of pain shot through Tristan's body as his ribs screamed. The minotaur, covered in its own blood, reached out with its good arm and grasped Tristan around his neck. The monster squeezed, and it was all Tristan could do to flex his muscles and avoid instant strangulation. The huntsman swung his sword down upon the arm of his captor and sliced it clean.

The Unhallowed roared back in agony, raising its stump in the air and spurting blood in all directions. Tristan dropped his sword and grabbed the lifeless hand still wrapped around his throat and wrenched it away. Heaving, he turned to Devereaux. Anger got the best of him and he flung his shield at it. The shield caught the false huntsman just above the eye and knocked the minotaur on its back amongst the weeds.

Stifling a cough, Tristan retrieved the ancient bone blade. He stalked toward the writhing beast and stood above it. Tears rolled down its swollen brown eyes. For a moment, pity overcame Tristan's heart, and he dropped his guard.

The minotaur smiled, then brought its hooves up and kicked at Tristan. The blow glanced off his cuirass. A weak attack, but it was enough to worsen his injury. Tristan growled in pain and brought his sword down one last time, into the heart of the beast. The force of the strike snapped the blade five inches from the tip, sending the broken shard off into the weeds. The monstrous beast shivered one last time upon the cold ground, then died.

Chapter 26:

A NEW ROSE

Tristan raced to his friend who still lay prone in the grass. Tristan checked him for injuries. There didn't appear to be any bleeding.

"Oak, Oak," Tristan said.

The huntsman's dark brown eyes flashed open, and he raised his eyebrows. "What happened?"

Tristan grabbed his friend's hand and helped him to his feet. "Devereaux betrayed us," Tristan said.

Just then, sizzling and crackling noises bubbled up from the corpse. The blue-black flesh of the creature sprung into sapphire flames from the center outward. Tristan and Okacheybay readied their weapons, but the beast did not spring back to life, only engulfed itself further into immolation.

"That him?" Okacheybay asked.

Tristan nodded.

"What is that in his chest?"

"I don't see anything," Tristan said.

"How can you not see it?" Okacheybay asked with half a laugh.

He walked over to the burning minotaur. As soon as Okacheybay's hand entered the flames and penetrated the exposed ribcage of the beast, the flames changed from blue to gold then back to blue as he withdrew something from inside.

Tristan couldn't see what his friend was examining in his massive palms, but the slim huntsmen smiled and nodded before walking over to him.

"What is it?" Tristan asked.

"Your treasure, my friend," Okacheybay answered, holding out a metal object.

Tristan took it and examined its beauty. The trinket was made of silver. It was diamond shaped. Round holes the size of his thumb were cut into each corner and the center. In the middle of each hole, golden thread suspended small gemstones: ruby, sapphire, topaz, and garnet.

"This must have been placed inside his body somehow," Tristan said.

"A truly remarkable piece," Okacheybay said.

Tristan scanned the battlefield. The air stood still and only the occasional chirping of swallows could be heard.

"Let's get back to the town," Tristan said.

Okacheybay helped Tristan recover his gear and the two set out for Vitalba. They arrived just before midday the next morning. Upon entering the gate, Tristan parted ways with Okacheybay and set off for the back of the village. His friend urged him to see a healer about his ribs, but Tristan insisted there was something else he had to do first.

He hurried along the busy streets of Vitalba, pleased to see the villagers back at their routines. When he neared the gardens, he saw Eldo sitting in his wheeled chair with something laid across his lap. Tristan strode up next to him and put his hand on the armrest.

"Eldo," he said.

"Ah, Tristan, was your search for the Goliath successful?" Eldo asked.

"Valere tell you about it?" Tristan asked.

"No, it was Jenelle when she brought me this," he said, holding up a modified crossbow that had been resting on what remained of his legs. "She made it after Garrov told her you still needed me to sentry the gardens."

"How's it work?" Tristan asked.

"Easy, I brace it against my chair like this," Eldo said, moving it into position, "and then I can reload, aim, and fire. This way I can guard the gardens, just like you suggested."

Tristan picked up the weapon and examined it. "How many children have come today?"

"Oh, only a half-dozen or so."

"There used to be so many more. I was always jealous of the throngs of kids playing here. I wanted to join them so badly, but my dad never allowed it. Anyway, I hope the crossbow serves you well. Janelle is becoming quite the craftsman. I bet Garrov will be pleased," Tristan said.

"Yeah, I wanted to thank him, too," Eldo said.

"He's not back yet."

"Oh?"

"Long story, for another time. I've got a meeting with that bear," Tristan said, pointing to the nearby cage.

Eldo looked over in that direction. "Need me to distract the guard again?"

"Nope."

Tristan returned the weapon and strolled directly to the cage, drawing the broken bone falchion from his belt. Tristan remained stone faced and silent. The guard opened his mouth to say something, then cast his eyes to the ground and shuffled out of the huntsman's way.

Tristan turned to the bear. "I'm back."

The bear watched the retreating guard for a moment, then said, "Did you find my words to be true?"

"Yes. You ready to get out of there?"

"Please," the plaintive creature answered.

Tristan slid the sword between the bars. He brought the edge down over the face, chest, and stomach of the poor animal. It groaned, snorted, and growled, and then the largest man Tristan had ever laid eyes on stepped out of the bloody bearskin, his massive beard stained and matted to his chest.

Tristan reached for the flimsy lock on the cage door and yanked it off with the satisfying sound of snapping metal. He swung open the door, and Maynard Kwan stepped into freedom. Tristan pulled off his shirt and wrapped it around the man's waist.

"You're a big fella, aren't you?" Tristan remarked.

"I was a warrior once," Maynard said, tying a knot in the sleeves.

"Why don't you come back to the Lodge with me?" Tristan said.

Maynard tipped his head and replied, "I would be grateful."

Eldo saw them from the gardens and waved his cloak at them, which they used to wrap the giant man up more.

Maynard followed Tristan back to the lodge where he could take advantage of the shower-cubicles in the back.

Tristan informed him where he could find food and clothes when he was done.

"Where are you going?" Maynard asked, as he stuffed himself into the small shower box.

"I need to speak with our lorekeeper, Aranka the librarian. Visit her when you are done. I'm sure she would be very interested to talk to you. I'll check in with you later," Tristan answered.

He thanked Tristan who then left for the library. The last thing he had to do was apprise The Council of what had transpired. He found her, busy as ever, amongst the shelves. Valere also sat at a nearby table, studying some documents.

"Tristan," he said. "Were you successful?"

Tristan placed the ancient bone falchion on the table in front of him. Aranka stopped what she was doing and joined them.

"Yes. The beast is dead. And Devereaux was working against us the whole time. Everything that happened since he entered the valley was orchestrated by Lord Dreadstone to transform Devereaux into what Oak called 'a minotaur' or something like that."

Aranka adjusted the spectacles on her nose. "That's a terribly painful ritual. One that takes years of preparation. Are you sure?"

Tristan described the amalgamated creature Devereaux became and all the other details including how he killed him and how he found the treasure inside his corpse.

"Oak was correct, then," she admitted.

Tristan shrugged. "Oak is always reading your books, Ranka."

"Indeed. Troubling, though, that Dreadstone was able to infiltrate our Lodge so easily."

Tristan folded his arms on his chest. "He should be destroyed once and for all."

Aranka grabbed a book from one of her shelves. "Is such a thing possible?

The sudden chirping of a dove at the library window drew her attention. Aranka's face washed over with confusion. She went to the window and put her ear closer to the fowl. It repeated the chirps and tweets.

"How many of them?" the librarian asked.

Valere and Tristan exchanged confused looks while the bird again filled the room with its melodic fluting.

"Did he escape?"

Even more vehement chirps emanated from the white-feathered fowl.

"How long before they get here?" she asked.

"Chirp-chirp," was the answer.

"What's going on, Aranka?" Valere asked.

She stared at the bird and said, "Lithie sent me a message. It seems three dozen or more hunters have escaped from Greyfell Tower. They're on their way here. I guess Thaul led a rebellion from inside Tatterdemalion's domain."

Tristan's spirits rose. "Is Emma among them?" he asked.

Aranka returned to the bird and asked. The bird chirped a reply and the library turned slowly to Tristan. "Doesn't appear so," she said.

"What about Thaul? Did he escape, too?" Tristan asked.

Aranka shook her head. "No. He was recaptured."

Valere hit the table in anger. "We have to go and—" he cut his sentence short.

"Yeah, I think it's time to go and rescue him," Tristan said.

Aranka began to turn around and say, "I don't know. We might—" then she too cut her sentence short.

"What?" Tristan asked with a modicum of irritation. "We need to go get him."

"That won't be necessary," Aranka said, slowly taking a knee.

Tristan was mystified by her behavior. "Why not? Here's our chance."

"I'm with her," Valere said, also taking a knee and facing Tristan.

"What are you two doing?" Tristan said, letting his annoyance show in his voice.

"Examine your chest, sir," Valere replied.

Tristan looked down at his cuirass. Where his red rose should have been, a gleaming white rose had replaced it. He touched it, dumbfounded for a moment.

"You are now the leader of the Lodge," Aranka said.

Tristan caressed the petals, saying nothing.

"We'll prepare a Prelation ceremony as soon as we can. It won't be the same without Thaul, but the huntsmen will need something to help them transition to new leadership, especially with all the new ones who will be coming in," Valere said.

Tristan stared at them. "I... I,"

"We'll take care of everyone," Valere said.

Tristan nodded. "I'll be in my room for a bit," he said.

"Understood," they said in unison.

A rush of power and possibility filled Tristan's heart with resolve. It threatened to overwhelm him, and the only thing on his mind was to share it with Mikhelena as soon as she returned. He exited the library and mounted the steps to the second floor of the Lodge, his fists clenched with pride. He threw open the door to his room to be alone with his thoughts.

Standing at the dresser, putting her belt and sword away, was Mikhelena. She started up at him but smiled.

"Miki, you're here! How?" Tristan said.

"Garrov was able to fix the wings not long after you left. They weren't as damaged as we first thought. The dwarves were quick about their work, not thorough. He and Filippos got them working again and we flew back to Vitalba just an hour ago," she said.

"I've got something great to tell you," Tristan said, taking her into his arms.

"Me, too," she said with a kiss on his lips.

"Look at my chest! I'm going to be the leader of the Lodge."

"You're also going to be a father."

THE END OF BOOK 3